CYNTHIA HICKEY

Christmas Cozy Collection

Cynthia Hickey

Copyright © Cynthia Hickey
Winged Publications

All rights reserved. No part of this publication may be reproduced, stored in a retrieval system, or transmitted in any form or by any means, with the exception of brief quotations in printed reviews.

This book is a work of fiction. The characters in this story are the product of the author's imagination and are completely fictitious.

ISBN-13:9798273259577

CHRISTMAS WITH STORMI NELSON

Two Short Christmas Stories
By Cynthia Hickey

A Thief for a Reason
And
A Christmas Deception

CYNTHIA HICKEY

A THIEF FOR A REASON

1

I dipped the cooled, cooked bacon into the chocolate, then thrust it into my mouth. Holiday cooking was my downfall. It always took me weeks to lose the five pounds I put on between Thanksgiving and Christmas.

"If you don't stop eating, we won't have anything to feed our guests." Mom plopped several cans of assorted beans and tomatoes on the counter.

"I have to do a taste test."

"You did that last week." Mom crossed her arms. "I can't help you with your list if I want to get my baking done." She glanced at her watch. "Guests will be arriving in five hours."

I sighed. Although I was excited to host my first Holiday Open House, I wasn't thrilled about the idea of a progressive-type affair where everyone went from house to house. I'd begged to stay home after the horde left our place, but Mom insisted I go along.

Yes, I wasn't as reclusive as I once was. Finding two dead bodies had a way of helping a person lose that affliction, but I had a deadline on my next mystery fast approaching. "Start your baking. I can handle this."

Mom scurried to the pantry. Ever since she opened her own bakery, Heavenly Bakes, my kitchen had been taken over by a baking machine. I told her she had the equipment at her store to do everything that needed doing, but she said she needed to experiment at home. She couldn't try new recipes out at the store. What if someone wanted to try the new concoction and it turned out horrible? Maybe if I baked it. I was the cook, she was the baker.

"I've made up gift bags." Angela, my sister, who sold face creams and cosmetics, entered the kitchen.

"You really want to do that after what happened at your first party?" Who could forget one of the guests dying because someone had put a high concentration of poison ivy in the cream?

"How else will I build my client list?" Angela glared. "People need to know that my product is perfectly safe."

I shrugged. I wouldn't be using it any time soon and feared we would all be receiving the product for Christmas. "Are the decorations finished?"

"Yes. The living and dining rooms look like a winter wonderland."

Which was a secret code for gaudy and over the top. At least I didn't have to spend the time doing it. Bacon done, I grabbed the can opener and opened what seemed like hundreds of cans.

Most of the neighbors would show up, get a look at

the crazy romance novelist who solved crimes, scarf down the food and move on. As long as they moved on, they could eat as much as they wanted. Maybe I could plead a headache and stay home before the next house in the progression.

As each dish was made, my refrigerator filled to capacity. Despite my reluctance to mingle, I couldn't squelch the flicker of excitement that sprouted in my stomach. I'd bought a new dress for the occasion and couldn't wait for my handsome detective/boyfriend, Matthew Steele to see me.

I finished the finger food with an hour to spare. I rushed past my sister and her two teenagers, who were putting the final touches on the decorations, and headed upstairs to my room. A long hot shower, scented body cream (not my sister's), a dab of makeup, and I stood in front of a full length mirror.

The black dress with red trim fit my slender figure like a glove. My red hair, straightened and hanging down my back, completed my holiday look. I'd even gone the extra mile and slathered on a shiny red lipstick. Matt would swallow his tongue when he saw me.

I headed through rooms full of white and gold decorations, noted the nativity in its place, and went to answer the ringing doorbell. "Hello, handsome."

Matt whistled. "Wow!"

I cocked my head. "Seriously? I've worn a dress before."

"Not like that one." He snaked his arm around my waist and pulled me close for a kiss.

"You've ruined my lipstick." I brushed away the evidence from his mouth with my thumb.

"Good. Doesn't hurt to let the neighbors know you're taken." He brushed past me and headed straight for the food table.

I shrugged and turned to hug my best friend, and Matt's sister, Mary Ann. "He's incorrigible."

"Try living with him." She glanced around the living room. "It looks great."

"I thought Angela would overdo it for sure, but it is beautiful. Don't forget to take a bag on your way out."

She glanced at the pink gift bags with white polka dots. "Not on your life." She laughed and left me holding the door for the next guests.

Thank the Lord for large Victorian houses. Soon, my rooms were filled with looky-loos and gluttons.

"I feel a headache coming on," I told Mom, biting into a forkful of red velvet cake. "It made me nauseous."

"Not so much you can't eat." She narrowed her eyes. "If you don't want to go, then don't. I won't force you. Oh!" She dashed toward a toddler who reached a chubby hand toward one of mom's cherished crystal ornaments.

Mother was one of the neighbors who argued about letting children attend the progressive parties. What did she think would happen?

The Snyders, a single mother with one too many children, stepped through the open front door. Clean and in their Sunday best, they glanced nervously around the room. I stepped forward to greet them. "Lucy, I'm glad you could make it."

"Can't turn down a free meal with this brood." She turned to her four boys. "Behave and don't touch anything."

They nodded and scampered away, filling their pockets with cookies. Lucy sighed. "I can't deny them some Christmas cheer. The holidays are lean for us this year."

As they were every year since her husband went to prison five years ago, if my guess was right. Maybe we could get the local church to adopt the family for Christmas. A week was enough time to purchase and wrap gifts. Matt would love to play Santa.

By the time the last guest left, my feet ached and I really did have a headache. Miraculously, all of Angela's gift bags were gone. I wished the recipients good luck. I closed the door, kicked off my shoes, and plopped on the sofa. I'd promised to call Matt later, and hoped I didn't fall asleep.

The twinkle of the tree lights filled the room with a sense of beauty and wonder. My gaze traveled down its branches and landed on the nativity, my favorite decoration. I bolted upright.

Where was the baby Jesus?

2

After totally destroying the festive piles of gifts under the tree and crawling around the living room floor for several minutes, I had to admit the figurine was gone.

I slipped my shoes back on and grabbed my red wool coat. Maybe I could find the culprit at the next house on the schedule. I teetered down the sidewalk in my heels and burst into the home of the Olsons. Their name still left me surprised.

Mrs. Olson, perpetually paranoid that another woman would want her shy, overweight, balding husband, left her the most unpopular person in the neighborhood. It wasn't unheard of for her to run women to the other side of the street at the end of her shovel.

I searched the room for Mom. She stood in conversation with Mary Ann next to a buffet table. "Wow," I said, staring at the roast ham and other dishes. "Mrs. Olson outdid herself."

"I thought you had a headache." Mom handed me a plate.

"Baby Jesus is missing." I plopped a spoonful of mashed potatoes covered with melted cheddar cheese onto my plate.

"Excuse me?"

"From our nativity. He's gone."

Her eyes widened. "Angela!"

My sister, recognizing "that tone" in our mother's voice, left the people she conversed with and hurried to join us. "Please, don't screech across the room. It's embarrassing."

"What did you do with Jesus?" Mom planted fists on her hips, leaving a smear of mashed potatoes on the black fabric.

"I left him at church." She wasn't a big church attender.

"Don't be snarky. The baby Jesus from the nativity is missing."

"He was there when I set it all under the tree."

I glanced around the crowded room. One of my neighbors was a thief. Tears pricked my eyes. After all I'd done for them, too. I'd formed a Neighborhood Watch, which, other than myself and the couple who lived next door were the only members, which had helped put two murderers behind bars.

"We have to find it." Mom set her plate on the table and marched straight to Matt.

He met my gaze over her head. I nodded, a signal to him that what she was saying was true, while at the same time, praying she was actually talking about the missing figurine and not how big my rear end would look this time next month after indulging in holiday treats.

Matt whispered something to Mom, then headed my way. "You're missing something? Do you want to file a police report?"

Silly man. He should know me better after almost a year of dating. "I'm sure it's something simple. I'll handle it. It isn't as if I stumbled across another dead body."

He paled. "You attract trouble, Stormi. It might be small now, but you have a way of blowing things up."

I held up a finger. "I have never—"

"Excuse me." Angela kicked off her stilettos and climbed on a kitchen chair, clapping her hands together like cymbals. "Your attention, please."

"Stop looking." Mrs. Olson smacked her husband's shoulder.

"Can I listen? She's going to say something."

"You may not. I'll tell you what you need to know."

He clapped his hands over his ears and stared at the floor. Matt and I exchanged shocked looks, then focused on Angela, who did her best to pull her dress down far enough to hide what God intended to stay hidden. She managed. Barely.

Once everyone quieted and were looking her way, she patted her hair, and pasted on a smile. "It has come to my attention that someone who visited our home, our home," she emphasized with a hand over her heart, "has made away with the baby Jesus. Now, I know that you all understand my predicament. I was the last person to touch the nativity, and now my sister, Stormi Nelson," she pointed a manicured finger at me, "is blaming me for the theft."

Murmurs of shock rippled around the room. Several people glared in my direction. What had I done wrong?

"Now, if Jesus isn't returned, my sister will feel the need to investigate, which always, results in her family almost being killed. I implore your Christmas spirit. Please, return the baby Jesus. Thank you."

She held out her hand. Detective Ryan Koontz, Matt's partner, helped her down. He flashed a startling white smile against his dark skin. I narrowed my eyes. Please don't tell me he was dumb enough to fall for my sister.

"Well, that was interesting." I popped a cherry tomato into my mouth. "I doubt it will work."

"Of course it will." Angela grabbed a stick of celery. "Whoever took the piece will be terrified not to return it. If they fail to do so, you'll be sniffing at their heels. That's all it will take to make someone return the figurine."

"I'm going to find out who took it before it's returned." I marched away from her, ignoring Matt's protests about my snooping.

I could find the culprit. I had experience. Finding a miniature Jesus had to be easier than finding a killer and far less dangerous.

3

I followed the group to the next house, checking each person for suspicious bulges in their pockets. It was hard to see whether the women carried anything in their fancy holiday clutches, and every man had the distinct outline of a cell phone. I transferred my attentions to the younger people.

Cherokee, my niece, laughed with her brother, Dakota. He could be a suspect. Just the other day he had commented how boring life was without a mystery to solve. I wouldn't put it past the scamp to hide Jesus just to get me to search. Then, there were the four hooligans that Lucy had to raise on her own. Not to mention at least three toddlers. Maybe I should have checked my toilets. Didn't they like flushing things?

I waited until everyone had entered the home of Tony and Becky Salazar. My neighbors were 'little people' with big hearts and the desire to please. I shook hands with Tony and bent down to give Becky a hug. "The two of you ready to do some neighborhood investigating?"

Tony grinned. "More than ready. We'll make the rounds while everyone fills up on cake and cookies." He lowered his voice. "We bought all the desserts from your mother's shop, although I wish she would stop treating us as if we have a handicap."

"I'll talk to her." Again. I followed the sound of moaning people happy with the sweets they were stuffing in their mouths.

The Salazars must have spent a fortune, and if Mom wasn't in love with them before, she was bound to be now. Cupcakes, a three-tiered white cake, and a multitude of cookies covered the red-draped table. Every single person held a plate in their hand piled with goodies.

I tried to mingle, but everyone became suddenly involved in a deep conversation while I strolled by. One man actually preferred talking to a silk plant to answering my questions.

Pouting, I retired to a vacant corner. Maybe I could learn something by merely observing.

Matt flirted with Mom, much to the aggravation of her boyfriend, Robert. Matt had a way of making whatever woman he talked to feel like the most important person in the room. I wasn't worried. I knew he was mine.

A nativity sat on the Salazar's mantel. Clearly made in Mexico, since Mary, Joseph, and Jesus had distinctive Hispanic features, the painting and detail were exquisite.

"Not going to steal mine to replace yours, are you?" Tony handed me a glass of punch.

"I'm admiring the workmanship."

"I carved that myself. Becky did the painting."

"Seriously? You two are talented. I'd keep a close watch on it if I were you."

"I intend to." He patted my arm and continued to greet each guest by name and with a handshake. The world needed more people as friendly as Tony.

I eyed the Snyder boys who stood a bit too close to the presents under the tree, in my opinion. The oldest, Jaxon whispered something to the youngest, Kyle. They acted very suspicious to me. I started to approach them when Angela stopped me.

"Everyone took one of my gift bags." Her eyes shimmered with tears.

"That's good, right?" And surprising, considering.

"No. They've left them next to the Olson's trashcan. They only took the bags to be nice."

"I'm sorry, Angela, really I am, but maybe you should consider another line of product to sell. Daisy's murder is too fresh in everyone's minds." I could still feel the itchy rash of the poison ivy, and that had happened two months ago.

"I'm not going to sell Tupperware!" She stormed away.

Did anyone sell Tupperware anymore? Surely, there was another makeup line she could sell. Regardless, I didn't have time to worry about makeup. I sidled closer to the Snyder boys.

Jaxon caught me creeping closer and herded his brothers outside. I shrugged. Not having a lot of experience with children, I really had no idea whether they were telling secrets, up to no good, or behaving normal. From the look in Lucy's eyes as she watched them go outside, I was going with up to no good.

"What's up?" I asked.

"I think I might know where your baby Jesus is."

"Let's go get it."

She shook her head. "I want them to return it because it's the right thing to do, not because I told them to."

"You have a plan?"

"I might. I could also be wrong, which means my boys will be angry with me, but I'll deal with that if it happens." She pulled me back into the corner. "We're going to set a trap. Do you think your boyfriend will help us?"

"I'm sure of it." I caught Matt's eye and waved him over. "We're going to catch us a thief under the age of fifteen. You in?"

He shoved a chocolate-chip cookie into his mouth. "Sounds like fun. Then, I plan on dragging Stormi under the mistletoe. My lips are feeling a total lack of the Christmas spirit."

My face heated as Lucy laughed. "I miss Mark so much it hurts, especially at the holidays."

I put an arm on her shoulder and winked. "Do you

want Matt to kiss you, too?"

She laughed. "Tempting, but no, he's all yours."

Matt scowled. "Stop poking fun and tell me about your plan."

4

Plan in place, Matt made the rounds, asking the guests to participate. Most were enthusiastic about the idea, and it was no surprise that Mrs. Olson balked.

"Why don't you just make the boy admit to taking the figurine." Mrs. Olson crossed her arms over her ample bosom, straining the fabric of her forest green tent, I mean dress.

"The boy's mother wants to teach him a valuable lesson," Matt said.

"A trip to the woodshed would be lesson enough." Mrs. Olson glared in the direction of the Snyder boys who still stuffed their faces and their pockets with Christmas goodies. "Make them turn out their pockets."

"We're hoping it won't come to that." I knew what kind of mother Lucy was. She had raised the boys right. If they took the figurine, they had a reason, however misguided it might be.

It was time to put the first part of the plan into action. I sidled up to the boys and pretended to study the dessert items. I sighed dramatically. "Look at all these wonderful cakes. I don't ever feel like eating them."

"Why not?" One of the middle boys, I couldn't remember his name, glanced up at me with a powdered sugar smile. "You're missing out."

"I can't eat when I'm depressed. I lost something very valuable to me today. A baby Jesus that had been in my family for a very long time."

The four boys exchanged glances, confirming my suspicions that they knew something about the theft. If they weren't the ones who had stolen the nativity, they knew who did.

I tried to drum up a fake tear, to no avail. So, I grabbed a napkin and dabbed at dry eyes, hoping they wouldn't notice the lack of moisture.

The youngest boy's chin quivered, and he glanced at his older brother.

Jaxon herded his brothers to the other side of the room, tossing over his shoulder that they didn't know anything. The little liar.

I moved back to Matt's side. "I played the sympathy card. I'm sure they took it, but they aren't admitting a thing."

"They will." Matt stuck two fingers into his mouth and blew. "Folks, sorry for the interruption, but we now have a live investigation. No one is allowed to leave this house until the culprit is apprehended. Each person will be interrogated before being allowed to leave. Now, if the thief will come forward and return the stolen item, the party can continue, and no charges will be pressed."

"That's a bit excessive for a holiday decoration, don't you think?" A man I didn't know stuffed a brownie into his mouth.

"Go to the store and buy another one. Why ruin everyone's fun," a woman said. "Stormi makes enough money with her trashy novels to buy ten new nativity sets."

I did, but that wasn't the point, and my novels weren't trashy. Why did people always assume that a romance writer wrote smut? "This is a family heirloom. Priceless and irreplaceable." I stabbed Jaxon with a stare. "God knows who the thief is."

The boy glanced at his brothers and avoided my gaze.

"I'll start with Lucy Snyder," Matt said. "In the kitchen, Ms. Snyder, if you please."

Tears welled in Kyle's eyes. He said something to Jaxon, who shook his head.

Surely, they would confess before long. Especially when they saw what happened in the next few minutes. My heart actually went out to them, for a second. The belligerent look on Jaxon's face erased any trace of sympathy.

I understood their pain and anger at their father's arrest, but the man had embezzled money from the bank he worked for. Not the children's fault, but they needed to accept the fact that when a person did something wrong, there were unfavorable consequences.

"I don't think they're going to crack," Mom said. "That oldest boy has a chip on his shoulder the size of Mount St. Helen's."

"He'll crack." If he loved his mother, he would confess. Oh, I prayed we weren't wrong as to who had taken the baby Jesus. I hated to think we were punishing the boy for no reason. But, what if we were wrong?

I moved to the kitchen. Maybe Lucy could give me more insight into her children.

She stood next to the sink, dabbing some kind of oil in the corners of her eyes. She grinned and blinked at me. "Clove oil. Works wonders when you need to drum up some tears. I haven't had this much fun in ages."

"Are you sure one of your boys took it?" I capped the bottle for her.

"I'm positive. Jaxon didn't, but he will always cover up for his younger brothers. I see guilt written all over their faces." She held out her hands to Matt. "Cuff me."

"Why?" He took a step back.

"More dramatic. The boys never saw their father cuffed and hauled away. I want them to know without a doubt what happens when you break the law. If I don't turn them from their bad ways now, I may never be able to."

"I don't have any cuffs with me." He shook his head.

"I do." Tony Salazar passed through the kitchen. "Sorry for eavesdropping, but we're out of punch."

I wanted to ask why he would have handcuffs, but decided it was probably best not to know. "Are you really sure, Lucy?"

She nodded. "I know it's a small thing, really, that they took, but the next time it might be a DVD, then a car. My heart won't be able to take it if they follow in their father's footsteps. My boys love me. They're protective of me. If they have it, they'll confess as soon as Matt leads me out of this room."

The handcuffs clanked as Tony handed them to Matt. He grabbed a jug of punch out of the refrigerator and headed back to the living room.

Lucy winced as Matt clicked the cuffs around her wrists, then took a deep breath and squared her shoulders. "Does it look like I've been crying?"

I nodded, real tears springing to my eyes. This was a woman willing to do anything for the sake of her children. I felt privileged to call her friend.

Those in the living room gasped as Lucy and Matt stepped out of the kitchen, me close behind. Without a word, Matt guided her toward the front door.

"Wait!"

5

Kyle raced to his mother's side, tears streaming down his six-year-old face. "I took it." He opened his palm. "I'm sorry. Jaxon told me to keep quiet or I would go to jail like daddy."

Tony handed Matt the key to the cuffs, and he unlocked them, then squatted down to peer into the little boy's face. "Can you tell me why?"

"Are you going to arrest me?"

"No, son." He took the figurine and handed it to me.

I gazed at the porcelain face. "Mom, can you get the wooden nativity out of the garage?"

She nodded and rushed away.

"Why did you take it, honey?" Lucy sat on the sofa and pulled Kyle down next to her.

"The preacher at church said that if we ask Jesus for the desires of our heart, he will give them to us. I wanted to put the baby Jesus under my pillow so daddy will come home." He buried his face in his mother's shoulder.

"Oh, sweetie." Lucy pulled him onto her lap. "All

you have to do is pray. You don't need to steal a figurine of Jesus. He's with you all the time."

"But I thought that since his birthday is coming that it would be more important if I could hold him."

My heart melted. Especially when I saw tears gathering in Jaxon's eyes. Not only his, but most eyes in the room shimmered.

Kyle looked up. "I'm sorry, Miss Nelson. I won't steal from you ever again."

"Me or anyone else." Mom handed me a cardboard box. "I have a gift for you, Kyle. Now, before you think it's a reward for stealing, I need to tell you otherwise. I set the box in his lap. "I do have an extra nativity set," I made a point of staring at the woman who had commented earlier that I could afford several. The one that had been stolen was actually Mom's, but meant the world to me and my sister. It took some of the shine off Christmas not to have the heirloom under the tree.

"This was my first ever, very own nativity set. Now, your mother is right in that you don't need a figurine of Jesus for him to be with you. He's with you every day, and most importantly on Christmas. But if it helps you to have this until your daddy comes home, then this is my gift to you. Do you understand that stealing is wrong?"

"Yes, ma'am." He opened the box and picked out Jesus from the pieces inside. "Is it okay to keep it in my room every day?"

I glanced at Lucy, who nodded. "Yes, it is."

He grinned and dashed to Jaxon's side. "I want you to have it. You're the man of the house right now and can use Jesus."

"We'll share it," Jaxon said.

The party dispersed, everyone returning to their homes. Despite the cold in the air, I snuggled on the front porch swing with Matt, cozy under a thick quilt.

"This has got to be the best Christmas I can remember." I laid my head on his shoulder. "It's amazing how children can bring back the true meaning."

"They're good boys. They'll be fine." Matt slid an arm around my shoulders. "It was a good plan you had, dangerous, but not like the ones in the past where I had to worry about you getting killed."

"I was afraid they were going to let you take Lucy out of the house. That Jaxon is a tough kid."

"He's had to be. It was sweet of you to give them a nativity of their own." Matt rested his cheek against the top of my head.

"I'd like to see whether the church will adopt them for Christmas." If not, I would do so myself.

"You're a gift, Stormi. A true gift. Merry Christmas."

"You aren't so bad yourself." I lifted my face for a kiss. "Merry Christmas."

The End

COZY CHRISTMAS COLLECTION

A Christmas Deception
A Nosy Neighbor short holiday mystery
By Cynthia Hickey

CYNTHIA HICKEY

1

I don't know why we have to leave town for Christmas." I was a creature of habit. A keeper of tradition. Going out of town to attend a Christmas masquerade did not fit in either category.

"Because it will be fun, Stormi," Mom said. "Don't be such a stick in the mud."

"I also don't understand why I can't go as myself." I sat on my suitcase, trying in vain to stuff a 19th century dress into a 21st century suitcase. "The theme is literary. I'm an author."

"It's literary characters." Mom pushed me off the suitcase and pulled out the green and brown dress. "Use a garment bag. You're crushing the petticoats. You're too pretty to be Jane Eyre, but the character suits you."

Gee, thanks. "Who are you going as?"

"Agatha Christie." She grinned. "I know I'm slimmer and not gray haired yet, but that's the fun of a masquerade. Your sister is going as Hester Prynne. You know, from the *Scarlet Letter*?"

Of course, I knew who Hester Prynne was. This was

also more like a costume party, but who was I to correct Mom's high school friend? I'd keep my mouth shut and let them call it what they wanted to. Matt was going as Edward Rochester, so I'd be happy anywhere as long as he was there.

"You can't be Katniss!" My niece, Cherokee, shouted down the hall. "You're too old."

"Ah," Mom said. "She's discovered what Matt's sister is going as."

"Go as Hermione," Mary Ann said. "Your brother is Harry Potter."

"My hair is too dark to be Hermione. Oh, you're ruining everything." Footsteps stomped past the door right before someone knocked.

"Come in."

Mary Ann, my literary assistant and sister to my boyfriend Matt, poked her blond head into the room. "The labels for the postcards are printed. Anything else before I run home and pack my last-minute items?"

"No, that's it. See you in an hour."

"An hour?" She whirled and dashed away.

"You shouldn't have had her work today," Mom said, zipping my suitcase closed.

"I told her it could wait, but she insisted." I carried my makeup bag into the bathroom and tossed my toiletries inside.

Matt said he rented an eight-passenger van for the trip and would pick us up at two. We'd be at our destination by six.

I didn't remember much of Mom's friend, having met her once when I was a teenager, but I did recall her being ... flamboyant. And dramatic. It was going to be an interesting few days. The party was on the twenty-third, and we'd drive home on Christmas Eve. It wouldn't be the same. I liked stretching my family celebration over the entire week, and it didn't involve a house full of strangers.

"Stop pouting." Mom tugged my hair when I re-entered the room. "You might actually have fun."

"Maybe." I dragged the suitcase off the bed and rolled it down the stairs, leaving it by the front door.

As if that were the signal for the rest of the household to hit frantic mode, everyone raced around as if there were a fire, shouting about the lack of time. I shook my head and checked the ice chest, making sure we had enough drinks and snacks for the ride. It wasn't as if I didn't give them half-hour updates on the time.

"Hey, beautiful." Matt entered the house and kissed me. "Ready for an adventure? I've always wanted to play the brooding hero with a checkered past."

"Silly." I kissed him again and motioned to the suitcases. "I'm ready. The others are finishing up. We'll only be about fifteen minutes late. I told them they only had that long so that they'd hurry."

"That's my smart girl." He flashed a dimpled grin that set my heart in overdrive. His arms snaked around my waist, pulling me close. "What do you say we send the others on ahead of us and we can conveniently forget to go."

"Tempting." I tapped his nose with my finger. "But Mom is looking forward to showing off her best-selling daughter. She'd kill me and that would ruin our Christmas."

He stuck out his lower lip. "You're breaking my heart."

I laughed and pulled free. "Load up the van, Edward."

"Yes, Jane." He grabbed my two bags and carried them out as if they weighed nothing.

"Ready." Angela wheeled two large suitcases down the stairs.

"You do know we're only going for a few days, right?" At least one of my bags was a carry-on size.

"I might change my mind on what to wear." She breezed past me, dumped her bags next to the door, and sashayed into the kitchen, leaving a trail of sweet-scented cologne in her wake.

"Wash off that smell before we all get in the van or you'll gag us."

She poked her head into the foyer, stuck out her tongue, then withdrew again. "I'm not going anywhere without my wine."

I rolled my eyes. Mom was going to have a coronary. No matter how hard she tried, she couldn't get my sister to leave behind her fast ways. It was very surprising that she actually chose a character from such a modest time in history to dress as.

Mom, followed by the teens, dragged their cases to the front door. Mom clapped her hands and grinned. "Now, if we can get through the next few days without Stormi stumbling over a dead body, we'll all have a Merry Christmas."

2

"My husband is trying to kill me." Mom's friend, Sylvia Duncan, opened the door with a flourish.

"Merry Christmas, Sylvia." Mom hugged her and breezed into the house so large it could fit two of mine. And my house wasn't exactly small.

"You never take me seriously, Ann." Sylvia fluttered hands covered with rings. "Martin has discovered that I'm leaving him and has vowed to kill me."

Mom smirked at me over the woman's shoulder. "Well, Stormi is adept at solving crimes, and her boyfriend is a cop. Matthew, please make sure Sylvia stays alive through Christmas."

"I'll do my best." He panted and dropped the suitcases inside the door, sending me a questioning look.

I shrugged. I had long ago stopped trying to figure out my mother's strange friends.

"Since none of you will take the threat against me seriously, I'll show you to your rooms." Sylvia lifted her nose in the air and stomped up the stairs.

I would be sharing with Mary Ann, Angela with Cherokee, and Matt with Dakota. Since Mom was a close friend of our hostess, she got a room to herself. Of course, the rooms were more like suites, each having their own bathroom and king-sized beds. Ours was done in blue and white with a cast-iron headboard complete with sheer valance. A tabletop Christmas tree with blue and silver ornaments graced a corner table. Beautiful. I would have to ask her for decorating tips for my Victorian. I tended to be sparse until something was needed.

"It kind of stinks that we're saving gift opening until we return home the day after Christmas," Mary Ann said, rolling her suitcase into the room. "I love presents."

"We'll survive. Tomorrow night is the party." It might actually be fun.

*

The weatherman had predicted an ice storm the night of the party, but it didn't stop the long line of guests from strolling inside, dressed like every literary character imaginable. I hung over the banister and watched as Sherlock Holmes escorted a sexy black spider through the door. Charlotte from *Charlotte's Web*, I presumed. Cute.

Sylvia, dressed as Scarlett O'Hara in the infamous green curtain dress greeted each guest with a smile. I could stand on the second-floor landing and watch the people stroll by all night. It would be way more fun than having to mingle and talk to everyone.

"Ready?" Matt crooked his arm. "There's quite a spread of food in the dining room. Lunch was several hours ago."

I sighed. "I'm as ready as I'll ever be." I smiled as Cherokee and Dakota, err...Hermione and Harry Potter, thundered down the stairs and past the twelve-foot Christmas tree in the foyer. I held my breath until they raced past, afraid they'd send the entire thing toppling.

A buffet table in the dining room held enough food to feed a small city. Turkey, ham, and a goose filled large platters. Every side dish to complement each meat stretched along several tables.

Sylvia strolled by, her hoop skirt swaying from side to side. "If you see Sherlock Holmes," she said, "who also happens to be my husband, tell him I need to speak with him in the library. That man is not going to get out of his host duties."

Uh-Oh, I'd seen the famous detective slip out to the backyard with the spider just moments before. Sylvia seemed to be enjoying a dalliance of her own as she patted the face of a Rhett Butler on her way to the kitchen.

I grabbed a flute of what I hoped was sparkling cider from a passing server and sat back to watch the show. The night promised to be more entertaining than an Oscar-winning drama.

I sipped my drink. Yuck. Champagne. I set it down.

"I hope they have something nonalcoholic to drink."

"They're bound to. There are several people under the age of eighteen here. Let me find you something, although the almond champagne is very good." Matt squeezed through the crowd to the beverage table across the room.

Sherlock and his curvy spider reentered the room and made a beeline for the foyer. The spider's face was flushed and her wig askew. Wait until Scarlett got a look at her.

Which took about two seconds. Sylvia stepped out of the kitchen with a tray of cutlery. Her eyes narrowed and she took off after them like a bowling ball from a cannon. Everything in me wanted to follow.

Instead, I peered through the crowd to see Matt talking to a man with a black face and wearing a trench coat. Was he supposed to be the invisible man? I glanced back to where Sylvia and the other two had disappeared. I had to watch the scene play out.

It took me a while to fight my way through the crowd. Why did everyone stand in my way and grin like fools? How many people had Sylvia invited?

I pushed through Hansel and Gretel and practically fell into the foyer. Drats. I'd lost them.

Just as I turned to rejoin Matt, a scream rippled down the hall.

3

I burst into the room, designated a library by all the books on the shelves, and tripped over a sexy spider with a bleeding head. Standing over her was Sylvia, clutching a bronzed bust of Einstein. I might not be law enforcement, but even I couldn't miss the tufts of Miss Spider's hair on the bust.

Sylvia screamed and dropped the bust. Einstein's head rolled across the oriental carpet. "I didn't kill her. I found the head next to her." She put a hand over her forehead and gracefully fell onto a chaise lounge.

Matt and several others tripped over each other almost falling into the room. My love took one look, felt for a pulse, then ordered the others out. He pulled his cell phone from his pocket and called 911.

"I cannot believe it." Mom squeezed past the crowd. "You managed a dead body after all. We aren't even safe at Christmas."

I held up my hands. "I had nothing to do with it." I pointed at Sylvia. "She was holding the murder weapon."

"Only because it cost me a fortune and was on the floor!" Sylvia glared from her resting spot.

"Who is she?" Matt asked.

I shrugged. "I saw her with Sherlock, who I think is Sylvia's husband."

"He is," she said with a scowl. "That ... spider is ... was his girlfriend. That's why I wanted a divorce."

"So, you killed her?" My eyes widened.

"Of course not."

"Where is your husband now, Mrs. Duncan?" Matt slipped his phone into his pocket.

"I have no idea."

"I saw all three of them head in this direction," I said, "and I followed."

"Of course, you did." Matt grinned.

"When I came in here, Sherlock wasn't anywhere to be seen."

"Cops are here." Dakota stuck his head in the room, then withdrew when Matt waved a frantic hand.

"I know your niece and nephew are probably used to dead people by now, but they still don't need to see this."

Agreed. I perched on a corner of the desk and did another sweep of the room. Black shoes peeked out from behind the forest-green curtains. "You can come out now, Mr. Duncan."

He groaned and stepped from his hiding place. "I didn't kill her. She's a party planner." He stood in front of Sylvia. "I hired her to plan our twenty-fifth wedding anniversary party."

"Then why were you hiding?" Matt asked.

"I left her in here, ducked into the restroom, heard a scuffle, and found her like this. When I heard Sylvia screeching down the hall, I hid. Stupid, and it doesn't make any sense, but I was still trying to be secretive."

Sylvia jumped to her feet and clasped his hands. "You were planning a party?"

"Of course, silly dumpling." He caressed her face. "That's why I didn't want a divorce."

"I thought it was because of my money."

"Somebody killed this woman." Matt shook his head. "Stay focused, people. Let's start with her name."

"Yes, let's." The oldest of two police officers said, entering the room. "I'm Officer Lincoln, and this is Officer Boxer. Officer Boxer will start interviewing the guests while I speak to those in here."

We were going to be here all night. I settled more comfortably on the desktop.

Officer Lincoln peppered us with questions. When he got to me, his eyes narrowed. "You're the writer. The one who writes about the crimes she conveniently stumbles upon. Well, Merry Christmas, you have another one."

"That's not called for. I didn't ask for this." I glanced at Matt for backup.

"She isn't the suspect here," Matt said.

The officer shrugged. "But, she's always around."

His words hurt. He was right. I did tend to find

murder victims. It was a gift, really. One I'd like to return. Still, I had a hand in bringing justice to the victims. I didn't intend to stop now because it was Christmas.

Instead of wasting more time defending myself to an officer who already had his mind made up, I studied the victim and the Duncans.

Sylvia and her husband seemed to have forgotten all about poor little ... "What's her name?"

"Who?" Mr. Duncan didn't take his gaze off his wife.

"The spider."

"Oh, Charlotte. That's why she thought it clever to be a spider. Get it?" He turned and grinned. "Charlotte Web. Her parents had quite the sense of humor."

Quite. Still, something didn't add up. I slid off the desk and headed toward the victim.

Officer Lincoln stepped between us. "That's far enough."

"I just want a closer look."

"Nope." He stayed firmly between me and her until two men in white coats wheeled in a gurney and removed the spider.

Something was definitely fishy. When they'd opened the door, I hadn't heard a single sound drifting down the hall. That many guests should make some noise, even if they were in shock. And why hadn't my sister stuck her nose in the library?

I glanced back at Einstein's dented head. Did brass

dent? Again, I tried to move and found my way blocked by Officer Lincoln. The man was as tenacious as a dog with one of those rubber toys you shoved peanut butter in.

I huffed, crossed my arms, and plopped into the office chair. The whole thing was hopeless.

Why was Matt smiling? Surely, he wasn't enjoying my predicament. How could I possibly be face to face with a mystery and not get involved? We were going to have to stay longer at Sylvia's. There was no other way. I had to have time to solve this.

Matt and Officer Lincoln conversed quietly in the corner, then ushered us all from the room. Officer Boxer, who was obviously the fastest interrogator on the planet, strung yellow tape across the library door.

They handed us business cards, asked us to call if we remembered anything pertinent, then hurried out the strangely empty house.

"Where is everyone?" I surveyed the foyer. "This should have taken hours. They didn't do a very good job questioning everyone."

"Leave the murder to the police," Matt said, slipping an arm around my shoulders. "It's Christmas."

I sighed. "But I don't feel as if they were thorough enough. I'll have to stay a few extra days and question the guests myself. Poor Charlotte deserves that."

He chuckled and kissed me. "That's my girl. Always out for justice."

Exhaustion caught up with me and settled over my

shoulders like a heavy woolen shawl. I gave Matt another kiss. "I'm beat. I'll see you in the morning."

I climbed the stairs to my room, surprised to see Mary Ann already tucked in. Why did no one seem to care about the poor dead woman?

4

Comfortable in my normal attire of jeans and a long-sleeved tee shirt, I splashed cold water over eyes gritty with lack of sleep and then tromped down the stairs to the kitchen. Christmas Eve, and I couldn't enjoy the day because of pity for a dead woman.

"Good morning!" Mom smiled from the kitchen island, then turned back to watch a woman in a white apron and chef's hat fold an omelette. It had to be killing her not to be the one at the stove.

"Mornin'." I perched on a stool next to her. "I'm thinking of going to the police station today."

"Can't." Her grin widened. "Roads are iced over. It looks like we'll be spending Christmas at Sylvia's."

I groaned and banged my forehead on the counter. Stuck in the middle of a murder investigation and stranded because of ice. What kind of cruel joke was this?

"Cheer up." Mom patted me on the shoulder. "You can snoop around this big old house for clues."

"I doubt the killer is still under this roof."

"But you don't know that, do you?"

She was right. I could focus on Mr. Duncan. He was still the prime suspect. I straightened. Or Sylvia. One could have killed Charlotte to keep her mouth quiet and the other to get her out of the way. I wasn't totally convinced Mr. Duncan was telling the truth about her being a party planner. "How many staff does Sylvia hire?"

"More than five, but less than ten, I think." Mom's eyes smiled over the rim of her coffee mug.

I was sliding off the barstool when Matt's arms wrapped around my waist, stopping me. He nuzzled my neck, eliciting a squeal from me when he gave it a playful nip.

"Where are you off to?"

I turned to face him. "I was headed off to ask questions about Charlotte."

He tweaked my nose. "We're iced in for a day or two. I thought we could spend quality time together."

"You can help me. It'll be the first mystery we solve where you aren't in the role of detective." I slipped my hand in his. "So, will you?"

He grinned. "Anything to spend time with you."

"Great." I started to leave the room but was held fast by his grip.

"After breakfast," he said, smiling. "No one is going anywhere right now."

I let him pull me into his arms. He had a point. Why not simply enjoy each other for a while?

After a wonderful breakfast of strawberry and cream cheese crepes, I led Matt to the library. We ducked under the yellow tape, and I grabbed a small notepad and pen from the desktop. It was time to take notes.

"Not too close," Matt said as I squatted next to the carpet. "Don't destroy evidence."

Seriously? I doubted the crime-scene folks were going to trek up the mountain. It wasn't like I was going to stomp over the ... blood stain?

I'd smelled blood before, and this didn't come close. This was a sweet smell ... like syrup. I peered closer. Corn syrup with food coloring? I opened my mouth to say something, then snapped it shut. Something wasn't adding up. I pushed back to my feet and made my way to the dining room.

I had stood here. Matt had gone to get me a drink, and he and the other man next to the table had looked and grinned my way several times. The room had been claustrophobic with people. Mr. Duncan and Charlotte, looking very cozy, had gone into the foyer. Several seconds later, Sylvia followed. Then, I had fought like a salmon swimming upstream through a crowd that seemed to be doing everything it could to prevent me from following her. Then, once I broke free, I heard a scream. I burst into the library to see Sylvia holding a bust of Einstein ...

I raced back to the library and grabbed the bust from where it had rolled in the corner. Not brass at all!

A very good plaster imitation, complete with a dent. If someone had hit someone with this, they would have barely felt it. Someone had some explaining to do.

I brushed past Matt as he said "uh-oh," under his breath. I'd question that later. First, I needed to talk to Sylvia. As I climbed the stairs, Matt rushed toward the kitchen. Curiouser and curiouser.

After banging for several minutes on Sylvia's door, and trying not to wonder what the hurried sounds of scurrying people might mean, she opened the door in a flowing red nightgown and robe.

"There are some things that needed clarifying."

She clapped her hands. "Wonderful! Let me get dressed and I'll meet you in the family room. We can talk while enjoying the beauty of the Christmas tree."

O-kay. I shook my head and made my way to the family room, surprised to see my family sitting there with foolish grins on their faces. I glanced over my shoulder to see whether they were smiling at me or someone else. Not finding anyone, I glared and crossed my arms. "What in the world is going on here? Has everyone lost their mind?"

"What do you think has happened, dear?" Mom leaned forward and stared into my face, her smile never fading.

I glanced around the room. At Matt's loving gaze that sent my heart into overdrive, to my sister's smug look and the amused ones of her children, to my mother's indulgent one. When Sylvia entered the room, her arm linked with her husband's, I knew I had solved the murder of a pretty little spider.

5

Once everyone was seated, I glanced at each in turn. "Whose idea was it?"

"In regard to what, dear?" Mom tilted her head.

"Faking Charlotte's death."

"How did you figure it out?" Sylvia plopped into a wing-backed chair. "We were so clever with our plan."

"First of all," I held up a finger, "I write mysteries, so I can tell fake blood from the real stuff. Second of all, I retraced my steps and discovered Einstein's head couldn't kill much of anything." I perched on the arm of the sofa next to where Matt sat. "So, why the charade?"

"Merry Christmas!" Mom clapped and bolted to her feet. "This whole murder thing was my gift to you. I know how much you enjoy solving mysteries and wanted to come up with one tailored just for you." She looked so proud of herself.

"This was my gift?" I scratched above my eyebrow to rid it of a twitch. "Everyone knew about it but me?"

"Yeah." Matt put his arm around my waist. "Don't

be mad," he whispered. "She went to a lot of trouble."

I sighed. A regular weekend for Christmas would have been the best thing, but having Mom go to so much trouble only showed how much she loved me. "So, who is Charlotte?"

"She's the gardener," Sylvia said. "Isn't she lovely? Nothing would have gone as planned had she been homely."

I rolled my eyes and kept my attention on Mom. The pleased look on her face was fading. I hurried to her side and gathered her in a hug. "Thank you. It was fun. Are we really iced in?"

"That part was God's work," she said. "A little help from the big man upstairs."

I resumed my seat on the sofa arm. "The two officers?"

"Friends of mine," Mr. Duncan said.

"Rhett?"

"That, my dear, is Charlotte's husband." Sylvia leaned back. "They were very happy to accommodate us in our little Christmas deception. I haven't had this much fun in ages."

"Did you have the party just for this?"

"No, silly. I love parties." Sylvia giggled. "Your mom came up with the deception."

Everyone looked so pleased with themselves. Well, everyone except Angela, but she was never pleased when attention centered around me. I decided then and there that my Christmas gift to them would be to act as happy about the gift to me as they were about giving it.

"Thank you, Mom. Everyone. It was very thoughtful and loads more fun than mingling with dozens of people I didn't know." I found as I said it out loud that I actually believed the words I said. I had had fun. A lot, actually. I grinned and stared at the blinking lights on the gigantic Christmas tree.

Front and center hung an ornament that flowed with an inner bulb. Carved in the center was a nativity, bringing to mind the real reason for the season. I leaned back into the solidness of Matt.

While Mom's gift was precious because of the time and effort she put into it, God's gift to us of his son was infinitely more so. I thought of the new baking ware I'd purchased for Mom for Christmas. Since she owned her own bakery, shopping for her was easy. But how precious was it going to be? I hadn't done more than thumb through a catalog for her gift.

Matt's gift was a three-day stay for two at a resort. I thought it perfect since he always wanted to spend one-on-one time with me. But, had I chosen it with my heart? I thought so, having thought of his feelings and wants.

"Mom, your gift was very thoughtful. I'll cherish it for years to come." My eyes welled with tears. "I really am thankful."

She shrugged and grinned. "It was kind of a gift to us all, since we all played a part." She straightened. "When we get home, we should host a murder mystery-dinner party!"

God help us all. Why did so many of our family gatherings revolve around someone dying?

The End

Check out the other Nosy Neighbor books, starting with, Anything For A Mystery.

Poinsettia Madness

A Shady Acres Mystery, Book 4

By Cynthia Hickey

1

"Shelby Hart, as beautiful as ever."

I straightened from planting the last poinsettia in a sea of red to face my ex. "Well, if isn't Donald Trayer." I lifted my chin. I wouldn't smile or shake his hand. Not after he'd ditched me at the altar months ago. Several Shady Acres residents watched, curiosity etched on their faces. It wasn't often a man other than my new love, Heath McLeroy, spoke with me. Unless it was a police officer, that is.

"How are you?" He tilted his head.

"Peachy. You?" What was he doing here?

"Well, I'm getting married." He grinned.

"To the woman you left me for?" What, he wanted a congratulations?

"No, that didn't work out. My bride-to-be is Sasha Woodrow."

I raised my eyebrows. Donald did get around. My best friend Cheryl Leroix kept me abreast of things that went on at the elementary school where I used to work. "What do you want? I'm busy."

"Well," he took a deep breath. "I, uh, can I have back the jewelry I gave you?"

At least he had the decency to look ashamed.

"I sold it at a yard sale."

"What?" He jerked, his face as red as the Christmas plants behind me. "Do you know how much they were worth?" He ran his hands through his hair. "I can't believe even you could be that stupid!"

"They weren't worth anything to me, and you had given them to me as gifts. That meant I could do with them as I pleased." I eyed the three pronged garden tool in my wheelbarrow. If he got aggressive…

"I ought to ring your…" he growled and turned away. "Of all the idiotic, hare-brained—"

Wow. His ditching me at the altar turned out to be the best thing that could have happened. I wouldn't have liked spending the rest of my life with such a sharp-tempered man.

He whirled back to face me. "You're lying. No one would have sold jewelry as expensive as what I gave you at a yard sale. This isn't over, Shelby."

"Drop dead." I planted my gloved hands on my hips. "Whatever we had is over and done with. I've moved on and you're doing the same."

He glared, then stormed away.

Someone must have alerted Heath because he rushed toward us. "Is everything all right?" He put a hand on my shoulder and glanced to where Donald had stormed away.

"It's wonderful." I smiled and waved a hand toward the onlookers. "I'm closing a chapter of my life for good. All you looky-loos can go away now. The show is over."

The crowd dispersed.

"My ex is getting remarried and wanted some of the things he'd given me back. I told him I sold them."

"I remember. He had given you a lot of jewelry." Pain clouded his eyes. "I'll never be able to give you that, Shelby."

"Maybe not, but you love me and only me. I won't have to share you with other women. That is far more precious." I caressed his cheek. "Want to help me put these tools away and string Christmas lights?"

"I'd love to." The pain faded, to be replaced by a twinkle. "Obviously you plan on hanging them everywhere."

"Obviously. You can't have too many lights at Christmas."

Heath grabbed the handles of the wheelbarrow and led the way to the far corner of the community to where my garden shed and greenhouse were. "Where did you get all the poinsettia's? I've never seen so many in one place."

"I ordered them. Alice gave me a Christmas decorating budget. I spent it all on flowers and lights." I grinned and unlocked the shed door.

Once we stepped inside, Heath released the wheelbarrow and pulled me into a hug. "Want me to kiss you hard enough to make you forget that jerk of an ex?"

I wrapped my arms around his neck. "That would be wonderful."

He lowered his head and engulfed all my senses until someone cleared their throat. I lifted my head.

Donald stood in the doorway. "I forgot to give you this." He handed me a box containing a watch and money clip I'd given him. "Some of us keep the gifts."

"They're yours. I don't want them." I stepped away from Heath. A rustling sound drew my attention to the window where purple-haired Birdie ducked out of sight. Nosy woman. "I asked you to go away. There should be no reason for us to ever have to see or speak to each other again." The pain of betrayal and humiliation washed over me as it had on what would have been our wedding day.

"You heard her." Heath motioned toward the door.

Donald shook his head, grabbed the box he had given me out of my hands, and muttered something about crazy women as he marched away.

I sagged against a work bench. Why did he still affect me so? Because I thought I'd loved him. I'd given him my heart only to have it trampled on. I glanced up at Heath. Now, I had a wonderful man and I was afraid to give him the same commitment.

"Come on." He held out his hand with a smile.

"Let's go string lights and turn this place as bright at night as it is during the day."

I slipped my hand in his and let him lead me to the storage shed where boxes and boxes of lights waited. I clapped my hands and ripped into the first one. "I hope we have enough."

"Sweetheart, you have more than enough." He shook his head. "You can cover every bush along the walkways."

"Don't forget the pool area. I wanted to decorate the maze, too, but I ran out of money."

"My back will be very grateful." He loaded a box onto a wheeled cart. "Alice gave me a list of repairs, but they won't take long."

"Thank you for helping me."

He winked. "I'd rather do this than fix toilets and leaky faucets."

By the time all the lights were strung, I lost count of how many strands, I barely had time to take a shower before the supper bell rang. I met up with Mom and Grandma on the way to the dining hall and flipped the switch near the door that would turn on the timer for the lights to come on at dusk.

"I heard Donald came by," Grandma said as we entered the hall. "Are you all right?"

"I'm fine. He wanted his gifts back."

"I'm not giving back the necklace I bought." She narrowed her eyes.

"There's no need to. He knows they're gone." I

headed for the buffet and filled my plate with a large salad, fried chicken, and fried potatoes. I needed the sustenance after the day I'd had. Plate full I joined Heath at our usual table.

It had once been designated the employee table, but my family and friends took it over as our place to sit. The other employees sat wherever they could find an empty seat. Except for Alice Johnson, the manager. She'd integrated herself into our group.

She now approached the table, clomping on high heels she couldn't gracefully walk in, and plopped next to me. "Shelby, this community has had enough drama. Please take care of past business off campus."

"He wasn't invited." I drizzled ranch dressing over my salad. "I don't think he'll be back."

"See that he isn't. The complex is at full capacity, for once. No more deaths, thefts, or exes, please." She straightened. "Much more of that and we'll get a bad reputation."

"Pish posh," Grandma said, waving her glass of wine. "It'll draw people. We'll be known as the community of excitement."

"I'm with Alice." Ted, Grandma's boyfriend and a retired cop, sat down. "The trouble Shelby gets into is enough to make me gray haired."

"Darling." Grandma ran her finger through his thick hair. "You already are."

"See what she does?" He grinned.

Mom patted my hand in a gesture of goodwill. "You

do tend to put everyone on edge, dear."

I sighed and concentrated on my food. After the last fiasco where someone was poisoning people with deadly plants from my garden, I swore off solving crime. Every time, either myself or someone I cared about came within an inch of losing their life. It wasn't that I went looking for murder and mayhem. But rather that it followed me like a homeless person to a free buffet.

Heath leaned close. "Don't listen to them."

"You agree."

"True, but I also want you to be happy."

Sweet Heath. I planted a kiss on his cheek. "Let's get through Christmas without someone dying and I'll be happy."

Seth Willis, police officer and beau of my best friend, marched to our table. "Shelby, come with me, please."

"Why? I'm eating." Seriously, the man was becoming a thorn in my side. While we were tip-toeing around friendship, he still thought me little more than a troublemaker.

"I don't want to make a scene."

"Fine." I stood, as did the rest of the table. It wasn't as if he could make an announcement for me to follow him and not have them curious.

Seth led us to a far corner near the fountain.

Birdie perched on a concrete bench, jumping to her feet when we came near. "The body is over there." She glared at me.

A body? My heart sank to my knees.

Heath grasped my hand.

Taking my strength from him, I stepped forward. A man's legs stuck out from crushed poinsettia plants. I took a deep breath and followed the legs up to the face. Donald! A string of Christmas lights were wrapped around his neck. My legs gave way and I crumpled to the ground.

Heath knelt and wrapped his arms around me.

Seth stood over us. "Do you know this man?"

"My ex-fiance." I forced the words from a throat clogged with tears.

"You were seen arguing with him earlier and quoted as saying 'drop dead'. Is this true?"

I nodded.

"You can't possibly think Shelby killed him," Heath said, his voice cold. "Don't you know her well enough by now."

"I'm taking you both in for questioning. Don't move."

"You didn't know him." I glanced at Heath's face, illuminated by multi-colored Christmas lights and looking anything but festive.

"Do something Teddy!" Grandma clutched his arm.

"There isn't anything I can do. She isn't under arrest, right Seth?"

"Just a person of interest."

This couldn't be happening. Yes, I was angry at

Donald. I'd said some hateful words. But, I would never kill anyone. A sense of de ja vu washed over me. The very first murder of a resident, Maybelle, had resulted in Heath and I being suspects.

I pushed to my feet and faced Seth. "You know I'm not capable of murder." I cut a sharp glance at Birdie. "I thought we were friends. I caught Maybelle's killer."

She lowered her head. "I only said what I saw and heard."

"Right. That I wanted someone dead."

"Did you say it?" Seth asked.

"Yes, but I didn't mean it literally."

"Do I need to cuff you and Heath or will you come peaceably?"

I sighed and headed for the parking lot.

2

At least Seth didn't put us in a holding tank. Instead, Heath and I waited for him in a small room with a table and three chairs. It would have been cozy, if not for the two-way mirror taking up one wall. Who watched from the other side? Boonesville, Arkansas wasn't exactly a booming metropolis with several police officers at their disposal. At my last count, they had three. The only one I knew personally was Seth.

Wait until Cheryl heard about him dragging me to the station. She was going to give him an earful.

"It might not be good for you to wear a smug look," Heath whispered.

"Oh, right." I cleared my face of all emotion. Still, I couldn't wait until my friend got a hold of Seth.

Seth entered the room. "You're looking happy for someone suspected of murder." He glared and took a seat across from us. "We don't normally interview suspects together, but we're shorthanded."

"You know we're innocent, so cut to the chase," Heath said, crossing his arms. "We've both been through this before."

Seth exhaled sharply. "I'm just doing my job." He opened a leather binder and pulled out a pen. "Where were you this evening around six o'clock, Shelby?"

"Eating supper in front of most of the community." Seriously? That's where he took me from.

"What time did you arrive there?"

"When the bell rang at five o'clock. I didn't have time to choke, uh, Donald, with a string of lights, then make it to the dining hall. I'm five foot two inches tall and weigh one hundred five pounds. It would have taken me a while."

"Heath?"

"I arrived there a little after five."

Seth sat back in his chair. "I know you two didn't do it, but you were the only ones handy that had a motive. Can you give me the names of those who were at the dining hall? That leaves everyone else for me to question."

"I don't know all the names of the new residents," I said. "But maybe Alice can fill in any blanks." I rattled off the names of those I'd seen, Heath added a few, and still Seth had more people to interview than made him happy.

"You're free to go." He looked so dejected I couldn't help but reach across the table and pat his hand.

"We'll catch whoever did this."

His head snapped up. "There is no 'we', Shelby."

Heath sighed. "Dude, when are you going to learn? Shelby can't help but get involved." He took me by the arm and led me from the room.

"It's personal this time," I said.

"You say that every time."

Well, it was this time. Someone I had once loved very much had died a horrible death. Despite my resolve to stay out of snooping, I couldn't stay out of this one.

We walked across the street to a small park where Heath called Ted to come and pick us up. While we waited, I picked at the splintered corner of the picnic table we sat at.

Tears stung my eyes. I'd gone from loving Donald, to disliking, to apathy, and now sorrow. The man had been a two-timing skunk, more interested in notches on his belt than in commitment. Still, no one deserved to die as he had and especially during the holidays.

A pall hung over the Christmas season. One I needed to help lift.

Heath put his hand over mine. "I'm sorry about Donald."

"I don't even know where to look for his killer."

"I should tell you to leave it to the police, but I know better. I'll help you, sweetheart. We'll question every single resident if we have to. Someone had to have seen or heard something. Call Cheryl and see if she knows the name of his fiancé. Maybe she can give us a lead."

"That's a good idea." I pulled my cell phone from the pocket of my jeans and dialed my friend.

"Oh, my gosh, Shelby. Are you all right? Sue Ellen told me Seth dragged you down to the station. Wait until I call him."

"I'm fine, and don't give Seth a hard time. He knows we're innocent. He wanted possible leads more than anything. Which, by the way, is why I'm calling. What is Donald's fiance's name?"

"Sasha Woodward. She's the art teacher here. I'm sorry I didn't tell you."

"None of my business. Can you text me her contact information?"

"You might want to question every teacher here under the age of thirty. He's been with most of them at one time or another since your split."

I closed my eyes, the pain of betrayal fresh again. "Send me their info, too."

"I'm taking vacation along with Christmas break and coming to help. I'll be there Saturday."

"No. These things I get mixed up in are too dangerous. I don't want to worry about you."

"Don't be silly. Look, one of my students stuck a permanent marker up his nose. Gotta go. See you this weekend." Click.

"See's coming to help." I folded my arms on the table and rested my head on them. Having my friends and family in harm's way was different than myself in dangerous situations. More than once, I'd found myself facing a killer. How many more times before I didn't make it out of those situations alive?

Ted and Grandma pulled up in his renovated 1957 Thunderbird. Like a diva from old Hollywood, Grandma waved a scarf. "Yoo hoo!"

I shook my head and climbed into the backseat with Heath.

Normally, we'd spend the time snuggling. This time, we sat lost in our thoughts.

Grandma chattered away, filling the silence. "Once people found out the dead guy was your ex fiancé, well, rumors and speculation filled the air." She glanced over her shoulder. "Everyone loves you, Shelby, but they also say that a jilted lover is capable of anything."

"Seth knows we're innocent," Heath said.

"Well, not everyone else believes the same." She pouted and turned back around, muttering something about ostriches with their heads in the sand.

I wasn't quite sure what she meant, but decided to leave it alone. There was enough going on in my head without worrying about her feelings being hurt.

Once Ted stopped in the parking lot, we all trooped to my cottage where Mom already waited. I glanced around for her boyfriend, Bob, but I guess we didn't have the pleasure. He tended to stay away when crime solving was involved.

"I've made coffee." Mom smiled. "I'm not going to

pretend that my daughter isn't going to get involved or that we won't be up half the night coming up with a plan."

"Finally," Grandma said. "You're learning how it's done."

Mom shot her a sharp look then poured the coffee, handing us each a mug. "I'm resigned to the fact that my daughter thrives on danger and that my mother encourages her."

"There is nothing wrong with wanting my grandchild to have a more exciting life than her mother who is content to sit behind a desk and wear her hair in a bun." Grandma set her coffee aside and pulled a bottle of wine from her canary yellow bag.

"Can we please be civil to one another?" I glanced from Mom to Grandma. "Remember how your bickering almost got us eaten by a bear."

Grandma waved a hand. "That was over a month ago."

Sometimes I felt like the oldest of us three. Mom dressed like a wall flower, hair tamed back from her face. Most often she wore a cardigan over a blouse. Grandma couldn't be more different. Animal prints, bright red hair, scarlet fingernails, and the ever present bottle of wine. Me...petite with hair bigger than I was. I think God chose three random people to go through life together. The only thing we shared, physically, was blue eyes.

Ever the peacekeeper, Heath said, "I think we

should focus on the task at hand."

"Agreed." Ted took the wine from Grandma. "Try coffee."

"Oh, pooh, Teddy. You know my fruit beverage helps me think clearly." She took back the bottle.

He shot me an amused glance. "I tried."

Mom handed me my fluorescent pink clipboard. "Let's get to work so we can go to bed."

"This is not something I wanted to get involved in again."

"Too late for that. You were going to marry the man. As awful of a person as he was," Grandma said, pouring wine into a glass, "he deserves justice. Now, who are the suspects besides you and Heath?"

"We aren't suspects." I groaned. Why didn't she listen to me? "Everyone who wasn't at supper is a suspect. The women he cheated with are suspects. Possibly the fiancé. She's the only one whose name we know. Sasha Woodrow."

"She sounds like a stripper," Grandma said.

Choosing to ignore her, I glanced at the others. "Who do we know that was not at supper?"

Ted pursed his lips. "Not many people turn down food that's included in their rent, but that Leroy Manning was absent."

Our neighborhood vampire, a man who was severely allergic to the sun, never attended meals. But, he was a good one to talk to. He saw more of what went on around here than anyone. I wrote down his name and put a star.

The others rattled off names and, if they didn't know the name, a description. We were getting nowhere fast. "I really want this solved by Christmas. I do not want to spend the holidays fighting off a killer."

"No guarantees," Grandma said.

"For once, I'm on Shelby's side in this crime solving business." Mom patted my shoulder. "Let's not ruin our Lord's birthday with bloodshed. We have a little under four weeks to solve this."

I bit my lip. A nearly impossible task with no suspects. "Cheryl is coming on Saturday with information on the teachers at the school that Donald had affairs with. I'm starting my investigation with them."

"You'll have to give that list to Seth," Ted said, giving me a stern look. "He tolerates you snooping, but he won't allow you to impede his investigation."

"No problem." I knew people would rather talk to little ole me than a cop. They'd tell me things they wouldn't tell him.

I made a column on my paper for teachers and scanned the list of other names. "What motive would anyone at Shady Acres have for murdering a man they'd never met?"

"None." Heath crossed his arms. "I think we should focus on the women he fooled around with."

"No wrath like a woman scorned and all that, right?" Grandma raised her glass in a toast.

"Right." Come Saturday, I'd be knocking on at least one person's door. My five-foot-eleven-inch best friend would be my bodyguard. Mild-mannered and not the least bit brave, it was her size that tended to steer people away from doing me harm. It had happened all through high school. "Anything else before we wrap this up?"

"There are five of us here on a regular basis. Six if you count Cheryl," Grandma said. "I think we need a club. Something cool to call ourselves. Like the Shady Acres Gumshoes. Yes, I like the name."

"You've had enough." Ted took away the bottle and the glass and handed them to Mom. "We aren't crime fighters. We don't need a club or a name."

"The newspapers need something to call us." She frowned. "So far, they've only mentioned Shelby."

"That's because I come close to being killed on a regular basis."

3

"Hello, everyone!" Cheryl stepped through the dining hall door at breakfast on Saturday morning.

Immediately every man with a heartbeat focused his attention on her. Tall, blond, and buxom, she usually could get them to do anything for her. Today was no exception. Four men rushed to take her suitcases.

Grandma glanced down at her chest. "I need a boob job."

Ted spewed orange juice across the white tablecloth. "Whatever for?"

"So men will do my bidding like they do her."

"Sweetheart, I'll do anything you ask, flat chested or not."

"Thank you, Teddy." She grasped his face in both hands and planted a big kiss on his lips.

I shook my head and rushed toward my friend, wrapping my arms around her. "Thank you for coming."

"Girl, the things you get into are the only excitement I get. Seth refuses to tell me about the cases he's working on." She took a seat next to me. "Where's your hunky hero?"

I shrugged. "Alice has him doing something important." I did finger quotes around the word important. "I made a list of the names you sent, but want your input on who to start questioning first."

"I can't wait to get started." She accepted full plates of food from two old men who could barely shuffle across the room. "Just as soon as I eat."

Seth marched through the door and straight to our table. "The list, Shelby."

Sighing, I forwarded him Cheryl's text. "Hello to you, too."

"Good morning, gorgeous." He ignored me and kissed Cheryl. "I'll be back for supper." And, just as fast as he arrived, he left.

"Why couldn't he just call?" I glared at his back.

"He didn't think you'd give him the list unless he told you in person."

"Why didn't you give it to him?"

Cheryl shrugged. "He didn't ask me."

Sometimes, I swore my friends and family personally tried to thwart my attempts at…anything. Why did I always have to be the one in the police department's crosshairs? "If we're going to be a team, I could use a little help with the tiny details once in a while."

"Team?" Alice joined us. "I want in."

"We're solving a murder," Grandma said. "You wouldn't be interested."

"Who says? I'm very interested in everything that goes on here." She pouted. "Oh, and Shelby, are you ready for tonight's Winter Ball?"

Yikes. Not only was I the gardener for Shady Acres, but the events coordinator as well. I'd completely forgotten about tonight's big event after Donald's demise. Questioning suspects would have to wait until tomorrow. "Except for a few minor details." Like decorations, a gown, food.

"Wonderful. Now, what about this team you're getting together?" Alice smiled.

"It's not really that. Grandma has loose lips. I'm going to solve the murder, if I can."

Alice grinned. "That's right. The dead guy is your ex-fiance."

"How do you know that?"

"Everyone knows." She rubbed her hands together. "What would you like me to do first?"

"Make a list of everyone who wasn't at that night's supper." That should keep her busy for a while.

"It'll take some work, but I can think of something." She leaped from her chair and rushed toward her office.

"Smart way to get rid of her." Grandma grinned.

"She might actually be able to help. Now, I'm off to visit the kitchen staff about food for tonight's party.

Cheryl, could you find me a gown to wear?"

"You got it, toots. I'll make sure you look gorgeous. I brought something perfect for myself to wear."

I'm sure she did. I headed for the kitchen and stepped inside the marble and stainless steel room. Joyce, the head cook stirred a pot on the stove. Lori Brown, her helper, sliced bread. A new guy, tall and rail thin, peered over from where he washed dishes.

"Well, hello, Shelby." Joyce smiled, more of a grimace. We had a shaky relationship since I'd once accused her of poisoning the residents. "What can I do for you?"

"With all the excitement," my heart lurched, picturing Donald lying in the poinsettia's, "I forgot about tonight's party. It's a formal winter affair. What can we whip together for the menu?"

"You're killing me here." She turned off the burner under the pot on the stove. "I've got in a shipment of salmon. How about a seafood buffet? We can decorate the buffet with white lights and glitter."

I gave her an impulsive hug. "Perfect. Thank you."

She stood as stiff as an English guard. "You're, uh, welcome."

Now, to find Heath and work on decorations.

I located him, mumbling, in the storage room. "Hey."

He straightened. "Just the person I need. Alice has the insane desire for me to build more benches along the walking paths."

"What can I do?"

"Brighten my day." He gave a lopsided smile that almost sent my heart flopping.

"Want to work for me instead?" I returned his smile.

"Honey, I'd clean toilets for you."

I laughed. "Nothing as bad as all that. I need a place to have tonight's Winter Ball, and decorations gotten out of the shed."

"Cutting it close." He wiped his hands on the legs of his jeans. "I have some garden heaters. Let's use the decorations we already have. Why not have the party in the courtyard by the fountain? We already have plants and lights. Keep it simple and elegant."

"Maybe you should be the events coordinator. That's a perfect idea." I slipped my arm in his. "Let's head over there and make sure everything looks good."

We strolled to the fountain. Someone had removed the crime scene tape. I groaned. "I need to find some new poinsettias."

"For tonight, take them from somewhere else. I'll bring in the furniture from the pool and other common areas. It'll be fine." He gave me a quick hug. "I didn't think about this being where Donald died when I suggested it."

"Don't worry." I blinked back traitorous tears. Sometime soon, I was going to have to re-evaluate my feelings about Donald's death and grief. "It will be good for something fun to happen here." Although, the fountain area was the second time a crime had occurred there, it wasn't the fountain's fault.

~

Dressed in an ice blue gown, faux fur stole around my shoulders, and my hair up, with rhinestone barrettes, I surveyed the magic of the courtyard. Heath had out done himself.

He'd turned off the multi-colored lights, leaving only the white ones and had somehow found fake snow to scatter around the ground. Glitter winked from the flakes. The buffet table sparkled with crystal and white dishes. Garden heaters kept the area a comfortable temperature. It was all beautiful and magical.

"Wow, Shelby." Alice stood next to me in a black gown. "You've outdone yourself."

"I had help, and thank you. This will really kick off the holiday season."

"You can't even tell a murder had happened here."

Gee, thanks for the reminder. My smile faded, and I wandered over to survey the seafood on ice. I'd have to thank Joyce. It couldn't have been easy to put this together on such short notice.

"You did good, girlfriend." Cheryl, accompanied by Seth, approached me.

"So did you. I feel like Cinderella in this gown."

"It's one of your grandmother's." She smiled. "Who knows how old it is. That woman must have kept every gown from the 1920s."

I laughed. "She isn't *that* old."

Cheryl waved away my comment. "You get my meaning. The woman hoards clothes. Now, let's mingle and see whether anyone saw something they didn't know they saw the night Donald died."

"Let me handle this," Seth said.

"Nope. These old men will talk to me. You stay in the background and look handsome." She tugged the neckline of her gown a little lower and sailed away.

Seth chuckled and grabbed a plate. "Can I get my food and then do as Cheryl said? I think it wise for me to be as invisible as possible."

"Definitely. You can see everything from the shadows by those hedges." I pointed to our right. "I'll mingle, too, and play the sad jilted ex-love."

"Have you considered getting a private investigator's license?" He moved away.

Hmm. Would I have to go to school? Take a test? Learn to shoot a gun? I was kind of happy just being a nosy nobody.

"You're the most beautiful woman I've ever seen." Heath wrapped his arms around my waist from the back and nuzzled my neck.

Flushed, I turned in his arms. "You'll mess up my hair and makeup, but go ahead and kiss me."

He obliged, leaving me warmer than the heaters could do. When he pulled back, he asked, "What's Seth doing in the bushes?"

"Spying on the residents and Cheryl who is wearing a very low cut gown in order to get the old men to tell their secrets." I led him to the entrance of the courtyard. "Greet the guests with me."

We smiled as one-by-one the residents of Shady Acres entered the courtyard. If one more of them said how sorry they were for my loss, I was going to scream.

"I need to talk to you," Leroy said, stopping in front of me.

"About the night Donald was murdered?" I lowered my voice.

He nodded. "Meet me at the far corner once you've finished saying hello to all these…nosy people."

I nodded and squeezed Heath's hand. "I knew he could help us. The man doesn't miss a thing."

"Make sure Seth is close enough to hear what Leroy says. I'll go tell him to find a hiding place over there."

Keeping a smile plastered on my face, I couldn't help but wonder where Alice was. As manager, it was her job to greet folks at our events. The last time she failed to show almost resulted in her death. I pulled my cell phone from a hidden pocket in my stole and texted her.

Where are you?

Snooping. Be right there.

Snooping what?

I said I'll be right there. Geez.

Fine. I put my phone away and kept my gaze trained on the path leading to the main building. Sure enough, Alice trotted toward me.

Grabbing my arm, she pulled me to the side. "Sorry

I ditched you, but once I arrived here, I realized I didn't have my list." She handed me a folded sheet of paper. "The people who didn't show up for supper the other night."

"Thanks. Can you take over as hostess now? I need to talk to someone." Without waiting for her answer, I hurried to where Leroy waited.

He grabbed my arm and pulled me into the bushes where we collided with Seth. Leroy exhaled sharply. "I should have known the cops would be here."

"You have something to say you don't want me to hear?" Seth crossed his arms.

"I don't like people. Only Shelby."

"Thanks, Leroy. I like you, too." I smiled.

"Stop with the niceties. What do you want to tell her?" Seth's eyes glittered.

"Fine. I was taking my nightly stroll the night that man was killed. He was arguing with a woman. A woman in a black cloak. Very theatrical, don't you think?" Leroy wiggled his eyebrows.

"Get on with it," Seth ordered.

"Whatever you say, boss. So, hearing the raised voices, I crept closer," he lowered his voice. "The woman said she was tired of playing second fiddle. That he needed to stop fooling around and choose already. He begged her to be reasonable. Before I knew what was happening, she'd picked up a big rock and bashed him in the head with it." He glanced at Seth. "I bet that isn't common knowledge, is it? That he was hit in the head?"

Seth shook his head.

"Then, she grabbed a string of lights from one of the bushes and strangled him."

"Did you get a look at her face?" Seth asked.

"No, but just as I stepped on a twig, which cracked like a firecracker, she ran off. Her hood fell revealing a very lovely head covered with blond hair."

4

"Blond?" Cheryl's eyebrows rose. "Every woman Donald had an affair with is blond. His fiancé is blond. There's speculation as to whether she's a true blond, but...well, you get the idea."

"Then our suspect list got knocked down to four." Of course, more tended to come along as an investigation got underway, but at least we had a place to start.

Seth shook Leroy's hand. "You've given us our best lead. Thank you for your help." Then, he turned to Cheryl. "Is it at all possible for me to work without you showing up?"

She grinned. "No. I'm as nosy as Shelby."

With a groan, he marched down the pathway and back to the party.

"What did you two do to Seth?" Heath asked when we followed. "He tossed back a tumbler of whiskey like it was water."

"I think he's realizing he can't win against us," I said, smiling.

"Poor guy." Heath put an arm around my shoulder. "Want to dance? Bob brought his record player and band music and crooner vinyls."

"That sounds lovely."

He swung me onto the dance floor to the tune of Frank Sinatra. I breathed deep of his cologne, closed my eyes, and leaned my head on his chest. It surprised me how safe I felt with Heath after only a few months. After Donald, I thought I'd never love again. I prayed Heath would be patient enough to wait until I could say the words.

After two songs, he led me to the buffet. "Let's eat. I can hear your stomach growling over the music."

"Mine or yours?" I grabbed a plate and handed him one.

"Okay, mine." He grinned and grabbed a slice of salmon with mango salsa. "I think this is the best meal the chef has put together yet. Great music, beautiful atmosphere, good food, and a gorgeous date. What more could a man ask for?"

"Not to be plagued by crazy women?" I pointed to where a beautiful blond woman in black leggings and a baggy sweatshirt stood next to the fountain.

She put her fingers to her lips and blew a piercing whistle until everyone else stopped and looked her way. "I want to talk to Shelby Hart."

"That's me." I handed my plate to Heath, then

stepped forward.

Cheryl grabbed my arm. "I'm coming with you. That's Sasha, and she's nuts."

I sure wished I could have one night with Heath that wasn't shadowed by drama or death. With my heart in my throat, I approached the crazy-eyed woman. "Let's step over here where we can talk in private." I led her to the other side of the fountain. Heath and Seth could still see us, but we weren't in full view for all the gawkers.

Sasha's brown eyes were red-rimmed. Smudged mascara gave them a hollowed out look. Even distraught, the woman was drop dead gorgeous. "You were once engaged to my Donald, right?"

I nodded. "But, he ditched me on our wedding day for someone else."

"Who? I demand to know." She gripped my arm and gave me a shake.

"Hands off, lady." Cheryl pushed her back.

"What's the Amazon going to do about it?" Sasha glared. "I want to speak to every cheating, wanton, woman that kept my Donald from giving me his whole heart."

Was this woman for real? "Do you have proof he cheated on you?"

She threw a cell phone at me. "It's full of women's phone numbers!"

"Look, Sasha. You're upset. Go home and sleep it off. Why dwell on the bad? The man you love is dead."

I picked up the phone from where it had fallen next to

the path and returned it to her. "Wait a few days and talk to these women reasonably. I'm sure you'll all have a lot of things to say to each other."

She tilted her head. "Wasn't he with you on the day he died?"

"Yes, but only to ask me to give back the jewelry he gave me so he could give it to you. I'm sorry to tell you I sold it all."

"He really meant nothing else to you?"

"I promise. Do you need someone to give you a ride home?"

She shook her head. "I haven't been drinking, just crying." She turned and shuffled down the walkway.

"I told you she was nuts." Cheryl crossed her arms.

"She's grieving. Let her be." I returned to Heath and my food. "Everything is fine." Not really. More than one woman would shed tears over Donald, myself included.

"Did she tell you anything I need to know?" Seth asked.

"No." I sat at one of the bistro-style tables. "You should probably keep an eye on the women on that list I gave you, though. Sasha plans on confronting each of them. She might be a bit unstable."

"Is she fine with you?" Heath sat next to me.

"I think so." I cut into my salmon. My appetite wasn't there, but I refused to let good food go to waste because a stranger showed up at a party. Still, my heart ached for her. I could, in a sense, empathize with her.

By the time the ball broke up at midnight, I was as exhausted mentally as I was physically. Back at my cottage, I hung up Grandma's dress and crawled into bed without putting on my pajamas. I lay on my back, tears trickling down my cheeks, and stared through the dark at the ceiling. Tonight, and tonight only, I would shed tears for what could have been. In the morning, whatever I once felt for Donald would be put away and the search for his killer would start in earnest.

~

The next morning I chose a simple breakfast of coffee and toast with Cheryl for company. "Who should we start questioning first?"

"I have a map." She spread a map of the city on the table. "We'll start with the closest and work away or vice versa. I'm leaving Sasha on the list. We need to talk to her away from here. She might know something if asked the right questions."

"Any idea who Seth is starting with?" I leaned over the map.

"I wish. We could start opposite him and get the facts first."

I glanced up. "We're helping, not impeding."

"Yeah, right." She grinned and sipped her coffee. "We need to get a move on if we want to sneak out without your grandmother."

"True." I stood and grabbed my purse. "We'll go the long way to the parking lot. Maybe she won't see us." I loved the woman, but sometimes she was more trouble than help. Especially during an interview of a suspect.

Like fugitives, we bolted out the door and around my garden shed to the parking lot. Grandma leaned against my Volkswagon, arms and ankles crossed.

"I was beginning to think you two ditched me."

"We didn't tell you when we were leaving." I pressed the car fob to unlock the doors. "Let me and Cheryl do the talking."

"Of course. I always sit and keep my mouth shut. I'm there to observe and notice." She slid into the back seat.

I rolled my eyes and climbed into the driver's seat. "I'm serious, Grandma. Don't mess this up or we won't bring you again."

"I have no idea what you're talking about."

I inserted the key and drove to the freeway. "Punch the first address into your GPS, Cheryl. You're the one guiding us."

"Gotcha."

We drove to the home of April Marks, a first grade teacher at Cooper Elementary. I remembered her from my days of teaching. A small, petite, curvy blond with an infectious smile. Don't let her looks deceive you, though. The woman could be as mean as a badger when provoked.

We stopped in front of a bungalow style home painted a cheery yellow with a white door and shutters. "Ugh," Cheryl said, "the house is as cute as she is."

"Stop it." I climbed out and headed for the front door, leaving the others to follow. We had four women to visit that day and couldn't waste any time. I rang the doorbell and stepped back to wait.

Within a few minutes, a sleepy April answered the door. "Shelby? What in the world are you doing here?"

"I'd like to talk, if that's all right."

She narrowed her eyes. "Is this about Donald? I may have been the one who broke up your wedding, but he left me for someone else."

Well, that was one question answered. "It's not about that. May we come in?"

She peered around me at the other two. "I don't like Cheryl. She scares me."

"She'll be on her best behavior. Please."

"All right." She opened the door and ushered us inside. "At least you aren't sending me text after text like his latest fiancé. That woman doesn't give up."

I glanced around the tropical themed room. "What does she want?"

"The same thing you do. To talk." She motioned for us to sit on the wicker sofa. "What do you want to ask me?"

"When was the last time you spoke to Donald?"

"At work on the day he died." She lowered her head. "He wanted back a necklace he had given me. I told him I'd give it to him the next day, but it was too late."

So, he was gathering up all of his gifts for Sasha.

Interesting. "Did you argue?"

"No."

Cheryl snorted. "Everyone heard you screeching about him being an Indian giver. Not politically correct, by the way."

"Well, he was. He gave me that necklace. Donald was a horrible lying cheat and he got what he deserved, God rest his soul. Would y'all like some tea?"

"We would not." Grandma twisted her lips between her fingers, trying desperately to hold back her words…and failed. "That was a mean and cruel thing to say about a dead man. A man killed in a vicious, twisted way. Maybe you killed him."

"Me?" April put a hand to her chest. "The man was a foot taller than me."

"He was found near a bench," I added. "Maybe you stood on that bench and wrapped the lights around his neck."

"Oh, please. You should be a fiction writer, Shelby." She crossed her legs. "Regardless of what I said, I loved Donald. We all did. Every stupid woman that got involved with him."

"One of you killed him," I said, taking note of the crossing and now uncrossing of her legs.

"It wasn't me. So, if you're going to ask me the same questions over and over, you should leave. I have lesson plans to make."

"Do you own a black cloak?" Cheryl asked.

"Yes." April frowned. "Why?"

"Just wondering." She stood. "We're done here. Oh, and the police will be by soon to ask you more questions. If you think of anything you forgot to tell us, here's my number." She scribbled it on the back of an envelope from the coffee table.

When she went to hand it to April, I caught side of something written on the other side. The address to Shady Acres. "Have you ever been to the place Donald was killed?"

"That place full of old people? No."

"Then why do you have the address written down?"

"Oh, that. Because, well, I'm looking for a place to put my grandmother."

"You don't put grandparents somewhere, Miss," Grandma said, scowling. "You help us. My money is on you, little girl. I'll prove it, too."

"Whatever." April tossed her head. "You can go now. I'm getting upset."

I sighed and glared at Grandma, before forcing a smile on April. "Thank you. Please do call if you think of anything. I'd like to find out what happened to Donald."

"Why?" Bright spots of red glowed on her cheeks. "The world is rid of one more philanderer. You ought to give flowers to the killer."

5

"She's a definite suspect," Cheryl said as we headed back to my car.

I nodded, figuring the other women on our list would dislike Donald as much as April. "Who's next?"

"Michelle Boudreau. She's…exotic looking. She's new to the school." Cheryl settled back in her seat. "You never had to worry about Donald with me."

"Because you're my best friend, right?" I cut her a sideways glance. "Or, are you comparing yourself to these women?"

"Both."

"Seriously? You're tall, blond, beautiful, and have majestic boobs. Of course Donald cast you several lustful glances." I'd elbowed him a few times for them.

She grinned. "Really?"

"Really. I'm the one who doesn't the fit the profile." Surprisingly, that no longer bothered me very much.

"Nope. You're the type every man wants to take home to Mom. Gorgeous, stylish, and well-mannered. No wonder Heath fell fast and hard."

"He did, didn't he?" I smiled and parked in front of a two-story Victorian. How could a teacher afford a place like this?

As if she could read my mind "Cheryl said, "There's speculation Michelle has a *night* job." She made finger quotes. "But no one can prove it. Another rumor is that she inherited."

I shrugged and opened the car door. How she came about her money was none of our business. "Let's get this over with."

I walked up the porch steps and rang the doorbell next to the navy blue door. I'd almost given her up as to not being home when the door opened and I stared into a pair of almond shaped, almost black, eyes. Even without makeup Michelle could grace the cover of Cosmo.

"If you're selling, I'm not buying."

"I'm not. My name is—"

She looked past me to Cheryl. "If I would have seen you, I wouldn't have answered the door."

Cheryl laughed. "Why do you think I hid behind the pillar?"

"Focus," I hissed. "Michelle, I used to be engaged to Donald Trayer and—"

Her lips curled, "So, you're the one who couldn't hold onto her man." She peered around me at Grandma who said she would stay outside and stand guard. From whom, I had no idea, but it left me free to question people without her interfering.

I bit back a groan. "Yes, that would be me. May we ask you a few questions?" Five minutes after meeting her and I despised the woman.

"Sure, I'm not doing anything. I'll tell you whatever you want to know about the weasel." She stepped aside and ushered us into a home that either Michelle was very talented in home décor, or she had hired an interior designer.

A small Christmas tree sat on top of an end table. All the bulbs and lights were white and silver. Even the tree skirt sported silver stars. The tree was the only tribute to Christmas I saw. The rest of the furniture was done in muted tones of salmon and sand color. Very modern.

"Want a coke?" Michelle raised her eyebrows.

We shook our heads. "No, just a few questions and we'll be out of your hair," I said.

"Have a seat."

We both perched on the edge of the sofa.

"Have the police been by yet?" I asked, trying to get comfortable on the hard cushion.

"Last night a good looking one came by. Unfortunately, he had the personality of a porcupine."

Cheryl bristled next to me.

I put a hand on her leg to settle her. "Since I knew Donald, I'm trying to find out a bit of how he died.

Would you mind telling me where you were on the night he was killed?"

"Having dinner with a man. No, I cannot give you his name. Our relationship is complicated."

He was married, she meant. I'd bet my car. "Any idea who might have killed him?"

She studied her sculpted nails. "Any female, I reckon. Oh, sure, we all fell for him at first, but then he showed his true colors. You should know that better than anyone." She speared me with a glance. "Maybe you killed him. You had a strong enough motive. Or, you had your giant freak here do the deed. I doubt you were strong enough, come to think of it."

"I'm stronger than I look." We were getting nowhere fast.

She gave a sly smile. "The other castoffs have formed a club. The Second Mistress Club. Not very original, I know, but you're welcome to join. We're meeting Friday night at Betty's Bar. Seven o'clock. That wimpy Sasha will be there, too. I have no idea why April invited her, but it's too late now. You can do your detecting then while we're all in one place. Cheryl is *not* invited."

I took that as a dismissal and stood. "I guess that's all. Thank you for your time."

"No problem. Good luck." She laughed, letting us see ourselves out.

"You aren't seriously thinking about going to their little get together are you?" Cheryl asked the moment we stepped outside. "You'll be a mouse among cats."

"I think I've proven I can handle myself in tough situations." I slid back into the driver's seat. "Jeanna next, right?"

I remembered her from my teaching days. A little older, but a whole lot looser than the other women. At least outwardly. Still, we'd gotten along all right for a while. Then, she'd stopped talking to me altogether.

"She lives in Boonesville Vista Resort. In other words, the trailer park."

"Has she always lived there?" The woman was pretty and athletic, but I couldn't see Donald interested in her. He seemed too big of a snob to date someone in a trailer park.

"No, she went bankrupt a few months ago. Lost everything. If you want to meet someone who really hates Donald, it's her." Cheryl shook her head. "Maybe you can find out why. She doesn't like you much either. Did you know you're the one Donald left her for?"

I snapped around to look at her. "Then why are we visiting her?"

"Because, the rumor mill has it that he got back with her right after leaving Michelle. It was Jeanna, you, Michelle, Jeanna, April, and then Sasha. I never could figure out why he dated Jeanna twice."

I raised my eyebrows. A very good point. I pulled in the entrance of the trailer park and parked beside a single wide near the back.

Rust dotted the corners of Jeanna's home. No grass

or flowers grew anywhere close by. I actually felt sorry for her demise, now that I knew why she didn't like me. Still, we had something in common. Maybe I could use that to get her to cooperate.

I glanced in the rearview mirror as a vehicle pulled behind us. "Uh-oh. Seth is here."

He got out of his squad car and knocked on my window.

With a sigh, I rolled it down. "Hey."

"What are you doing here?"

"Looking for Jeanna." I hated the mirrored sunglasses he wore.

"Questioning her?"

"Don't ask questions you don't want the answer to," Cheryl said. "You know exactly what we're doing. Besides, Shelby got invited to a club these women belong to. We're only looking to get more information about that before she commits."

Oh, good thinking. I smiled. "Considering one of these women might be a murderer, it's wise, don't you think?"

His face gave away no sign of what he thought or felt. After an interminable long few seconds, he gave a curt nod. "Getting inside like that might actually help us."

"So, can we go in now?"

"She isn't home. Either that, or she isn't answering the door."

"She won't while you're parked there either,"

Cheryl said. "Go away. We'll see you back at Shady Acres in an hour. Shelby, park in front of a different trailer and we'll wait."

I eased forward the moment Seth stepped back. "You sure do know how to handle him."

"He likes when a woman takes charge."

"Sure he does." I laughed.

"Well, not really, but we'll argue a little when we get together, and then we'll make up. That's why I boss him around. The making up is great." She wiggled her eyebrows.

"Eew." I kept an eye on my rearview mirror, hoping Jeanna would make an appearance soon.

Half an hour later, a Toyota truck that had seen better days pulled under the awning of trailer number eleven. "Text Seth and tell him we'll be late." I shoved open my door and hurried toward Jeanna, followed by a texting Cheryl, and a suspiciously silent Grandma. Cheryl ran into me, almost knocking me off my feet, when I stopped. I glared over my shoulder.

"Sorry," she mumbled.

"Come on in," Jeanna said, frowning. "Michelle told me you were making the rounds."

There went the element of surprise. We followed her into a worn, but immaculate mobile home.

"It isn't much, but it's home. Sit. I've fresh lemonade." Without waiting for consent, she poured four glasses and handed us each one before sitting across from us. "No, I did not kill Donald. Am I sad he's dead? Absolutely not. Where was I on that wonderful evening? Here, watching TV and doing lesson plans. No alibi." She smiled over the rim of her glass. Her eyes cold and hard.

"You can see what I've fallen, to. Donald took all the gifts he had once bought me and given them to you, dear, sweet Shelby." She tilted her head. "Have they been passed on to another?"

"I sold them. He did come for them on the day he died."

She laughed without mirth. "That is priceless. Poor, financially broke, Donald. Did you know his money was gone? Flittered away like butterflies on butterflies. Now, I'm living in this dump and he's relaxing in the morgue."

"Not exactly relaxing." I frowned and sat my untouched drink on the coffee table. I wasn't thirsty enough to drink anything this crazy woman handed me. "Someone killed him."

She cocked her head. "And you want to know if it was me." She exhaled heavily. "If only I'd thought of it. What restitution!"

"It wouldn't have brought you money."

Her eyes widened. "No? I guess you haven't heard. Dear Donald left money to all of us in his will. Even you. Once his assets are liquidated, we'll each have a hundred thousand dollars."

"You said he was broke."

"He is broke, cash wise. Everything is tied up in

real estate. He may have been the principal of an elementary school, but his parents were loaded, until Donald got his hands on the family fortune. All that's left to do now, is for his lawyer to sell off everything." She smiled. "Any plans for your share?"

"You're getting money, Shelby." Grandma clutched my hand.

I didn't want a cent of it. "Charity, I guess."

"Still the sweet little Shelby despite everything you've been through. How quaint. If only there were more of you in the world."

"We didn't come here so you could belittle Shelby," Cheryl said, setting her glass down with a thunk. "We came to catch a killer. My eye is on you."

"Oh, I'm so scared."

"We're all victims here, Jeanna," I said, standing. "You aren't the only one Donald hurt. Instead of bashing each other, we should work together to find out who killed him."

"You go right ahead. You seem to have a knack for that sort of thing. Me? Well, I'll sit back and wait to get my share of his money. It's small compensation for the humiliation, but it's something." She tossed her long blond ponytail over her shoulder. "I was the first. That makes it that much more degrading."

I stared at the broken woman in front of me for a minute, taking note of the flicker of pain in her eyes, then turned to leave. "I'm sorry for your loss. It's obvious you still care a great deal for him."

A long line of cursing followed us out to the car.

"Wow. That woman is definitely capable of murder." Grandma cast a look over the roof of the car. "We're lucky she didn't poison our drinks."

"You drank the lemonade?" My mouth dropped. After all the poisonings during the last murder she would take something from a suspect?

"Sure." She winked and got in the car. "It was good."

6

The next morning, after several hours of raking leaves, I headed for my favorite thinking spot in the maze. It hadn't always been my favorite. Not when a killer had chased me through the tall hedges a few months back. But, that was behind me now and I enjoyed the quiet and beauty of the gazebo in the center.

After a day spent with desperately unhappy women, I needed solitude. Plus, I knew Seth would be hunting for me to see whether I had learned something about Donald's death that he hadn't.

I lay on my back on the wooden bench and stared up through the slats toward the late afternoon sky. In the distance, the bell signaling supper rang. I'd grab something in my cottage. The peace of my surroundings outweighed the need to eat.

I closed my eyes and let my mind sift through the day's events. Not one of the women Cheryl and I had visited seemed to hold a smidgeon of fondness for

Donald. Except...Jeanna. Unless I was wrong, she still loved him despite his faults. Did she love him enough to kill him? Perhaps. They were all equal suspects in my book.

A heavy footfall sounded to my right. A twig snapped.

I bolted to a sitting position and peered down the darkening paths. Biting back the urge to say "hello" as so many stupid heroines did in horror movies, I leaped from the gazebo and raced back toward the cottages.

"Whoa." Heath grabbed me and pulled me to a stop.

I smacked his chest. "You scared me half to death."

He gave a crooked smile. "What are you doing out here alone close to dark? After checking your cottage, I knew I'd find you here."

"Worried?"

"Yes." He took my hand. "After the last few months, I don't take any chances with you. Seth is fit to be tied, convinced you've been killed and your body hidden because you don't know when to mind your own business."

As we walked home, our entwined hands swung back and forth. "I've been avoiding him, trying to wrap my head around the women I spoke to today. So much hate flowed through the day."

"Let's go to the movies so you can get away from it all." Heath squeezed my hand.

"A date?"

"Yeah." He smiled. "Maybe dinner, too, since you

skipped."

"That sounds wonderful."

We grabbed burgers, then went to the drive in to watch an action flick. We even managed to squeeze in some kissing. By the time I fell into bed after midnight, nothing filled my mind but how blessed I was to have a man like Heath by my side.

A loud knocking on the door woke me the next morning. I shuffled to the door and opened it to find a scowling Seth on my doorstep.

"I get the feeling you're avoiding me," he said. "I brought coffee." He held a tray containing three cups.

"Is Cheryl here?"

"Sleeping." I waved for him to come in.

"No, I'm awake." She pulled her hair back into a ponytail as she entered the living room. "Ah, a man after my own heart."

After grilling us about where we were last night, me out with Heath, and Cheryl shopping with Mom, Seth pulled out his ever-present notepad. "Now, what did you learn yesterday from our suspects?"

"They all hated Donald," Cheryl said with a grin. "And they've formed a club."

"I already know that."

"That's pretty much it," I added. "Until the club meeting, I doubt I'll learn anything new. Although, I suspect Jeanna still has feelings for the man."

"Why do you say that?"

"It's just a feeling." I sipped my coffee. "I think any

one of them are capable of murder if provoked enough."

"Have the meeting here. I want to eavesdrop through the window."

I looked at him as if he'd grown another head. "Not the first time I'm invited, Seth. Maybe the next time. I'm not thrilled to have any of them know where I live."

"It wouldn't be hard for them to find out. Your name is on the mailbox."

True. I sighed and focused on caffeine.

"We'll tell you everything we find out." Cheryl patted his hand.

"You weren't invited." I looked up. "I can't attend the first meeting with you in tow when one of the women definitely doesn't like you. Besides, the club is for Donald rejects."

"Sasha is going." She frowned. "She wasn't a reject. I can always say we dated. No one would know otherwise. We could have been discreet."

"I agree with Cheryl," Seth said. "I don't like you going into the lion's den alone."

I shook my head. "I go alone or not at all."

"Fine," they said in unison.

I went to my room and quickly tugged on a pair of faded jeans and a long sleeved blue flannel shirt before rejoining the others.

"Now that that's settled, let's go eat." I stood and stared at them until they followed.

Breakfast was uneventful, thankfully. Full of egg

and bacon croissant, I went outside and climbed into my golf cart to make my rounds around the grounds. The fountain beckoned like a beacon.

The early morning sun glinted off the water pouring from the stone maiden's urn. I parked and slid out. No crime scene tape fluttered around my poinsettias, it had been taken down before the Winter Ball. One of the red flowered plants didn't take to the dirt like the others. I knelt to repack the dirt around its roots, hoping an extra dose of vitamins later would revive the plant.

As I planted my palms on my knees to stand, I noticed something shiny partially under a rock I'd dislodged with my foot. A pearl button. I used a fallen petal to pick it up. Definitely a button off a piece of woman's clothing. A clue? I hoped so, although I knew the chances of finding the item the button had fallen from would be near impossible. Still, the owner might have replaced the button and wear the item again. I slipped the button in my pocket and climbed back into my cart.

"Shelby!"

I turned to see Alice tottering toward me. "You need to stop wearing heels." I clamped a hand over my mouth. It was time someone told her, but I wasn't sure it should be me.

"Why?" She planted her fists on her hips. "They make my legs look nice."

"But…you aren't very…graceful in them." I wanted to say those words since the moment I met her.

She narrowed her eyes. "Of course, I am. I'm a lady."

"Maybe you should wear kitten heels instead of stilettos." I smiled. "Can I do something for you?"

"Rather than insult me, you mean? Yes. I need a ride to the maze."

"Hop in. What's going on in the maze?"

"I really liked the last time you had a party there and thought we could do a magical Christmas treasure hunt. Your ideas are starting to get a little mundane. Our events need livening up."

Gee, thanks. "I'm always open to suggestions. If we did our events once a month instead of every weekend, they'd be better."

"That might not be a bad idea since all units are now rented. Let's do this last Christmas one and we'll go month-to-month. I want to hide gifts around the maze for people to find. It'll be expensive, but fun, don't you think? I like it much better than a simple gift exchange. Of course, we'll have consolation prizes."

Of course. We wouldn't want anyone to feel left out. "Instead of a treasure hunt, which we've done, why not a Christmas carnival with booth games? We could still use the maze as one of the games."

"That's an excellent idea. Why, we could have a kissing booth. The old ladies would pay a pretty penny to kiss Heath." She cut me a sideways glance. "I'll let him know it was your idea."

"That particular game wasn't." I increased our

speed to where she had to grab the handle bar above her head. "If you're going to charge for the games, you need to have a reason. What will the funds be used for?"

"Purchasing gifts for under-privileged children."

That was an idea I could get behind. "Even easier would be a Christmas tree in the dining hall with the names of these children and what they need. Then, we could have a gift-wrapping party with refreshments."

"You just don't want a bunch of women kissing Heath."

True, no matter how old they were. "I'm thinking of the cost."

She sat silent for a few minutes. "Turn around. I like that idea better."

I grinned and headed toward the main building. The ugly green dragon of jealousy slid back into its burrow. I knew I shouldn't be worried about women over the age of sixty purchasing a kiss from my boyfriend, but with all the hatefulness going around, I couldn't help feeling that way. In a few weeks, I might think differently. Maybe in the spring we could do the carnival. Something like that would take a lot of planning.

I dropped Alice off and headed for the greenhouse. Inside, I checked the herbs which would no longer grow outside because of the cooling temperatures and hung some upside down to dry. Others, I placed on a towel and carried to the kitchen for Joyce to use in her cooking.

"Good morning," I sang as I entered.

"What's so good about it?" Joyce slammed a pot on the stove. "My new helper scorched the potato soup I was preparing for lunch."

"Sandwiches?"

"I suppose." She sighed. "Why is good help so hard to find?"

"I have no idea." I gave her what I hoped was a reassuring smile. "Where are Lori and Steve?"

"Inventoring the pantry. Even they can't mess that up, I hope." She wiped her hands on her apron. "Oh, nice. Fresh herbs." She took them from me and placed them on the cutting board. "I'll make baked chicken with a pesto sauce for supper. You're a good gardener, Shelby."

"Thank you. Has anyone said otherwise?"

She shrugged. "Just murmurings about how death follows you. A bunch of hogwash. Don't worry your head."

I leaned against the counter. "It does seem to follow me, though. Hardly a month goes by without someone dying by nefarious means."

"It's a curse." She waved a knife at me. "It has nothing to do with you. It's this place. Someone built a wonderful community, filled it with people from all walks of life, and voila! Murder and mayhem. You do a good job catching the bad guys, even if you do get confused sometimes. I still can't believe you thought I was poisoning people."

"I am sorry about that."

She waved away my comment. "It did make sense. I had the means, if not the motive. You be careful, Shelby Hart. You won't always be lucky. You need God on your side."

"I didn't know you were a Christian."

"Well, there's a lot people don't know about me on account of my bad temper. Think about it, Shelby, and keep your nose where it belongs."

"Thanks. I'll do my best." I'd been told that more times than I could count, yet couldn't seem to tear myself away from a new mystery.

"Sorry to hear about your ex."

"Thank you, but we were over a while ago."

"I guess you're on the hunt again, right?"

I nodded.

"I'll be praying, and I'll get the prayer chain at church active, too. God's word says He looks out for the foolish. Only He knows why. Don't be a fool and press your luck."

7

I smoothed the skirt of the simple sheath dress I wore, squared my shoulders, and entered the reserved room at the restaurant. Four heads turned to stare.

"You came," Michelle said. "I wasn't sure you would."

"I'm never one to turn down a party." I forced a smile and took the vacant seat next to Jeanna. "Besides, we all have something in common."

"Not me." Sasha sniffed and examined her nails. Several scratches marred her right hand. "I wasn't ditched. Death took Donald from me, not another woman."

"You took him from me!" April slammed her glass down. "Or was it Jeanna? I can't remember."

"Let's not squabble." Jeanna sighed. "We're here in remembrance."

"I thought we were here to bash a dead guy." Michelle smirked.

"Why are we here, exactly?" I picked up the menu.

"Camaraderie," April said. "Isn't that a hoot? Except for Jeanna and Sasha, the rest of us can't stand the guy."

"But, we all used to love him," I added. The words tasted bitter in my throat. But, if I wanted to get the other ladies to talk freely, I'd have to encourage them. I really hoped the evening wasn't a waste of time and one of them moved up the suspect ladder.

The waitress arrived to take our order. After the others all ordered salads, I changed my mind from chicken fried steak with gravy to a salad. Groaning inwardly, I handed over my menu.

"You don't fit," Sasha said, tilting her head. "You aren't a blond. What did Donald see in you? You're tiny, skinny, and have uncontrollable hair."

I shrugged. "I was told I was the type he wanted to take home to his mother." God, forgive me, but I enjoyed the stunned expressions on their faces. These women put cattiness to a whole new level. I refused to allow them to get to me.

"The kitten has claws," Michelle said, clapping.

Sasha grabbed her purse. "I cannot believe I'm sitting here listening to this. Of course, Donald loved me. We were engaged!" She waved around her ring.

"Doesn't mean anything, toots." Michelle seemed to be enjoying herself. "He was once engaged to Shelby, too. I guarantee he had someone else on the side while you wore his ring."

Sasha narrowed her eyes. "I'll kill her. Who is she?"

"I have no idea. I'm only speculating."

Interesting. Other than anger, Sasha didn't look surprised that Donald may have had another woman besides her. I decided to pay a little more attention to the grieving fiancé. "What happened to your hand, Sasha?"

"Rose bush. That's a passion."

Hmm. I noticed she didn't say her passion. I'd recently read somewhere that if a person doesn't 'own' their words with me, my, or I, they're most likely lying. "As a gardener, I know firsthand how dangerous plants can be. I hope you cleaned them well. They might scar." Fingernails were worse than thorns any time.

"I wish I would have killed him," Jeanna whispered. She gasped and straightened, then glanced around as if to determine whether anyone heard.

I pretended not to. Instead, I suddenly found the contents of my purse very interesting.

"What are you rummaging for?" Michelle leaned across the table.

"Lipstick." I pulled out a tube that had definitely seen better days.

She laughed. "You're a strange one, Shelby Hart. I wish we could be friends. We'd have a lot of fun."

I almost asked why we couldn't be friends, but the food arrived. All the skinny women dug into their salads like they hadn't eaten in a week. Myself included.

Occasionally, someone would say something nasty about the deceased or each other, but for the most part the get-together was congenial. I didn't learn a thing other than the fact that Sasha was a liar about how she hurt her hand. I needed to get the women at the scene of the crime.

"Shady Acres is having a gift-wrapping party for under-privileged children. Interested?" I peered over the rim of my water glass.

They glanced at each other, then nodded.

"I believe in giving," Michelle said. "We're all teachers and love children. Count us in. Maybe I'll meet myself a sugar daddy who will die and leave me his money."

I frowned. If they were going to prey on my friends, I would uninvite them. "This is a party and charitable event, not a nightclub."

"Lighten up. Just making conversation." Michelle tossed her napkin next to her plate and stood. "Well, it's not been fun, and I have things to do. Ciao." She slung her red purse over her shoulder and left.

That was our clue. The rest of us followed soon after.

I sat in my car and watched as the other women climbed into theirs. What a waste of time and unpleasant gathering. A knock on my window interrupted me.

"I don't think anyone told you," Sasha said after I

rolled down my window. "Donald's funeral is tomorrow at ten a.m." She sighed and stepped back.

I nodded and started my car. This was not something I wanted to do alone. Heath would go with me for moral support without hesitation. But was it a good thing to have my current boyfriend attend the funeral of my ex?

~

"Of course, I'll go with you," Heath said in my cottage later. "I'm here for you whenever you need me."

I planted a kiss on his cheek. "You're the best. Have I told you that?"

"Not recently." He gave me a crooked smile. "How did your get-together go?"

"It was awful. To die with so many people hating you…I can't imagine."

Seth knocked, then entered. I really needed to get in the habit of locking my door.

"What did you learn?" He sat in the chair across from us.

Cheryl came down the hall and perched on the arm.

"Hello, to you, too. I didn't learn anything more than that Sasha has suspicious scratches on her right hand. She said it was from a rose bush."

He jotted down what I had said. "That's it?"

"Sorry. The funeral is tomorrow. Every one of those women are bound to be there. Oh, and I invited them to the gift wrapping party for underprivileged children. I thought they should visit the scene of the crime. The killer is bound to trip herself up."

"Crimes of passion are hard to solve," he said. "I'm not sure this was pre-meditated."

I thought for a moment. "You think the killer saw Donald talking to me and lost her mind?"

"Yes." He settled back in the chair. "I've been thinking about this case, a lot, and talking to Ted, which means your grandmother. She reminded me of the saying 'hell hath no fury like a woman scorned'. Plus, Donald was murdered with a string of Christmas lights. The killer didn't come prepared. They used what was at hand."

I agreed. The murder didn't seem planned. Since it had occurred on the same day Donald had visited requesting back his gifts, I was of the same mind as Seth. The killer had seen Donald speaking with me and acted in anger and rejection.

Heath squeezed my hand. "It wasn't your fault."

He always knew what I was thinking. I rested my head on his shoulder. "It hasn't been a very nice Christmas season so far."

"Let's change that. As soon as the funeral is over, it's all about the season, the gifts, Jesus, and family. No more murder investigating. Seth, it's all yours."

"Agreed. Shelby, you've been a big help, but this is my job. You make sure the people here are happy. That's all you need to focus on."

"All right." I was more than happy to step aside on

this one.

"Yoohoo!" Grandma and Ted waltzed into my cottage. "You young people are up late."

"Just chilling," I said, motioning for them to sit.

"I'm resigning from the case."

"Oh, pooh. I was ready to get involved."

"You can come to the funeral tomorrow. Snoop to your heart's content."

She clapped. "I love funerals."

"That isn't something you should say out loud, Grandma."

"Oh, well. I have a new dress I can wear. Do you think it'll be an open casket?"

"I'm sure it will." I gave Ted an imploring look.

"I can't do a thing with her," he said. "Ida is one of a kind." He put an arm around Grandma's shoulder.

"You're so sweet." Grandma kissed him, leaving a lip print of fuchsia on his forehead.

"I'm beat. Good night." I stood and gave Heath another kiss. "Y'all can stay and chat if you want, but I'm going to bed. Lock the door when you leave."

"I'll pick you up at nine-thirty," Heath said.

I headed to bed and dreamed of angry women teachers, poinsettias, and Christmas lights.

~

The next morning, I donned a pair of black slacks and light grey blouse. It was too cold for a dress, in my opinion. Grabbing a black trench coat from the closet, I knocked on Cheryl's door. "Ready to eat?"

"Coming." She stepped out in a navy maxi skirt and blue and black striped blouse. "I hate funerals."

"Good. You'll balance out my crazy grandmother." Huddled against a brisk wind, we rushed to the dining hall.

Alice met us at the door. "Heath will not be able to accompany you this morning. Since he did not know the deceased, I have not given him the day off. He is needed elsewhere. The kitchen sprang a huge leak and flooded my office." She raised her eyebrows as if daring me to argue.

"O...kay." I cut a sideways glance at Cheryl who made circular motions behind Alice.

"Good. He ate early and is already at work." She marched away in sensible kitten heels.

I chuckled and headed for the buffet. While she acted as if we were no longer in competition for Heath's affection, I saw the way she looked at him when she thought I wasn't. I didn't blame her. A man who looked like Chris Hemsworth would turn any woman's head. But, his outward appearance was only a bonus. It was his kindness and his heart that kept me around.

"She loves to boss you around," Cheryl said, piling a plate with eggs and bacon.

"She's the boss. That's her right." I added fruit to my already full plate.

Cheryl groaned. "You eat as much as I do and hardly weigh as much as my right leg."

"I'm small boned, and take after my grandmother who has the metabolism of a hummingbird."

"And drinks like a fish. I bet you my next paycheck that's a mimosa she's holding in her hand."

I glanced to where Grandma sat, a wineglass in hand. "I don't know what to do about her. I mean, she's...wild. I feel as if I'm the adult here."

Cheryl laughed. "You are. I hope I'm as full of life as Ida when I'm sixty something. I asked her the other day how she stayed so active. She told me wine and chocolate."

I did love my grandmother. "Help me keep her under control at the funeral. She acts more like they're parties than a memorial service."

"I'll try not to encourage her."

We made our way to the end of the buffet, grabbed our eating utensils, and headed for the table.

"Ready to catch a killer, girls?" Grandma raised her glass in a toast. "They always show up at the funeral of their victim. This could be our day."

8

Sandwiched between Grandma and Mom, with Cheryl following, I entered the main room of the funeral home. At the front, sitting on an ornate pedestal, was an oak coffin surrounded by so many floral arrangements the air reeked. I hadn't known Donald had been so popular. The room was filled to capacity. The four of us, to Grandma's consternation, had to take seats in the back.

"You were engaged to him," Grandma said. "That should allow us to sit up front. I can't see a thing from back here."

"You can hear just fine." Mom patted her knee. "Besides, the killer always sits in the back according to the movies."

"Right." Grandma settled back and grinned, then scanned the room with narrowed eyes.

I closed my eyes and prayed Grandma would behave. Prayed. Huh. Something I seemed to be doing more and more often. Maybe heading into dangerous situations on a regular basis, as I tended to do, would restore a faith I once had.

While I knew Mom believed, she never talked about it. Grandma, on the other hand, did, but all in the name of God forgiving her for her outlandish behavior on a regular basis. Still, it was a subject I needed to visit soon. I needed healing from Donald's betrayal if I was ever going to have a future with Heath.

I took a deep breath to settle my thoughts and studied those in attendance. The jilted women and grieving Sasha were in attendance, as were many others I knew from my previous job as a teacher. A few admin from other schools, and faces I didn't recognize filled the rest of the chairs. Seth, trying to look inconspicuous in a dark suit, stood in a far corner with another man, a police officer, I assumed.

No one looked out of place.

A minister approached the podium and gave a short, but stirring message on leaving a legacy. He spoke about Donald's role in the education of our youth.

Sasha broke into loud sobs toward the end and rushed to the coffin, draping herself over the body. Her behavior seemed strange to me. I hadn't gotten the impression she was over the top in love with Donald. Sure, she cared for him, but she was as angry as the rest of them.

I gave a sad smile, noticing I didn't lump myself in with the others. I'd forgiven Donald, it seemed. After all, nearly a year was a lot of time for the cracks in a heart to fill in.

"Holding up okay?" Mom leaned close.

"I'm fine." Murder had hit closer to home this time, but I would be all right.

Heath slid into the seat next to me. "I bugged Alice until she relented." He took my hand.

Tears sprang to my eyes. I did not deserve such a caring man. "Thank you."

"You would do the same for me."

I'd like to think so. But, I wasn't sure. When his ex-fiance had shown up as an interior designer for Shady Acres, I hadn't been nearly as accommodating. I wasn't sure I could have paid my respects to a woman catty enough to try and convince me Heath couldn't be trusted.

Everyone lined up to pay their respects to the deceased. When my turn came, I glanced inside the coffin, said goodbye, and apologized for not finding his killer. Then, that chapter of my life closed and I headed to a building in back where a potluck was to be served.

Still drawn together by their common bond, the jilted ladies sat at the same table. They waved my party over. Once we sat, Seth included, all seats were taken.

Michelle eyed Heath with a predatory study. "You must be Shelby's new squeeze."

"I am." He smiled. "Heath McLeroy." He offered his hand to shake.

She returned the shake, holding his hand longer than necessary. I rolled my eyes and glanced at Cheryl.

"He's not on the menu, Michelle. Neither is Seth here. He's mine." She linked her arm through Seth's.

Michelle shrugged. "There are plenty of others for me to find. Take the man standing alone. He's cute enough. Not handsome, but still attractive. Those are the most easily influenced. Like Donald. Not homely enough to be desperate, but not good looking enough to be arrogant. These men are disposable. Watch and learn."

She swung her hips in the man's direction, faked a trip, and dropped her purse, all while falling into his arms. Of course, he caught her, then knelt to gather her spilled things. She tossed us a grin over her shoulder.

"She's despicable," Grandma said. "I bet she killed Donald."

"Shh." I motioned my head to the other women, but too late.

"You think Michelle killed him?" Jeanna's eyebrows rose. "Why?"

"Didn't you hear her? Men are disposable." Grandma stood and headed for the table loaded with casseroles.

Sasha watched her leave, then turned to me. "Are y'all trying to find the killer? I mean…I've heard of your success in the past, but never guessed you'd get involved in this one."

"I'm not." I stood. "Grandma is living a fantasy. Heath?"

"Wait." Sasha held up a hand. "You seriously aren't

involved?"

"Well, I'd like to catch the person who did this, but I'm not actively looking. If I stumble across a clue, I'll turn it into the authorities." I dragged Heath to the food. "She's full of questions."

"Her fiancé was killed. Of course she's curious."

"Seems suspicious to me." I eyed all the different types of potatoes, choosing one with cheese and crushed potato chips on top. Then, I chose a fried chicken breast and a slice of cornbread. Nothing packs on the pounds like a Southern potluck.

By the time we returned to the table, Michelle was gloating. "I've got his phone number," she said. "He's very sweet."

"Try not to kill him," Jeanna muttered.

"Why would I do that?" Michelle's smile faded. "Are you insinuating I killed Donald?"

"Shelby's grandmother said it first."

"Oh, good grief. Just because I play with them then throw them away doesn't make me a killer."

Sasha cocked her head. "Weren't you upset when Donald left you?"

"Of course, but only because I do the leaving." She stared at April. "What's wrong with the little mouse at the end of the table?"

"It's a funeral!" April tossed down her napkin and dashed from the building.

"Maybe she did it," Grandma said.

"Stop speculating." Mom glared. "You're causing

problems."

Grandma crossed her arms. "There's nothing going on here. We might as well go home."

I agreed. I had a Christmas tree to decorate and children's tags to hang on the branches. "I'm ready whenever y'all are."

We clamored to our feet and made our way to the vehicles. I chose to ride with Heath, leaving Mom to drive Grandma, and Cheryl to ride with Seth. Even though I'd said I wouldn't investigate anymore, I wanted a chance to mull over the conversation at the table without Grandma's chatter.

Once Heath drove onto the highway, I said, "Who is your top suspect?"

"So, we are investigating?"

"No, just discussing."

"Michelle. She's a piranha. But then, quiet April might have. Still waters run deep, they say. Of course, Sasha has a temper simmering under that cool exterior. Then, Jeanna was wronged twice, right? So, yeah, I have no idea."

I laughed. "You're no help."

~

After changing into a pair of yoga pants and long tee shirt, I met the rest of my family and friends in the dining hall to set up the tree before supper. A stack of children's names and needs written on angel shaped tags, collected by Alice from a charitable organization, sat on a table. There were so many names, there wasn't much room for ornaments.

"Let's hang the tags with bows after stringing the lights. That's all we have room for. The children are the main cause anyway." I picked up the top tag. A five year old girl wanted a doll that looked real and a stroller. I tucked it into my pocket.

The next one was a three year old that wanted a Spiderman doll. I shoved that one in my pocket, too.

Heath chuckled. "If you keep doing that, there won't be any left for the rest of us."

"I wanted a boy and a girl. Now, I'm finished." I grinned and stepped back while he strung the lights. "With as many people living at Shady Acres now, I don't expect a single tag to be left on the tree."

"If there is, I'll cover them. No child deserves to not have something under the tree on Christmas morning."

"Helping children is the best idea Alice has ever had."

"It was your idea to do the tree," she said, coming up behind me. "Thank you. We'll have the wrapping party next weekend. We've plenty in the budget for paper and bows, but I'm going to ask the party store to donate as much as possible." She riffled through the names. "So many. It breaks my heart." She sighed.

"We'll give them a good Christmas, Alice." I put a hand on her shoulder. "There are wanted toys, clothes sizes, shoe sizes, everything we need to know."

"I'll make an announcement at supper for people to be generous. You'd better get a move on. Joyce doesn't like to serve the food late."

A quick glance at the clock showed we had an hour. Plenty of time. Once the lights were on, Mom, Grandma, Seth, Heath, Ted, and I had the tags hung in ten minutes. The tree looked pretty with angels hanging everywhere, white lights twinkling and red bows.

Heath slipped an arm around my waist. "It's beginning to look a lot like Christmas," he sang.

"Silly." I stood on tiptoe and kissed him. "Know what I want for Christmas?"

"I'm dying to know."

"A night out with you, away from everyone else. We're always surrounded by my family."

His hold tightened. "I agree. That sounds wonderful. Let's make it an entire weekend. I'll book a cabin in the mountains for the weekend after Christmas."

"Heaven."

"Not to spoil the romance," Seth said, "but I thought you might want to know we got DNA back from under Donald's nails."

I pulled free of Heath's embrace. "Whose?"

"They aren't in the system. We'll be taking DNA from all the jilted lovers. We're getting close." He grinned.

Hope that we'd find the killer by Christmas leaped in my heart. Seth was going to catch the murderer, and I wasn't going to be in danger. What a wonderful holiday season!

As the residents filed into the dining hall, they made a beeline for the tree. Alice didn't have to make an announcement to guilt them into picking a name. All the names were gone before the last person sat down to eat.

Tears filled my eyes. I really did live amongst a wonderful group of people.

Bob Satchett, Mom's boyfriend, held a sprig of mistletoe over her head and kissed her. Her face turned a pretty shade of pink. I never would get used to such an unlikely pair getting together, but they were discreet. I needed to tell Mom it was okay by me. Dad had been gone a long time now. She deserved to be happy.

Ted grabbed the mistletoe and hung it over Grandma. She grabbed his face in her hands and planted a long kiss on his lips. I laughed when Seth then grabbed the plastic sprig and did the same with Cheryl.

"Our turn." Heath rushed forward.

The new kitchen help, Steve Olson, grabbed the mistletoe and sneaked a kiss from Alice. She gasped and slapped him. It didn't matter. He laughed as she stomped her way to her office.

Before I knew it, that little sprig had made its way around the room, filling the room with smiles and laughter. This was Christmas. This was joy. I wanted it all year long.

"Oh, I wish it was Christmas every day," Grandma said, echoing my thoughts. "Don't you, Teddy?"

"No, it's too expensive." He grinned, giving me a

wink. He mouthed the word 'ring'.

He was buying Grandma a ring! I bounced in my seat, beyond thrilled.

My simple gift of copper insulated bottles that kept wine cool would be pale in comparison. I glanced at Heath. What could I buy for the best man on the planet?

Heath gave me that grin that melted my heart and I knew what he wanted. Three little words.

9

I pulled down a box from the top shelf of my closet and dug through the ugly Christmas sweaters given to me over the years. I chose one with a reindeer's head that had lights around his antlers. The lights ran off a small battery and blinked. The sweater was perfect for the gift-wrapping party.

Cheryl and I stepped out of our rooms at the same time, pointed at each other's sweaters, and laughed. Her's was a snowman whose stomach was stretched abnormally large over her chest.

"I know it's a little…tight, but it's the only ugly sweater I have." She tugged at the hem.

"It's ugly for sure. You're bound to win the contest."

'No, I won't. You're lit up like a deranged Christmas tree."

We entered the dining hall where earlier Heath and I had set wrapping paper, tape, scissors and bows on every table. Christmas music played from a radio. Laughter and conversation flowed like fine champagne. The Jilted Ladies, I really needed to think of them as something different, congregated around the same table. The Christmas tree, bare of all its angels, sported only lights and red bows.

I rubbed my hands together, excited to participate, and joined my family at the table we usually sat at for meals. I gave Heath a kiss and a smile. "Merry Christmas. I'm going to tell you that every day. This room is filled with the spirit."

He pulled me into a one armed hug, his other busy holding a ribbon in place for Mom. "I'll take it."

"Nice sweater." His had dancing reindeer across a star-studded sky.

He laughed and released me. "Your gifts are under the table."

"Thanks." I pulled out the clothes and toys I'd bought for my two 'angels'.

Joyce and the kitchen staff brought out hot cider and hot chocolate, along with trays of Christmas cookies. Then, they joined the rest of us in wrapping gifts.

Grandma turned off the radio and started singing 'Silent Night'. Everyone joined in. I couldn't imagine a better Christmas party anywhere. Here, we were joined by a common goal—to provide a Christmas to a needy child. No one could stay unhappy in such circumstances.

"Did you think about the killer last night?" Grandma asked, shattering the illusion of peace.

I gave her a stern look and caught the gaze of Sasha who strolled by, a cup of cider in her hand. I smiled and waved. She glared and continued.

"Please don't ruin the party. I told you I left everything in Seth's hands. He's waiting on DNA results."

"Oh, pooh. I'll have to find something else for us to dig into after the holidays." She cut a long strip of silver ribbon. "I know you thought almost being eaten by a bear would curb the gumshoe bug that bit me, but it hasn't."

Mom sighed and kept her head bent over her wrapping. "We're doing the Lord's work here. No talk of death and murder."

"I'm pretty sure it was God that made me a thrill seeker, Sue Ellen." Grandma sniffed. "Who am I to deny his creation?"

Good grief. I tried not to laugh, I really did. But I couldn't help myself. My grandmother has some of the strangest ways of looking at things. "I'm going to get hot chocolate. Anyone want any?"

Everyone nodded. I slipped the scissors into the back pocket of my jeans so I'd have them when I returned, and headed for the dessert table.

"Shelby?"

I turned to face Sasha. "Merry Christmas."

She forced a smile. "Could you come help me with

something, please? I bought a...rather large gift and can't bring it inside without help."

I eyed the pearl buttons on her snowy white sweater. "I'll get Heath." I turned to get him.

"No, no. You'll do." She grabbed my arm to stop me.

I shrugged. "Okay." I followed her outside, waiting for a chance to escape. "Where is it? I don't see anything?"

She heaved a sigh and pulled a small derringer from inside her sweater. "Let's walk the maze, shall we?"

I pulled out the button from my jeans. The same jeans I'd worn the day I found it. Opening my hand, I showed her. "You killed Donald?" My voice rose. Surely someone heard me?

"Not here. Proceed please." She prodded me in the back. "I wondered what happened to that button. They're antique, you know."

I glanced over my shoulder. No one seemed to know anything was amiss. With a groan, I headed through the cold night to the maze. I wrapped my arms around my middle and stopped at the entrance. "Where to?"

"The gazebo. Oh, yes, I know all about your favorite place to think. I've been watching you, Shelby Hart. From the moment I saw Donald reconnect. Now, move."

"You could have just let me go. I had no idea you were the one."

"Sure, you did. I saw the look you gave me back there."

The woman was nuts. "What look?"

"The one after the old lady started talking."

"That was a look of frustration!" I marched forward. Once we got to the gazebo, I needed to find a way of getting to the scissors in my pocket before she shot me. "Why the gun? You used lights on Donald."

"I'm not a killer. I lost control. The lights were handy. He put up quite a fight, once the initial shock wore off. Poor fool. He didn't know how good he could have had it, married to me." She giggled. "Too bad you're going to have to die wearing that sweater."

"Yeah, too bad." Except, I didn't plan on dying that night.

Once we got to the gazebo, I turned, pressing my back against the planked siding. "Was your fiancé really worth all this? He was nothing more than a cheat and a lier. If you put down the gun and walk away, I'll tell the others you went away for the holidays."

"Right. Then the cops will hound me for the rest of my life."

"Look, Sasha. They're going to hound you anyway. You killed one person, and now you plan on killing me. I have friends who are police officers. They won't stop until you're behind bars."

"Oh, sweetie." She gave a smile that chilled my blood. "I don't plan on going to jail. After I kill you, I'll shoot myself. There's no reason to go on without

Donald. Not after what I've done. My life is ruined.

"When I saw him talking to you that day, I thought he wanted to get back with you. Rage filled me. I vowed he wouldn't make me a laughing stock as he did the rest of you. When he said he needed to talk to you again, I followed him. The garden was nice and dark that night, lit only by Christmas lights. It was actually kind of romantic."

"In a sick twisted way maybe. All he wanted from me was the gifts he'd given me during our engagement. He said he was getting married and needed them for his new fiancé."

"Really?" She put her free hand over her heart. "How sweet. But, it was a lie, too. He was so far in debt. I offered to help, but the man was too proud. Turn around, please."

"I don't think so. If you're going to shoot me, you can look in my eyes while you pull that trigger." I reached behind me for the scissors, wrapping my fingers around them.

She raised her gun hand.

I lunged forward, stabbing her in the forearm.

She screamed and dropped the gun.

As we scrambled for possession, sweet little Sasha spewed obscenities so vile, I swore my ears started bleeding. I kicked out at her, catching her in the thigh. She was a little bigger than me, but I was a whole lot madder.

She grabbed my hair and yanked me back.

"Ow!" I swung at her jaw, connecting with a solid right fist.

She tackled me to the ground. "I'll just strangle you." Her fingers wrapped around my throat.

"Nope." I pulled my legs up between us and kicked off.

She went flying, landing on her back.

I jumped on top and straddled her, pinning her arms to her sides. "Now, you can be reasonable and stop trying to kill me, or I'll knock you out cold. Which is it?"

She spit in my face.

I grabbed a fist-sized rock and bashed her in the head. She went limp and I rolled off her, struggling to catch my breath.

I glanced at the night sky. "Okay, God. We haven't spoken in a good long while, but I'm getting kind of tired of this."

Taking a cue from Sasha's own handywork, I pulled a strand of lights from the gazebo and trussed her up like a Christmas hen. I brushed off my clothes and took a few steps toward the entrance.

"You're just going to leave me here?" Sasha whined. "It's cold."

"I don't care." The knuckles on my hand hurt, my head hurt, and she'd torn some lights off my sweater. She could rot in the maze for all I cared. I picked up the gun and scissors and kept walking.

I'd just stepped from the maze when Heath and Seth

raced toward me. Heath planted his hands on my shoulders, while Seth took the gun and scissors from my hands.

"What happened? Where's Sasha?" Heath asked.

"Tied up in the maze. She's certifiably nuts." I rested my forehead on his chest. "What took you two so long?"

"Seth showed up and said the DNA results matched Sasha's. I told him I'd seen you talking to her. We looked and couldn't find either one of you. We put two and two together. After searching the grounds, the only place left was the maze." He pulled me close. "Let's get you warm."

While Seth waved another police officer to follow him into the maze, Heath led me back to the dining hall. Ted shook his head when we entered and continued wrapping. Poor man. I used to be his headache before he retired from the force. Now, it looked as if I was Seth's problem.

Mom thrust a cup of hot chocolate into my hand while Heath lowered me to a chair. The rest of the Jilted Ladies crowded around.

"It was Sasha?" Michelle asked, eyes wide. "I never would have pegged her for a killer. I thought it was April."

"Me?" April frowned. "I wouldn't hurt a fly."

"That's why I thought it was you. It's the quiet people who are the craziest."

"At least no one thought it was me," Jeanna said.

"I did," I said. "For a moment. You still love him. I thought it might have been a crime of passion. But then, I suspected all of you."

Michelle laughed, attracting the attention of most of the residents. "No wonder you make the front page of our town paper so much. You're a riot!"

"Yeah, that's me." I sipped the chocolate, feeling warmth seep back into my bones.

"Back away. Let me through." Grandma squeezed through the women to my side. "You should have had me go with you. We could have tag teamed her."

"She asked for my help, then lured me like a lamb outside." Sometimes, I felt like the dullest crayon in the box.

We all turned as Seth and the officer dragged a handcuffed Sasha into the room. Seth sat her forcibly into a chair and left the other man to guard her. "You all right?" He asked.

"I'm fine. She ruined my sweater." I stuck my finger in a hole where a light had once been.

"It was ugly anyway." Seth grinned. "From the looks of the two of you, it must have been quite the fight."

"We rolled around on the ground like a couple of animals." I glanced with satisfaction to where the side of Sasha's head was matted with blood. "She's tougher than she looks."

"So are you apparently." He clapped a hand on my shoulder. "Do you need an ambulance?"

"No, just a hot shower."

"A glass of wine wouldn't hurt," Grandma said. "It'll loosen you up."

"No thank you." I held out my hand to Heath. "Let's leave this place. The others can clean up. I've had enough festivities for one night. Seth, I'll be in tomorrow to fill out my forms."

With Heath's arm around me, we shuffled back to my cottage. It didn't take long for all my bumps and bruises to make themselves known. Heath drew me a bubble bath, poured me a glass of diet soda, and kissed me. "Thank you for making life interesting."

I smiled. "My pleasure."

Epilogue

Christmas morning dawned crisp and bright. My suitcase, packed and ready for the weekend rested in the corner of my bedroom. Through the bedroom door, the twinkling lights on my tabletop tree cast flickering colors along the hardwood floor. I tossed off my blankets and shuffled to the front room.

Heath, Cheryl, Mom, and Grandma were already gathered around the tree, cups of coffee in their hands. Heath handed me one, along with a kiss. "Merry Christmas, sleepyhead."

"Merry Christmas," I murmured. "Presents?"

Under the tree were several gaily wrapped gifts. Some I'd put there, others I hadn't.

"Let's toast to the birthday of our Lord," Mom said, raising her mug. "And thank him that my crazy daughter is here to enjoy another holiday."

"Here here!" I clinked my cup against hers. "Who wants to play Santa?"

"I will." Heath started handing out gifts. When he'd finished, he took his and sat on the sofa next to me.

"Ida, you go first."

"Oldest first, huh?" She grinned and ripped into the gift from me. "I've wanted the wine cooler bottles for ages. Thank you, Shelby."

"I know I shouldn't encourage you, but I couldn't resist." I smiled.

Mom got her several pairs of outlandish colored leggings, Cheryl gave her a journal, and Heath presented her with a faux fur stole. Grandma couldn't be happier. "Thank you all for the gifts, but I have to be honest and say Teddy's to me last night is the best by far." She wiggled the 2-carat diamond ring on her finger.

"I love the earrings Bob gave me." Mom flicked the ruby in her ear. "You need to get to know him better, Shelby. He's very sweet."

"We're poker partners, Mom. I know him very well, and yes, he is."

After the others had opened their gifts, I presented Heath with a small box. He raised his eyebrows and opened it. Inside, rested a single sheet of paper on which I'd written the words, 'I love you'. If he knew me as well as I thought he did, he'd know how much those words actually cost me.

He grinned, his eyes shimmering. "I was going to wait until this weekend, but…" He pulled a box from his pocket and stood, pulling me to my feet. "Shelby

Hart, I know you've been wounded. I know commitment is hard for you. I know what it cost you to say those words, well, sort of say them," he gave a crooked smile. "So, I'm not asking for this to happen right now. I'll wait forever if I have to, but will you wear this ring and proclaim to the world that you're my girl? The woman who will someday, Lord willing, be my wife?" He lifted the lid.

Inside sparkled a simple solitary diamond of a princess cut. He knew me so well. I lifted eyes filled with tears. "Yes, someday, I will marry you. I can't promise when."

He chuckled. "Just try and live long enough, okay?"

I giggled. "That I can promise to try and do." I caressed his face. Early morning stubble rasped against my palm. "Thank you for waiting, for being so patient. You've made this the best Christmas ever."

He lowered his head and kissed me to whoops and hollers from the other three. I tuned them out and wrapped my arms around his neck. Thank you, God, for the gift of Heath.

The End

Get the next book [Deadly Greenhouse Gases](#)
Get the first book, [Beware the Orchids](#)

COZY CHRISTMAS COLLECTION

Caper Steals Christmas
A Tiny House Mystery, Book Six
By Cynthia Hickey

Chapter One

I hung an ornament on the Christmas tree in the newly erected community hall. Now, we could have gatherings all year round, and our Christmas party would be the first big event.

The building took up the space where half the playground had been dug up after some serious issues with the local drug dealers a few months ago. Rather than repair the playground, we simply moved it over and built the community hall. Since the owner was my uncle, I could pretty much do anything I wanted with the place.

"CJ Turley," A voice scolded from behind me. I turned and smiled at my friend, Mags Snyder. "You know the tree should have some kind of a theme. This looks like a child decorated it. You've every color of the rainbow and then some."

I frowned, scrunching my nose. "These are my grandmother's ornaments. I like the ornaments to be a little of everything. You'll remember I did offer to let you take care of the décor, and you declined." I hung an obscenely large bulb at eye level just for spite.

Mags groaned. "I hope somebody steals that thing."

I whirled back to face her. "Take that back. Some of these are antiques." Maybe I shouldn't have used Grams's things, but I couldn't put a tree in my tiny house big enough for more than three or five bulbs. I wanted to share my treasures with those around me.

"Well, I think it's gaudy."

"It's gorgeous." Eric Drake, local park ranger and my boyfriend, entered the building as Mags continued her criticism. "But not as lovely as my girl." He lowered his head and kissed me.

"Hello to you, too." I smiled.

"Do you know where your dog is?" He stepped back. "Because she's causing trouble, chasing the new tenant's cat, or so they've complained."

I groaned. Caper only wanted to play, but not all four-legged, or two-legged, creatures for that matter, reciprocated my feisty pup's feelings. "Can you catch her and lock her in the house?"

"Already done. Just wanted you to know that house number fifteen isn't happy."

"Thanks. I'll stop by there when I'm finished here." I stepped back and surveyed the tree again. It was perfect. Grabbing my jacket, I headed for the door. "See y'all later."

A brisk wind blew off the mountain rising above Heavenly Acres. The winter sun sparkled off Blue Lake. I really loved where I lived, despite the recent crimes that had begun over the year I'd worked here as manager. Things had settled down for the time being, and life was good.

I climbed into my red and white golf cart and drove around the loop to house number fifteen. Hoping the couple who lived there, Lee and Kim Westford, were reasonable people, I hopped from the cart and knocked on their front door.

A fluffy white cat blinked at me from the windowsill. The pretty thing didn't look any the worse after Caper's romp with her, which eased my nerves.

Mrs. Westford, a slightly plump, well-dressed woman in her mid-fifties, answered the door. "What are you going to do about that dog?"

Okay, not reasonable. "I apologize. Caper is not normally away from me. Is your cat alright?"

"No thanks to that mutt, Sugar is just fine. I had to give her extra salmon to make up for the stress of the chase. When we rented this house, you assured us we could reside here in peace."

Caper was not a mutt. Well, I didn't know if she was purebred or not, but in my heart she was a show dog. "I'll do my best to fulfill that promise, Mrs. Westford." I glanced over to where the bored-looking feline licked its paw. "Sugar is very pretty."

"She ought to be. She's a Norwegian Forest Cat

with a long bloodline and cost us a thousand dollars. She's won awards." The woman actually lifted her chin and sniffed like an aristocrat.

Wow. I couldn't imagine spending that much money on an animal. "She, uh, looks worth every penny." No wonder they had to live in a tiny house. They probably spent all their money on the cat.

I shoved aside the uncharitable thought and turned to leave. Before I was off the porch, Sugar darted between my legs. I windmilled my arms and fell, bouncing down the steps. I'd call Caper and the cat even.

"Sugar," Mrs. Westford darted past me after the white ball of fur streaking down the road.

"I'm okay. I can get up by myself." I rolled my eyes and groaned. Nothing felt broken, thank God.

By the time I limped to my cart, Mags was speeding my way on her cart. "That cat is in your Christmas tree."

Oh, no. My ornaments! Sugar was starting to be a real pain in my behind, and that had nothing to do with my tumble down the stairs.

Shoving aside my aches and pains, I sped back to the community center. Thank goodness the tree still stood, but a white paw flicked out from inside the tree and batted at the large bulb I'd hung last.

"Mrs. Westford, please remove your cat from the tree." I put my hands on my hips and glared at the woman who sat, smiling, in a padded chair.

"She loves Christmas trees."

"These are my personal belongings that belonged to my grandmother. I'd really appreciate your cat not breaking them."

"Very well." She unfolded herself from the chair and carefully retrieved Sugar. "Have you considered a higher fence at the entrance here? I'm afraid Sugar can climb over or under the one we have."

"Mrs. Westford, I cannot put in a new gate for a cat." I fought the urge to roll my eyes again.

"This is going to be a long six-month lease." Back straight, she marched from the building.

I agreed with her. Six months would seem like an eternity if there were more days like today.

Less than two minutes later, Mrs. Westford returned. "Where is her collar?"

"Excuse me?"

"Sugar's collar is missing." She shoved the cat into my arms and made a dash for the tree. "I don't see it." Her frantic searching knocked several ornaments from the tree. One shattered, and the large bulb rolled across the floor and lodged under the tree.

"Be careful, please." I tightened my grip on the squirming animal and received a scratch for my trouble. "Could she have lost it on the way here? Do you have another one?"

She narrowed her eyes. "That one is crusted with diamonds!"

"Why in the world would you have a diamond

collar on a pet?" A jewel thief had once switched the rhinestones on Caper's collar to diamonds, but that was to hide the jewels in plain sight, not because my dog was spoiled.

"We bought it as a reward when she won her first ribbon." She took the cat from me. "She earned it."

"Let's fetch my dog and retrace her steps. Caper has a talent for finding jewels." Unfortunately for me in the past. I eyed Sugar. "Maybe we'll take her home first."

I drove Mrs. Westford to her house to drop off the cat, then she rode with me to retrieve Caper.

My little spaniel wasn't a genius or anything, but she definitely seemed to understand me when I talked to her. "Please hold out your wedding ring to her so she'll know we're looking for diamonds."

"Are you serious?" Mrs. Westford's eyes widened.

"Yes, ma'am."

Scowling, she held out her hand for Caper to sniff, recoiling as my pup's nose touched her skin. "I detest dogs."

"Be nice or she won't help." I knelt. "Find the diamonds, girl."

Caper barked once, wagged her tail, and took off with her nose to the ground. Diamonds, cats, and squirrels were what got my dog excited.

"What's going on?" Mags stopped next to us.

"An expensive collar fell off the cat's neck," I

said. "She has a name, you know. Her name is Sugar." Mrs. Westford clamped her lips together. "You sent Caper to find it?" Mags grinned. "That'll work. Hop in."

Mrs. Westford took the seat next to Mags, leaving me to hang onto the back. It wasn't the first time. Most of the time I actually enjoyed it, but my body was violently protesting my thumps down the stairs. I started to think I might have bruised my tailbone.

Caper slowed and glanced back at us, then continued forward again. She ran a circle around house number fifteen, then darted for the park, empty of children on the cold day. She squeezed under a bush and barked.

Bingo. I hopped off the cart and rushed toward her. "Okay, let me see." I pulled her out.

In her mouth was a collar with half the diamonds missing. "Looks like someone got scared and tossed this." I glanced around the area.

With no rain in a few days, there weren't any footprints. I didn't need anyone to know we had a diamond thief among us. Again.

Who and how did they know the diamonds on the cat's collar were real? And how did they manage to remove so many in such a short amount of time?

Chapter Two

Mrs. Westford yanked the collar from my hand. "I cannot believe this is happening."

Neither could I, to be honest. Theft and murder were getting old. At least it was just a collar. Hopefully, the woman had taken out insurance on something so valuable. Animals tended to get their collars hung on things when running around outside. "Time to call Davis."

Mags' grandson-in-law was our local detective. He wouldn't be happy, or surprised, about another mystery at Heavenly Acres.

Mr. Westford arrived at the community hall at the same time as Davis. While he had a worried look on his face, the detective looked more resigned than upset.

I went through the spiel of what had happened up to finding Sugar in the Christmas tree. Before I could finish, Davis had moved on.

Sighing, he parted the branches on the Christmas

tree, lowered himself to his knees, and looked up, then circled it twice. "I don't see anything."

"It's here." Mrs. Westford held up the collar.

Davis blinked a few times. "I thought it was missing."

"It was." She shook her head. "We found it with half the diamonds missing."

"If you hadn't been in such a hurry to be through with this," I said, "you'd know that I didn't have time to tell you the whole story." Seriously, was I that bad to be around that he couldn't stay long enough to hear all the facts?

"Sorry." Davis crossed his arms. "Mrs. Westford, kindly finish." When she did, he asked, "Do you have insurance on the collar?"

She looked taken aback. "Why would you ask?"

"Something that valuable should be insured."

"Yes, we have insurance," her husband said.

"But that doesn't bring back the fact this collar was a reward for Sugar's first blue ribbon. That is something we cannot replace." Mrs. Westford glared at me. "If it wasn't for your dog, this wouldn't have happened."

I raised my brows. "Your cat came here on her own. If it weren't for Caper, you wouldn't be holding at least some of the diamonds." I snuggled my pup under my chin. "You're a good girl," I crooned.

"Isn't there a leash law here?" Davis glanced from one to the other.

"Yes, but the cat ran out when I had the door open talking to Ms. Turley about her dog's horrible behavior." High spots of color appeared on Mrs. Westford's cheeks. "She's a high-strung animal and doesn't like a leash. The dog wasn't on one earlier."

Which reminded me. How did Caper get out in the first place? Since she seemed to find trouble when let loose, I always left her in the house, on her lead line, or on a leash with me. "May I go, please?"

Davis nodded. "I'll come by your place when I'm finished with the Westfords."

I stepped outside and glanced to house number seven where Eric lived. Seeing his jeep and his side-by-side parked out front, I headed in that direction. He opened the door before I reached the steps.

"Hey, gorgeous."

"Hey, yourself." I tilted my head. "Did you let Caper out earlier? Before you told me about her chasing the cat?"

"No, I saw the two running around, then Mrs. Westford flagged me down. Why?"

"Because I distinctly remember shutting her in my house." I went on to explain the rest of the day's happenings.

"Come on, Hershey. We're checking out CJ's house." He stepped aside so his chocolate lab could join us.

"You really think someone let her out?" It didn't make sense. Why? Usually when someone messed with my dog, it was because I'd poked my nose where it didn't belong.

He shrugged. "Let's go find out." He put an arm around my shoulders. "I was kind of hoping we could get through the Christmas season without a mystery."

"That would've been nice." I leaned into him, grateful for his warmth. "It's so cold today."

"Yeah, February cold, not December. No campers across the lake, so work is slow. Gives me time to get some things done around the house," he said, walking me home.

"What can you possibly do in a tiny house?"

"I've been watching shows. You know I like to cook, and one episode showed a tiny house with a pantry and spice rack that pulled down from the ceiling. I'm going to build one."

"Wow. That sounds amazing." I wanted one. I already had one in the floor storage where I kept things I didn't use much, but every inch of a tiny house could be utilized if one knew how. Maybe I needed to watch less true crime and watch what Eric watched to get ideas of my own.

"Stay outside." He put a hand on the mace clipped to his belt and pushed my door open. Unlocked. Had I forgotten again?

He glanced back and raised his eyebrows, holding the door open for the dogs to enter first.

My mouth opened and closed. "I got nothing." I really couldn't remember if I'd locked it in my excitement to decorate the tree.

Not hearing any barks or growls, Eric and I stepped inside. Nothing seemed out of place. I was good at putting things away when I'd finished with them. A house this size could clutter very quickly, so I could tell it was exactly as I'd left it. Strange. "Why let the dog out and not take anything?" I glanced around to locate my cat, Sherlock. He sat on the windowsill barely sparing us a glance.

"Are you sure nothing is missing?"

"Pretty sure. I don't keep anything valuable here." After the first rash of thefts, I'd rented a safety deposit box at the bank. Of course, I didn't really have a lot of valuables to begin with. My friend, Ann Lowery, cop turned private detective, rented my grandmother's house. I did have a few mementos there, but nothing someone would want to steal. I plopped on the sofa. "This has something to do with the diamonds." I heaved an exaggerated sigh and slumped. Sherlock leaped onto my lap. "Someone used Caper for their own rotten gain." Again. Why did this keep happening to me? "Sherlock could have escaped and been lost."

"Chin up, sweetheart." Eric sat next to me. "This is mild in comparison to some of our other adventures. Want me to call Anne?"

I rolled my head to face him. "Do you think we need to?" Anne always got roped into being my bodyguard when danger loomed over my head. "The Westfords seem to be the target this time. Someone just used my dog as a distraction." The thought made me feel a little better. No involvement meant no danger to me or my friends. "Want to stay for supper?"

"Sure. What are you fixing?"

"A hearty potato soup for a cold day like this."

A knock sounded at the door. Knowing Eric the way I did, I stayed put and let him answer. Always the gentleman, my man. He opened the door and let Davis in.

"Tell me again your version of the story, and you'll be done." Davis sat in the chair across from us.

I repeated what I'd told him. "That's it. Oh, and someone let my dog out as a diversion."

"What?" His eyes narrowed.

"I distinctly remember leaving Caper in the house when I went to the center so she wouldn't be under foot. Someone let her out. She chased Sugar. Sugar went home. I went to the Westfords, the cat got out. The cat ran to the center and climbed in the tree. Mrs. Westford retrieved said cat and noticed the collar was missing. We returned Sugar to the house and fetched Caper. You know how she loves diamonds." I smiled. "Then we found the collar with half of the diamonds missing. Voilà. End of story."

"Did the cat have the collar on when she darted out the door?"

"I don't know. She's pretty fluffy. It could have been easily hidden in her fur."

The pieces were clicking in his brain. "How far

behind you was Mrs. Westford?"

"She arrived at the building before me."

"Hm." He pushed to his feet. "Okay, let me know if you remember anything else."

"I will."

Eric escorted him out, then leaned against the door. "He's got a suspect in mind already."

"Good. I'm content to sit here." I propped my feet on the coffee table and crossed my ankles, then remembered I was supposed to be fixing supper and let my feet fall to the floor. With two dogs and a big man, moving to the small galley kitchen took some maneuvering. I loved this little house, but if I were ever to get married, I'd have to move back into Grams's house.

I couldn't help but wonder whether Davis would check the financial records for the tenants of house number fifteen. Not that I would ever have enough money to buy a thousand-dollar cat or a diamond-encrusted collar, but if I did, I wouldn't have anything left after. I glanced over my shoulder. "Do you think the Westfords could have done this for the insurance money?"

Chapter Three

I couldn't help it. I'd lain awake late into the night pondering how to find out whether the Westfords were trying to commit insurance fraud. Getting involved really was an addiction for me, one I had no idea how to break.

Ugh. I climbed out of bed and padded downstairs for a cup of coffee, doing some fancy footwork to keep from tripping over Sherlock who insisted on rubbing against my ankles.

I popped a pod into the coffee maker and stared out the window over the sink. The day looked as cold as yesterday. Frost covered the ground. Winters were slow not only for Eric, but also for myself. As manager of the campground and tiny houses, my main job was to lease the homes, or sell in some cases, and do one or two rides around the campground each day.

Some people might think my life boring, but I loved the simplicity of it. Coffee finished, I added creamer and folded down the two-person table from the wall. I set my laptop on top and booted it up to check for emails.

No new inquiries for rentals. Not a surprise this close to Christmas.

I closed my laptop and headed back upstairs to get dressed. Fifteen minutes later, I clicked a leash on Caper, checked and double checked that my front door was locked, and headed for the campgrounds in my cart with Caper wagging her tail beside me.

Just because there weren't any campers didn't mean there wouldn't be something that needed doing—kids partying, etc. It warranted me checking. Eric helped, but he had a much larger area to patrol.

I took the path past our little glass-walled chapel. The building was my pride and joy since its restoration. The cross that lit up at night could be seen from almost everywhere in the community and campgrounds. Everything looked fine.

Wait a minute... I stopped the cart and looked closer.

The chapel door hung open a couple of inches. I might forget to lock my own front door, and while the chapel was never locked, the door was always closed. I sighed. If people didn't take better care to keep the weather and critters out, I'd have to rethink the open-door policy.

"Come on, Caper." I led the dog inside the chapel and stopped to listen. No running footsteps, no slamming of the door to the storage room. All seemed in order, but I ventured forward anyway.

Footprints appeared halfway down the aisle. They led through the side door and disappeared. Whoever left them had gone into the woods behind the chapel. I called for Caper to follow, then let the footprints lead me.

It didn't take long for me to see the first sparkling, dropped diamond winking at me from the dried fallen leaves. Would the jewels leave a trail like Hansel and Gretel's breadcrumbs? Since I didn't know how far ahead the jewel thief might be, I returned to my golf cart. As I continued the drive to the campgrounds, I called Davis with my phone on speaker. "You know that path behind the chapel?"

"Yes."

"I found a diamond on the ground."

Davis sighed. "Please tell me you aren't getting involved."

"I'm not. I'm doing my job, noticed the door to the chapel was left open, followed the—"

"All right, I get it. I'll meet you at the chapel in twenty." Click.

I'd have to hurry to circle the campground. What I really wanted to do was stay at the chapel and follow the glittering trail. That would only result in more disapproval from Davis, and I'd had enough of that to last me a lifetime. It had been a very busy year.

I sped around the grounds, then circled back to the

chapel. The campground was asleep for the winter, and I hadn't spotted any signs of kids goofing around after hours. If I had, then Eric would step in, since enforcing the rules was his job. Breaking them was mine. I grinned and hopped off the cart to greet Davis.

"Come on, I'll show you." Rather than lead him through the chapel, we went around. "See?" I pointed to the gem.

"You only found this one?" He bent and used a cloth from his pocket to pick up the stone.

"Yes, I didn't go any further. I've learned my lesson about venturing out on my own."

"Sure you have." He glanced up the trail. "Let's see if we find any more."

Yay, he was letting me come along. A rare treat, indeed. I mean, I would have followed regardless, but it's nice to be invited.

"Stay behind me and be quiet."

Good ole Davis. Sweet as always. I took the end of Caper's leash to prevent her from running ahead and followed the detective, scouring the ground for anything sparkly.

We found nothing. The dropped diamond wasn't part of a trail.

"Keep your eyes open," Davis said. "The thief might be back."

"For the rest of the diamonds?"

"Maybe. The collar is at the station, but the thief doesn't know that."

"You think the Westfords are committing insurance fraud, don't you?" I arched a brow.

"What makes you think that?"

"A gut feeling."

"Don't ask any questions, CJ." He marched down the path, refusing my offer of a ride, saying walking helped him think.

Very well. I still needed to drive the loop of the community.

Roy Olson, our local handyman, stepped out of his house and waved for me to stop. "Number fifteen is really getting on my nerves."

"What are they doing?"

"They want me to build a see-through cat tunnel that goes up and around the house." He crossed his arms.

"That isn't your job."

"They seem to think I'm their personal servant. I need you to put your foot down. I'm hired to do repairs, that's it."

Yep. It was going to be a long six months. "I'll talk to them." Cat tower. Ridiculous. Plus, the Westfords were renters, not owners. They couldn't do major construction to the house, and I seriously doubted whether the other tenants would want a cat tower if the house wasn't rented.

I secured Caper's leash to the cart and approached the Westfords' front door. I knocked and stepped back, prepared to scoop up Sugar if she tried to escape.

A laughing Mrs. Westford opened the door. "Yeah?" She seemed to have gotten over yesterday quick enough.

"I must inform you that we cannot fulfill your request about the addition." There. That sounded official and authoritative.

"This place really doesn't care about the happiness of its residents." Her smile faded.

"You are renting, Mrs. Westford. That type of construction could prevent us from renting the house to someone else after you've vacated the property."

The woman stared at me, stony-faced, for a moment, then she slammed the door in my face. "Lee, you'd better figure this mess out so we can leave this horrible place," her voice echoed through the door.

Figure out what? How to retrieve their collar? The insurance money? Or something else entirely? I decided to keep a close eye on the occupants of number fifteen.

"What cha doing?" Mags pulled up alongside of me.

"Come back to the house and I'll tell you."

Back home, I made coffee for the two of us and told her about finding the diamond and the silly request of the Westfords. "Want to help me spy on them?"

"Do I? Silly question. Winters bore me to tears. With your Uncle Larry working such long hours at the youth center, he doesn't have a lot of time to spend with me." She blew into her mug. "What do you want to do first?"

"Stakeout?" I wiggled my brows. "It'll be cold, but we can wrap up in blankets."

"Let's do it."

Chapter Four

"This is like old times." Mags snuggled down in a thick quilt. We'd "borrowed" Larry's car since the Westfords wouldn't recognize it.

"Not enough time has passed for old times to fit here." I wrapped my hands around a thermos of hot coffee and stared at number fifteen.

The occupants still moved around inside at ten p.m. Sugar sat in the window. I'd bet she could see us, knew what we were doing. I shuddered. The cat might be beautiful, but her owner gave me the creeps.

"Say what you will." Mags cut me a sideways glance. "I miss having a mystery to solve."

"You're rarely the one almost killed."

"Nonsense. I'm usually right there with you. Except for the flight over the mountain. I'm too old for that."

I chuckled. Only Mags was allowed to mention her age. Not yet sixty, Mags wasn't old, at least I didn't think she was. Eccentric as she was, Mags was my best friend. I preferred older people, really. Especially after tending to Grams for so many years.

The door to the house opened. I squinted to see better. Mr. Westford closed the door and strode toward the front of the grounds, shoulders slumped against the cold. Who went for a walk this late on a frigid night?

"Come on. Let's follow him, but be quiet." I carefully opened my door.

Mags pretended to lock her lips, not that it would work, given past events. Still, she'd be silent for a few minutes before she couldn't help herself.

Staying low and keeping to the shadows as much as possible, we kept our eyes on Lee. The man stepped outside the gate and glanced both ways up and down the highway.

"He's waiting for someone," Mags whispered.

"Shh." I pulled her behind the dumpster and put a finger to my lips. Thank goodness it wasn't hot weather. The last time we'd hid here, we were surrounded by very unpleasant odors.

Lee pulled a cell phone from his pocket. "Where are you? Kim is going to notice me gone soon. I'd really like to put an end to all this." He listened for a few seconds. "Fine." He whirled and stomped back into the community.

I shrugged at the wide-eyed Mags. Who was on the other end of the conversation, man or woman? I motioned Mags forward and followed Lee back to his house.

His wife immediately started screeching, "Where were you?"

Uh-oh. The man wasn't very good at sneaking around.

"Just walking, dear. I've got a lot on my mind."

"You need to be worried about our investment in that collar." Her shadow through the curtains crossed its arms. "We're broke, Lee."

"I'm well aware of that, dear. That's one reason I've got a lot on my mind. Good night." His shadow headed up the stairs, I presumed.

"I'm not finished talking to you," his wife said.

We weren't learning anything here, other than the fact that things weren't rosy in the Westford household. Feeling bad for eavesdropping on a private, if unhappy moment, I pulled back.

A yeow sent me lunging forward. A white flash darted past me. Sugar had escaped when Mr. Westford either left or returned.

"Now what?" Mags asked.

"We catch the darn cat and return her. I'll say I was doing my last round before going to bed." As manager, it was plausible.

I gave chase, Mags quickly falling behind. Sugar ducked under house number six where the Flower family resided. Lucy would kill me if I woke up her kids.

"Here, kitty, kitty, kitty." *I'm going to wring your*

neck.

Sugar hissed and swiped at me. Of course, she wasn't declawed. My hand burned where her nail scratched.

"You like fish? I've got a can of tuna with your name on it."

The cat sprang away from me.

I sighed and crawled from under the house and continued my pursuit, passing Mags who now leaned against the car sipping her coffee. "Thanks for the help," I said, rushing past.

"No problem," she called after me. "I'm here if you need me."

I rolled my eyes and raced after Sugar as she headed for the community building. Now I had her. There was no way she could get inside. My shoulders slumped as she jumped and squeezed through a partially open window. Would I have to lock the building after hours? I'd hoped to provide a place for the teenagers to hang out of the cold.

Pushing open the door, I stepped into the dim room, lit only by the twinkling lights of the Christmas tree. "Here, kitty, kitty, kitty." *Please don't be in the tree again.*

She wasn't. Instead, she happily sharpened her claws on an easy chair in the corner. Destructive little beast.

I closed the window, turned on the overhead light, and unplugged the Christmas tree, already forming the notice I'd hand out tomorrow about how to leave the clubhouse before leaving. After shutting off all means of escape for the feisty feline, I headed to the corner.

"Come on. I've had enough of your shenanigans." As I stooped down to pick her up, my gaze landed on the back of chair where the upholstery had pulled away from the frame. How had I not noticed that before? I seriously doubted a cat could have torn it away.

I peered behind the fabric. Aha. A gift box. One of the fake presents I'd set under the tree as part of the décor. I pulled it out and opened it.

Loose diamonds blinked up at me.

Something hit me in the back of the head. The last thing I saw before blacking out was diamonds scattering across the polished wood floor.

The first thing I saw when I woke was a single diamond staring me in the eye. I put a hand to my head, relieved not to find any blood on my fingers, and inched to my feet before picking up the gem and dropping it into my pocket.

I groaned and stepped outside. Not seeing any sign of the trouble-making cat, I shuffled to where Mags still waited, although she'd moved to the car's interior.

"What happened to you?" She asked as I slid into the driver's seat.

I explained. "Did you see anyone?"

"No, but I closed my eyes for a few minutes." She pressed the button on her watch. "Look at that. It's after eleven. Way past my bedtime."

"I got hit in the head, but I'll call Davis in the morning." I drove home, which took all of two minutes.

"Should I stay with you?" Concern flickered across Mags' face.

"I'll be fine." It barely hurt, although I'd most likely have a dickens of a headache in the morning. "Call me at eight. If I don't answer, call the morgue."

"Not funny, Clarice Josephine." She shoved open her door and got out. "I'm going to call you every half an hour."

"Please don't. I'd really like a good night's sleep. I didn't get a nap like someone I know."

"Don't pout. It causes lines around your lips." She closed the door and entered her house.

Since I wasn't an idiot, I didn't go straight to bed when I got home. It was hard to resist teasing my friend. Instead, I let Caper out to do her business and leaned against the railing of my postage-stamp porch.

Whoever hit me hadn't targeted me. I was simply in the wrong place when they came to retrieve the diamonds. What bothered me was the fact I hadn't heard them enter the room. There were only two places to hide in the clubhouse. The bathrooms. The kitchen area wasn't closed off.

Had they taken Sugar, or had the cat ran out when my attacker did? I glanced toward number fifteen. I had to know whether the cat made it home safely. Pain in my rear or not, it was my tenants' beloved pet.

I reached into the house, grabbed Caper's leash off a hook, then clipped it to her collar. I wasn't going anywhere without a warning system, and my dog was perfect for the job. A few minutes later, I stood in front of number fifteen and stared at the open door.

Chapter Five

Here we go again. I'd landed smack dab in a mystery I didn't want.

Gravel crunched behind me. I gasped and whirled.

Eric crossed his arms. "Mags called me. Why are you out here after getting knocked on the head?"

"I wanted to make sure the cat made it home. Instead, I see an open door. I was just about to call the police."

Appeased, he pulled me close. "Are you okay?"

"A dull headache. Nothing serious." I leaned against him, called the local police, and was told Milton, one of the officers on duty, would arrive soon. "Should we look inside?"

"No." Eric rested his cheek alongside mine. "We wait."

I understood going inside would contaminate a potential crime scene, but curiosity tugged at me like a laser beam. I stretched, trying to peek over the steps.

Eric chuckled. "Relax, Milton is here."

The officer pulled to a stop in front of the house. He shook his head as he strolled toward us. "CJ Turley, do you ever stop nosing around?"

"Trouble seems to find me." I grinned. "You police officers might get bored without me."

"You do keep us on our toes." He climbed the steps and paused in the open doorway.

I followed and peered around him. The house looked as if the occupants had merely stepped out and forgot to close the door. "Where's the cat?"

Milton glanced over his shoulder. "Outside if the door was left open long enough."

Caper yanked the leash out of my hand and raced to a nearby bush. She set up a frenzy of barking, sure to wake not only the dead but the living as well. "Caper, hush." I grabbed the end of her leash and pulled.

She yelped, then resumed barking harder. I separated the branches of the bush and spotted a very irate Sugar. "Found the cat."

"I'll get her." Eric reached down and smooth-talked the feline until she curled up in his arms and purred.

I glanced at Caper. "She doesn't usually act this aggressive toward another animal. These two must have gotten into a scuffle."

Milton exited the house and pulled the door closed. "Everything looks fine inside. They must have not closed the door properly. Anything else?"

Sighing, I told him about getting hit in the head.

"Lead on." Milton gave an exaggerated bow.

I went with Milton while Eric returned Sugar to her home. "The diamonds had been stuffed into that chair." I pointed to the one in the corner.

"Did Davis tell you there are teeth marks on the cat's collar? Have you checked your dog's pooh for diamonds?"

"You think Caper stole the collar and ate the diamonds?" I raised my brows. "Then why would someone hide the diamonds? Why hit me?"

"I don't have all the answers. It's just a theory. But that dog of yours has a thing for diamonds." He scoped out the room, then declared it empty.

True. Caper enjoyed sparkling things. "Now what?"

"We keep trying to find out what happened and keep you out of trouble." He flashed a grin and ushered me outside. "I'd make this a crime scene, but it's so contaminated now it would do no good."

"Don't go to any trouble on my account. It's not the first time someone cold-cocked me." I doubted it would be the last considering my penchant for snooping. Maybe I should start wearing a helmet when I leave the house. Since I'd been up long enough not to be concerned about falling asleep, I curled up on the sofa, covered myself with a crocheted blanket, and fell asleep as soon as my head hit the pillow. When I woke, both fur babies lay on top of me, I stretched, then padded my way to coffee. Couldn't start my day without it, especially since I'd had a very long day and only a few hours of sleep.

The Westfords' car sat in front of their house, so I made plans to let them know about the open door. I'd leave the fact that my dog might have been the first thief of the collar to Davis. My tenants didn't seem like fans of mine, so no need to increase their dislike.

Glancing to where Caper waited at the door to be let out, I couldn't help but wonder whether she was guilty of taking the collar off the cat's neck. I grabbed my coat and stepped outside so she could do her business. "A simple imprint of your teeth will tell, won't it?" I gasped.

If she were guilty, I wouldn't have to pay, would I? I couldn't replace one diamond much less half a collar's worth. "Oh, Caper, you've been a naughty girl." I called her back into the house and resumed my wakeup routine.

After showering, getting dressed, and eating toast and jam, I shrugged back into my coat, locked Caper in the house, double-checked the lock, and drove my cart to house number fifteen. Nine a.m. was a decent hour to knock on someone's door, right?

Before I got out of the cart, Danny, Roy Olson's son, ducked around the corner, then dashed across the street. The sixteen-year-old hadn't been in trouble since I took the job, but his behavior bordered on suspicious, like the time he'd stolen my laptop. I gave chase, cornering him against an empty rental.

"Hello, Danny."

"CJ." His features fell.

"What are you up to? I want the truth. I'm too busy for games, and if you're up to no good, I'll tell your father."

"I'm trying to solve the mystery." He scuffed the toe of his shoe in the dirt.

I tilted my head. "How do you know about that?"

"I overheard Mags talking to Larry."

"By listening outside her house?"

He exhaled heavily. "It's Christmas break. I'm bored, so I wander around. I can't help it if folks leave their windows open."

"You wouldn't hear anything if you stayed on the road. Get in." I motioned my head toward the passenger seat.

"Are you going to tell my dad?" He moved as if walking the Green Mile.

"Not this time, but I am taking you home." Summer break was easier on the boy since I'd hired him to mow the grounds here and at the camp. I'd try to find something constructive for him to do during the winter.

I stopped in front of his house, the largest in the community. It wasn't as large as the Flower family's house, but Roy did everything for Heavenly Acres that I couldn't. "Did you hear anything?"

Danny's face lit up. "I sure did. I overheard Mr.

Westford telling his wife that everything was going according to plan."

"That isn't much." I frowned.

"She replied that if that nosy manager would mind her own business, things would be smoother."

Aha. That would be me. What kind of plan did they have going?

"Then they started arguing about someone that Mr. Westford keeps sneaking out to see at night. That's when I left. I didn't want to hear anything gross."

"I don't blame you." I smiled and drove back to number fifteen once Danny slid from the cart. I'd used his eyes and ears before to help gather information, but if he were going to do it again, I needed to know at least, so I could watch out for him.

With no more interruptions, I knocked on the door. Mrs. Westford yanked it open. "What now?"

"Good morning," I sang, determined to be cheerful despite her surliness. "I'm here to inform you that your door was left open late last night, and nobody was home. I called the local authorities who came out to investigate. We found Sugar under a bush and put her back into the house." My grin widened. "I thought you would want to know."

"Lee?" She turned around. "You left the door open last night."

"Sorry," he called from the loft.

"Thank you." Mrs. Westford made a move to close the door.

"Is there any news on the diamonds?" I wanted to keep her talking to see whether she'd give me a clue as to whether she was behind my attack.

"No. Besides, it's no concern of yours any longer."

"Actually, it is." I told her of chasing Sugar into the clubhouse and finding a bag of diamonds. "Someone knocked me out and took them. You wouldn't know who, would you?"

"Are you accusing me of something?" Her eyes narrowed. "If Sugar was out, then you would also know we weren't home. Didn't you just tell me my door was left open?"

I shrugged. "Doesn't mean you couldn't have circled back. Have a good day."

That ought to flush her out, if she was responsible and/or committing insurance fraud. I'd found that antagonizing a suspect seemed to make them careless. The Westfords were the only suspects I had—the only ones the police had, too, unless Davis was withholding information from me. The only time he readily shared was if we were working together.

Maybe it was time to pay a visit to Ann. Since the prior cop was now a private investigator, she had access to information I didn't.

Chapter Six

"Hey, CJ," Anne greeted me with a smile when I rang her doorbell. "I wasn't expecting you."

"I took the off chance you'd be home." I removed my coat and hung it on the antique coat tree by the front door. "I have a favor to ask."

"I've heard of the latest mystery you've gotten involved in."

Ah. I'd forgotten about her boyfriend at the precinct. "I'm wondering if you can find out what Davis knows, and if there's any dirt on the Westfords."

"Sure. Want some tea?" She headed for the kitchen.

Returning to Grams's house always seemed a bit surreal to me. I'd spent five years caring for her as cancer slowly wasted her body away. That's probably why I couldn't live here yet. "That sounds wonderful. Thanks."

Tea in hand, I sat on the familiar tweed sofa and

told Anne everything that had transpired over the last couple of days. "Milton suggested Caper took the collar. That would mean the theft after was one of convenience. Which might blow my theory of insurance fraud."

"Not necessarily. Who could have taken advantage easier than the Westfords?" Ann sat across from me.

"I can't think of anyone. Anyway, I've accused her. Now to wait and see what happens."

Anne rolled her eyes. "Deliberately inviting danger."

"How else can I find out?" I wiggled my eyebrows. "I've been lucky so far."

"Luck has a way of running out."

True. "Let me know if you find out anything."

"I'll know something, even if only a little, by tonight. Want me to bring over a pizza?"

"That sounds great." I headed home to do some household chores while I waited. Mags was peeking out her front window, It wouldn't be long before she came over to see where I'd gone. It took two minutes. I wasn't even out of my car.

"Come into the house," I said, stepping out of my car. "I'll make coffee."

"Great. I'll fetch the leftover cake." She rushed back to her house.

By the time she returned, lemon pound cake in hand, I'd already let Caper out to relieve herself and waited on the porch for my friend. "I'm assuming you want to know the latest."

"I have to admit I'm surprised to see you out and about after being attacked." She pressed her lips together and sniffed. "You should have asked me to go with you."

"I only visited Anne." I popped a pod in the coffee maker.

"To have her dig up information?"

I nodded. "On the Westfords." I told her about the teeth marks on the collar. "I'm expecting Davis to take an imprint of Caper's mouth at any moment. I've openly accused Kim Westford of hitting me. The ball is rolling."

"Why not make it roll faster?" She grinned. "Throw a Christmas party at the clubhouse and have those interested draw names. Make sure you get Kim's. Then, make sure the gift you give her has something to do with her faking the theft. That ought to do it."

I laughed. "You have an evil mind, my friend." The idea did hold merit. "What could I give her?"

"A book on insurance fraud. Fiction, of course. If she's guilty, she'll get the picture."

"You should have been in law enforcement." I handed her a mug of coffee and prepared my own.

With one week until Christmas, I'd have to move fast to plan a party. "Could you ask Larry what kind of budget he'd let me have? I need to work on fliers and put them up right away."

"Sure. You know he can't refuse you anything." She carried her coffee to my table for two and sliced the cake. "You were already going to have a party. Why haven't you started planning?"

"I got sidetracked with the whole missing-collar thing." Now, time was running out, and I prided myself on community get-togethers. Once a month was what I aimed for.

A knock sounded on the door. I opened it to see Davis. "Hello."

"I need an imprint of Caper's teeth."

"What took you so long?"

He shook his head. "Milton has a big mouth." He pulled a flat piece of...something soft from his pocket. "I put bacon grease on it to make it more enticing. Here."

I took the whatever it was. "Afraid she'll bite you? Caper doesn't have a mean bone in her body." I knelt and placed the thing in her mouth. She bit down. "Good girl." Poor thing looked offended when I removed it. I handed it back to Davis and fetched my pup a real treat.

"How's the head?" The corner of Davis's mouth twitched. "Knock any sense into you?"

"Ha ha." I wrinkled my nose. "Don't you have work to do?"

"Yep. Mags, Amber and I would like to have you over for supper tonight. You and Larry."

"That sounds wonderful." She smiled over her

cup. "I'll bring dessert."

"I'm counting on it." He planted a kiss on her cheek and left.

"To think he wasn't always my favorite person," she said. "Regardless, he can't know of our plan to trap Kim Westford."

"He's more likely to get the tip from you than from me." I resumed my seat at the table and opened my laptop. "Let's do a potluck. As people respond to my invitation, I'll pair them up for the gift exchange."

"Or—" She held up a finger, "Why not do a week-long thing? A Secret Santa exchange, revealing the final gift at the party. You could really make Kim sweat."

"You're a genius." My fingers flew across the keyboard. Half an hour later, I'd sent out emails to every resident and printed a cute flier to hang on the community board.

"Larry said you had all the money you need within reason." Mags slid her phone into her pocket and pushed to her feet. "Let me know if you need anything else from me. I have to go bake a chocolate cake."

"Doing it potluck style won't cost much. We'll supply paper products and drinks."

"Let's have an ugly Christmas sweater contest, too. Those are always fun."

By the time Anne arrived with the pizza, and Eric showed up, since we usually ate supper together, I had an affirmative response from everyone. Even the

Westfords.

"You look pleased with yourself," Eric said, kissing me.

I explained why. "Now I need to find the perfect book for my secret pal."

"Mega meat." Anne set the pizza on the table. "Why wasn't I invited to this party?"

"You don't live here," I said.

"No, but my landlord does." She opened the box and plopped a slice on a plate.

"Why do you want to steal the joy of Christmas by giving a gift to someone that will only upset them?" He held up a hand to stop my protest. "I know she's a suspect, but…it's Christmas."

"If Davis is right about Caper being the original culprit, my dog might have already stolen Christmas. Especially, if I have to pay for the missing diamonds."

"You won't have to. You never had them, they've gone missing, yada yada," Anne said. "You can't fault a dog for chasing a cat."

"Especially *that* cat," I muttered, reaching for a slice of mega meat. "Did you find out anything on the Westfords?"

"They filed for bankruptcy. Lost a big house, a second car…they're involved in cat shows up the Yazoo. They've spent a lot of money on that cat."

"And intended for the diamonds to be their saving grace." I pursed my lips. "Steal them, get the insurance money, and have all that money back. But why not put rhinestones on the cat's collar and keep the money? No one would know the difference."

Anne shrugged. "People are weird."

Sherlock growled from the windowsill. His tail flicked back and forth like a pendulum.

Eric parted the curtains. "Sugar is out again."

"I ought to let Sherlock out so he can father some mixed-breed kittens. Wouldn't that rile Kim Westford?" I grinned. "I'm getting tired of chasing down that cat for people who can't take proper care to lock her inside."

"That's the pot calling the kettle," Eric said, smiling.

"Hey, I lock Caper up now. Someone else let her out this time." And I still hadn't found out who or why, other than to create a diversion. "If she was let out for the sole purpose of stealing the collar, then someone knows of her love of diamonds. This was all planned."

"Wasn't it mentioned in the newspaper during the diamond thefts?" Ann's brow furrowed. "Someone is following your infamous career in troublemaking."

"This must be 'pick-on-CJ' day." I bit into the pizza. A pepperoni slid off onto my chest. Great. A greasy stain on my favorite sweatshirt. I sighed and scrubbed at it with a napkin. I refused to let their jokes upset me. I'd solved worse crimes and lived to talk about them. This time would be no different.

Chapter Seven

The sound of my front window shattering jolted me awake. Caper darted downstairs, her barks ringing in my ears.

No shuffling for me that morning. Having something crash through a person's window woke them up faster than two cups of coffee. I dashed down the stairs after Caper and scooped her up before she could run across the broken glass.

A rock with a sheet of paper wrapped around it lay in the middle of the room. A blast of cold air came through the broken window.

"Hush, Caper." I closed her in the bathroom, then called Eric before heading back upstairs to get dressed in something warmer than my pajamas. By the time I came back down, my man stood in the living room, staring at the rock.

"If you get me a broom, I'll sweep this up." He bent and picked up the rock, unwrapping it. *"Stay out of it*," he read. "Maybe they don't know you after all." The corner of his mouth twitched.

"Ha ha." I handed him the broom. "Funny how this comes right after our conversation last night. Maybe someone stood outside the window and listened to us. It could have been Lee or Kim coming for Sugar."

"Makes sense. Someone must have heard us talking to know you were involved. Call Davis."

After I made the call and swept up the glass, Eric and I headed outside to search for clues. The lack of rain had left the ground hard as cement. No footprints appeared under the window.

I stepped back to the road's edge and raised my hand as if to throw something. "I think they were about here." Where would they have run to? I'd rushed down the stairs. They couldn't be far.

Hands on my hips, I surveyed the area while Eric studied the ground. "Eric?" I took off after a man in a dark hoodie. "Hey!"

He glanced back. I didn't recognize him. His eyes widened, and he took off at a run toward the front entrance.

Eric passed me with little effort. I was fast, but nowhere near as speedy as my six-foot-two boyfriend. As he caught up with the fleeing suspect, Davis pulled up.

"That was fast." I bent over, trying to catch my breath.

"I was close by." He marched to where Eric held onto a struggling teenager. "What's going on?"

"These freaks started chasing me," the boy said.

"Why'd you run?" Eric released him.

"When two strangers yell and come after you, you run." The boy straightened his hoodie.

"Why are you here?" I straightened.

"I spent the night with Danny Olson. Cheez." He glared.

Davis narrowed his eyes. "Know anything about a rock through this woman's window?"

The boy paled. "No."

"Did you see anyone outside besides you?"

"Sure. I saw a man jogging. He wore black sweatpants and a gray hoodie."

"What's your name?" Davis pulled a small notepad from his pocket.

"Ryan Johnson."

"Tell me everything you can about this man."

"That's it. He was jogging. I didn't think anything wrong about it. Look, I got a job, and I'm going to be late."

"Hold on." I glanced around the area, instinct telling me the boy lied. "How do you plan on getting to town? I don't see a car."

The boy whirled and sprinted for the road. Davis and Eric gave chase, leaving me to wait behind. I'd had enough exercise for the day, thank you, and it wasn't eight o'clock yet.

A couple of minutes later, Ryan was brought back by Eric and Davis, handcuffed, then put into the backseat of Davis's car. "The jogger paid him twenty dollars to throw the rock," Davis said. "He'd never seen the guy before. He stopped Ryan when he left the Olson house."

"The jogger could be anyone." Although I couldn't picture Lee Westford jogging. "If you got close enough to take money, you saw his face," I said through the car window.

"It was just a guy." Ryan hung his head.

"We'll question him some more," Davis said. "I suggest you board up your window and let me handle this. Things are escalating."

I nodded and stepped closer to Eric. "Want me to make pancakes?"

"Is that your way of bribing me to take care of the window?" He grinned.

"Yep."

"I'd do it for nothing." He put an arm around my shoulders, leading me home after Davis pulled away with Ryan in the back of his car.

"I know you would, but I doubt you've eaten."

"Nope. I threw on some clothes and came the instant you called me." He turned me to face him. "I'll always come to your rescue."

A slow smile spread across my face. "I know you will."

His kiss drove away the morning's cold, warming

me from the inside out. When we pulled apart, I leaned my forehead against his chest. I could stay there forever if not for the plaintive grumbling of my stomach.

We strolled hand-in-hand back to my place. I glanced at number fifteen. "Remember when house number ten was where all the action happened?" That lot still sat empty. "Obviously, it wasn't the house. It's time to put a new tiny house on that spot."

"Silly girl. It's always the people." Eric grinned.

I nodded, but after so many bad people living on that lot, I'd had the house removed. I wasn't superstitious, not really, but that house had seemed to be cursed. "Now, I need to get inside number fifteen and see whether Lee owns a pair of dark sweatpants and a grey sweatshirt. See if he has running shoes."

"I still can't see him jogging anywhere."

"Neither can I." The pudgy man looked as if the most exercise he got was from the sofa to the fridge. "But I want to make sure." Somehow, I needed a really good excuse for entering the house. As manager, I could at any time if I gave the resident a day's notice. Maybe it was time for an inspection.

Chapter Eight

In order to make things "fair," I sent fliers to every resident who rented about a cursory checkup in two days. No one cared. It was in their contract after all.

Bad thing was, my idea increased my workload. Good thing was, I got to see everyone's Christmas decorations, which I loved. Not that they could go full-out in such small spaces, but every bit of Christmas cheer brightened my spirits. Until I reached house number fifteen.

Mrs. Westford waited on the front porch, Sugar in her arms. "Make it quick." She stepped back from the door.

Darn. I'd hoped she wouldn't be home. Hard to snoop with her looking over my shoulder. "I will." I flashed a smile, hoping it looked genuine, and stepped into the house. They'd sure managed to fill it with clutter since moving in. I thought Mags' place was crowded with knickknacks, but this house with all its porcelain cats had hers beat.

"How do you keep Sugar from knocking over your things?"

"She is very sure-footed."

I headed for the bedroom at the back. Number fifteen was one of the few houses without a bedroom loft. "Does Mr. Westford enjoy jogging?"

"You're joking, right?"

I faced her and shrugged. "We're thinking of starting a jogging club. Just curious."

"The man goes to work, comes home, kicks off his shoes, and sits on the couch until bedtime. Then, after I'm supposedly asleep, he sneaks out to meet his mistress. Foolish woman." She laughed at my expression and sat on the sofa. "Of course, I know about her. I'm not blind."

I opened my mouth, then snapped it closed. Their marriage woes were none of my business. I riffled through the clothes in the closet, dug through the hamper, and didn't find any sign of sweats or running shoes. I couldn't spend too much time snooping, or Mrs. Westford might get up and come see what I was doing.

"Thank you. I look forward to seeing you at the party." I brushed past her, having second thoughts about whether the Westfords stole their own diamonds or not.

It was apparent neither of them jogged. I needed to find out whether Davis had gotten a description out of Ryan. It wasn't fair that the detective expected me to divulge every tidbit of information I dug up, but he could withhold from me. Law enforcement or not, he should share.

I was also having second thoughts about gifting Kim Westford a book on insurance fraud. Christmas was a time of kindness. I'd find another way to bait the Westfords. I rubbed my hands together. Time to go shopping. After picking up Mags, I headed to town. "I'm excited now."

"You're a strange one, CJ." Mags shook her head. "But I'm not one to turn down shopping in a gift shop."

Neither was I when it was for someone else. I didn't like clutter in my own home, but this shop carried porcelain cats.

I picked up a kitten ornament, an adult coloring book picturing cats, and a sleek twelve-inch sculpture. That would be the final reveal. I also couldn't resist two dog ornaments, one that looked like Caper and one that resembled Hershey. Cute and whimsical.

Mags bought enough animal miniatures to fill Noah's ark. "These are for me. I need to find fine teas for Tammy Olson. I drew her name for the exchange."

"Want to go to the coffee shop? My treat." I rarely turned down the opportunity for a frozen mocha. "Maybe you can find a special teacup for Tammy."

"Sounds good. We can sip our drinks and discuss the next step in Operation Fraud."

Mags bought several flavored herbal teas, then

joined me with her coffee at a round table. "That man keeps looking at you."

I turned in my chair. "Which one?" The place was crowded.

"Blue jacket with his back to you," she whispered. "He keeps glancing over his shoulder."

My phone buzzed, distracting me from the man whose face I couldn't see. I glanced down to read a text from Ann saying she had the jogger's description. Mid-thirties, white, dark hair, medium build, brown eyes. I sighed. That fit a lot of people. It also fit the man who apparently kept watching me.

I glanced up and met his dark-eyed gaze. When I narrowed my eyes, he turned back to the cup in his hands.

"So, how are we going to draw out the thief?" Mags tilted her head.

"Shh," I whispered. The man who'd been glancing at her stiffened and sat back in his chair at Mags' question. "I don't think this is the place to talk."

"People talk business around here all the time. No one cares what others are conversing about."

"He does." I stood. "Come on." I headed for the door and directed Mags around the corner of the building. I peeked around the corner to see the man exit the building and glance both ways. He was looking for us.

I withdrew and plastered my back against the block wall. When the man strolled by us, I grinned.

"Hello."

His eyes widened and he increased his pace.

"Did you have something to say to me?"

He kept walking.

"I don't think he likes the fact you figured out what he'd been doing," I said.

"Then he should have been more subtle." Mags hitched her shopping bag on her shoulder. "Let's get our treasures home. We can talk there."

We picked up sub sandwiches for lunch and went to my house. "How are you going to hand out your gifts?" Mags asked. "I haven't decided. I can't very well walk up and hand them to Tammy."

"Why not ask Rose Flower to take it and not reveal who sent the gift?"

"Good idea. Tammy might think Lucy is the Secret Santa. It will totally throw her off."

"I'm going to set mine on Kim's porch each night before going to bed." That way, I could also get a good look around the grounds. If I was lucky, I might spot our jogger up to no good.

"Have you heard anything from Amber about who Davis thinks is guilty?" I bit into my Italian meat sub.

"She won't tell me anything other than his original suspect doesn't look like a suspect anymore. Whatever that means."

I frowned. "That means he no longer thinks the Westfords are guilty."

"That puts us back at square one."

"Yeah." I set my sandwich down. All Lee was guilty of was seeing his mistress, a woman his wife knew about. Caper might have pulled the collar off the cat, but someone else knew the diamonds were real. How? Did the Westfords go around talking about how much the collar was worth?

"The cat show." I snapped my fingers. "That has to be where the outsider discovered the collar's worth." I searched the web for the next cat show. Tomorrow. "Want to see some fancy cats? I guarantee the Westfords will be there. It isn't too far of a stretch to expect the thief to be there, too."

"Sure. It might be fun." Mags grinned. "We should bring our cats and show those fancy felines what a real cat is."

I laughed. "Sherlock would not be pleased. He hates the carrier." I bore some scars to prove it. "From the photos, it looks fancy. People dress up."

"Like cats?" Mags' brows rose.

"No. In nice clothes." I rolled my eyes. My friend would wear something bright and monochromatic. Mark my words.

Mags stood and tossed her sandwich wrapper in the trash. "I'll be ready in the morning. Don't do any investigating without me."

"There isn't anything to do until the cat show. I'm going to study cats so I don't sound like a complete idiot tomorrow."

"Good luck." She laughed and went home,

leaving me shaking my head at her not-so-funny attempt at humor.

After cleaning up from lunch, I curled up on the sofa with my fur babies and my laptop to learn what I needed to pretend I knew something about cats other than that they purred and landed on their feet. The show the next day had the list of entries. Sugar Westford would be participating.

Good. Hopefully, I'd catch sight of someone overly interested in the Westfords' loss of the collar. Wouldn't the thief be interested in knowing how much information the police had? Wouldn't he want to know if there were any suspects?

I propped my feet on the coffee table and started researching. Yep, something would pass hands at the show, and I intended to be there when it happened.

Chapter Nine

The next morning, I dressed in wide-legged slacks, black flats, and a sparkling sweater. Since I'd never gone to an animal show, I had no idea whether I was overdressed or under.

After making sure Caper's and Sherlock's stomachs were full, I stepped outside. Mags strolled across the street in a bright fuchsia sweater dress with matching gym shoes. Around her shoulders was what I hoped was a faux mink shawl. I laughed. "Glad you didn't disappoint in your attire."

She preened. "I know how to dress for the occasion, young lady."

I stifled another laugh and climbed into the driver's seat. I'd already texted Eric where we were going, knowing he'd receive the message when he got to where he had service. Sometimes getting service on the mountain was impossible.

"Did I tell you when I went to leave my Secret

Santa gift for Kim, Lee was leaving? Again."

"I'd never stand for that behavior from my man."

"Neither would I."

"On a more pleasant note, I'm very excited," Mags said, petting her shawl. "Once I'm familiar with these shows, I may enter Callie. She's a purebred calico, you know."

"Maybe you could enter her into the Moggie category." I snorted. Mags' spitting cat was definitely not moggie material.

"What's that? The cat version of a muggle? You know, non-cat as opposed to non-magical? Non-magical people are called muggles…" I waved my hand in dismissal as I realized she had no idea what I was talking about.

"It's where the cat is judged on temperament." I grinned.

"Oh, she would win that for sure."

"Really? Callie makes Sugar look like a meek kitten. You do not have a nice-tempered cat."

"I suppose Sherlock would do better." She crossed her arms.

"I'm pretty sure he's a mutt, but he does have a nice personality." I pulled into the parking garage after an hour of Mags' cold-shoulder treatment. "Keep your eyes and ears open. I guarantee you the thief is here."

"I know what I'm doing." With a swish of her shawl, she exited the car and marched toward the entrance.

Running to catch up with her, I apologized. "Callie is a very fine cat."

"Hmmph."

"You no longer agree?" I bit my lip to keep from smiling.

"I'm done with this conversation. Let's catch a diamond thief." With great dramatics, she flung the double doors open, struck a pose, then strolled in as if she walked the red carpet at the Oscars. Crazy dress or not, I now felt very dowdy.

Heads turned, some stared, others looked as if they should know who Mags was, then shrugged when they couldn't place her. My friend should have been on the stage, the way she loved the spotlight. "Where do we start?" She whispered. "I can only act as if I know what I'm doing for so long."

"Let's find the Westfords." I paused in front of a tabby so still when its owner dangled a feather in front of it that I thought the cat was stuffed.

"Prince is very obedient," the woman said. "He always earns high marks."

"He's gorgeous." I smiled and continued to where a flat-faced, white cat hissed and swatted at everyone that walked past. Definitely not moggie material there.

We passed cats of all colors and breeds, in all stages of readiness for their moment in the judge's eye. We found the Westfords in the back of the building. Sugar sported a pink bow on her head and a new collar around her neck. I doubted the sparkling gems were real this time.

"I could have used you last night, Lee," Mrs. Westford glared at her husband and ran a brush through Sugar's hair. "You knew today was important, and not only to me and Sugar. I thought you wanted to recoup our losses with another big win."

"I do, but I feel claustrophobic in that tiny house." He studied the nails on his right hand. "I told you I have everything under control."

"Is it the house or me that makes you claustrophobic?" She clamped her lips tight when she noticed us.

"We came to wish you luck," I said, "but if this is a bad time—"

"No, it's fine." Kim resumed her brushing. "Sugar needs calming, though. Give her a pat and move on. I don't mean to be rude, but I need to focus."

I raised my brows and glanced at Mags, then patted the top of Sugar's bow. The cat ignored me like her owner and licked her paw. "Good luck." I forced a smile and stepped away.

"No matter how nice you try to be to her, she's rude." Mags sniffed and pulled her shawl off her shoulders.

"She's having a difficult time with the stolen diamonds and a cheating husband." I sent up a prayer for mercy for the woman. I might be testy too if I was going through what she was.

I stopped in an out-of-the-way corner and studied

the crowd for anyone seeming overly interested in the Westfords. I spotted the man from the coffee shop almost immediately. He stood behind a table on which sat the biggest cat I'd ever seen.

"That's a Maine Coon," Mags said. "My next cat."

"That won't fit in your house." But it was gorgeous. "It looks as if our eavesdropper is here legitimately."

"Doesn't mean he didn't steal the collar. Let's see how he acts when he recognizes us." Mags strode toward him.

The man's eyes widened, but since he couldn't very well leave his cat unattended, he couldn't run.

"What a marvelous creature." Mags scratched behind the cat's ears.

"Thanks." His gaze flicked to me. "You showing or looking? Cats for sale are in the other building."

"Just looking, not buying." I smiled. "Our neighbors are showing, and we're here for support."

"Right." Mags winked at me. "They've been through some trials lately." She leaned closer to the man. "Thievery and infidelity."

I didn't think it possible for his eyes to widen further, but they did, going almost googly-eyed. "We shouldn't gossip, but are you acquainted with the Westfords?"

"No." He answered rather quickly. "Only seen them at these type of functions."

"Thank you for watching Frederick." A woman in her sixties squeezed up to the stand.

"The cat isn't yours?" I arched a brow at the man.

He gave a quick shake of his head and melted into the crowd. Recognizing suspicious behavior, and going with my gut instinct, I went after him. "Hey."

Shooting me a glance over his shoulder, he ducked into the men's room. Drat. Making sure no one was watching, I followed him in, leaving Mags to guard the door.

"Seriously, woman?" He paled.

"Why are you so interested in me and the Westfords?" I crossed my arms and looked as stern as my miniature frame would allow.

"I'm not."

"Sure you are. At the coffee shop, you were very interested in the conversation I had with my friend. Now, you're here and you don't have a cat."

"Neither do you." He tilted his head.

"Are you the jogger who paid a boy to throw a rock through my window? Did you steal the collar that belonged to the Westfords' cat? Who are you?" I narrowed my eyes.

"Stay out of it. This doesn't concern you." He growled and shoved past me, knocking me to the floor.

My head hit the tiled wall behind me. I didn't even want to know what germs I might be sitting in. When Mags didn't come to my rescue, I used the strength of my legs to press my back against the wall and push to my feet. No way was I going to touch the floor with my bare hands.

After making sure I wasn't bleeding, I washed my hands and turned as a man entered. He jerked back and peered at the Men's sign on the door. "You're in the right place," I said. "I'm the one who is lost." I flashed a grin and stepped out.

Where was Mags? My heart skipped a beat. That man hadn't taken her, had he?

I dug my phone from my pocket.

"Can't talk. Chasing Mr. Jogging Man through the showroom." Click.

Where was the showroom? I thought we were in it. I asked someone wearing an official-looking vest.

"This is the prep room. The showroom is through those doors." She pointed across the vast room. "You're only allowed in the bleacher section, not the floor. The show starts in half an hour."

I nodded and rushed after my friend. She should never have taken off after the guy on her own. He had to be at least twenty years younger and a lot stronger. What if he turned on her?

I stepped into a room devoid of people. Either there weren't a lot of spectators at a cat show or folks waited until the last minute to pick their seats. I stood and listened, straining to hear past the silence for any sign of Mags.

There. The pounding of running feet.

I headed on a sprint in that direction, catching a

glimpse of Mags, dress hiked around her knees, racing across the red show ring. I guess no one told her that area was off limits. Making sure no staff was around, I took off after her. "Mags."

She stopped, breathing hard. "Thank the good Lord. I'm winded. You go." She pointed with one hand and handed me her Taser with the other.

I grabbed the Taser and ran.

Jogging Man barged through a set of heavy back doors. "Stop. I only want to ask you some questions."

He flipped me an obscene gesture and slammed the door behind him. Rude.

I went through the doors a little more carefully then he had. My head still ached a little from meeting the men's-room wall. I didn't want another concussion. Why did bad people think hitting me over the head was the way to go?

As I stepped outside, Jogging Man, now on the back of a motorcycle, sped past narrowly missing me. He had to be the one responsible for hiring Ryan. Whether he'd actually stolen the diamonds or knew the Westfords was left to be discovered.

I entered the main room. Cats and their owners took up position behind podiums. A quick scan of the small crowd in the bleachers located Mags easy enough, thanks to her bright-colored dress. I made my way to her, careful to stay on the outskirts of the show ring. "What were you thinking?" I shook my head. "He knocked me to the floor in the bathroom. He could have done the same or worse to you."

"You let him get away, didn't you?"

"He sped off on a motorcycle. I couldn't exactly keep up."

"Do you think he knows the Westfords?"

I shrugged. "No idea, but I'm pretty sure he paid Ryan to throw the rock. What I don't know is why, unless he's involved, which he must be." My shoulders slumped. We were getting nowhere fast.

She snapped her fingers. "I have an idea. At the party, we'll talk about what happened today close enough to the Westfords so they can hear."

"Yes." I smiled. "They'll think we know more than we do. If one of them is behind all this, it might draw them out. I'd really like this solved before Christmas."

"That would be nice. We don't want a cloud hanging over a special day." With a satisfied smile, she focused on the happenings below us. "Oh, good. Sugar got a blue ribbon. That should make Kim Westford happy enough to answer any questions you might want to ask. Are you delivering another gift tonight?"

"Yes, the last one before the party, but I go late so she doesn't see me. Questions will have to wait." I was pretty sure her good nature would carry over until the next evening. I no longer thought her capable of stealing the diamonds. My money was on her husband. Caring for a wife and a mistress had to be expensive.

All I had to do now was prove it.

Chapter Ten

The evening of the community Christmas party, I donned a red sweater with a felt reindeer head covering the front. Right in the center of my chest was a blinking red bulb to serve as the reindeer's nose. I might not win for the ugliest sweater, but I doubted this sweater would ever see the light of day again.

Eric picked me up in a sweater the color of pea soup with dogs wearing Santa hats running across the front of his chest. "I put the last of the supplies in the clubhouse. Ready?" His eyes widened as I turned on Rudolph's nose. "The men are going to be staring at your chest all night."

"What little I have, you mean." I wiggled my eyebrows and linked my arm in his. "Let's go catch a thief."

He grinned. "That has become your favorite sentence lately."

"Better than let's go catch a killer. This is much

safer."

Our laughter carried us across the road and to the community center. The party would start soon, but I had time to make sure any last-minute details were in order.

Mags and my uncle, Larry, arrived first, followed by Amber and Davis. They weren't members of the community, didn't expect to participate in the gift exchange, but did bring food. Davis figured I was up to something and wanted to be there to get me out of any trouble I might find.

"It's a party, Davis." I rolled my eyes and took the potato casserole from his hands. "Try to enjoy yourself, and don't look like a cop, please." He'd scare away the thief.

Soon, the laughter and excitement of the community's children filled the room, drowning out the adults' conversations. I eyed the stack of presents under the tree, grateful for Larry's donation for gifts for the children since they weren't part of the Secret Santa exchange.

The Westfords arrived last and sat at a table. Davis watched them with narrowed eyes, as did I. From their body posture, they weren't pleased with each other. I prayed a fight wouldn't break out and ruin the party atmosphere.

Soon all the tables filled with people and plates piled high with food. No one seemed to be acting suspicious at all. Maybe Jogging Man was the sole person responsible for the theft. I shrugged. The Christmas party would have taken place either way. I took my seat next to Eric and decided to enjoy myself and let what would come...come.

"People aren't doing anything but eating." Mags stabbed a meatball with her fork.

"Maybe we were wrong about the Westfords." I glanced up to see Davis's reaction to my comment.

He kept his focus on his plate, but a muscle ticked in his jaw. Interesting.

"Do you have a prime suspect yet, Davis?"

"Why do you insist on calling me by my last name? You know my name is Bill." He scowled.

"Habit." I grinned. "Well?"

"Yes, I have a suspect, and no, I'm not going to tell you anything more." He resumed eating.

"Maybe I won't tell you what I know." I dug into my pasta salad.

His plastic fork slapped against his paper plate with a dull thwack. "Since you've mentioned it, you'd be breaking the law by not saying anything."

"The two of you are more entertaining than a movie," Eric said, laughing. "But you might want to keep your voices low. You're attracting attention."

"CJ makes me lose all reason." Davis shook his head. "What do you know?"

I lowered my voice and leaned forward to tell him about Jogging Man. "I wasn't able to get his name."

"You were attacked and didn't tell me?" High

spots of color appeared on Eric's cheeks.

"No, I simply fell when he pushed past me."

"What's the difference? You were injured."

"Barely."

"Save it for later," Davis interrupted. "You said this guy followed you to the coffee shop?"

"Did he?" I glanced at Mags.

"He came in after we did," she said, "and took a seat at the closest table. But we didn't know he would be at the cat show."

"Could he have followed you there?"

"Possibly," I said. "We were busy looking for the Westfords. You know, to wish them luck."

"Right." Davis smirked and rose to his feet, then carried his empty plate to the trash bin.

"You really do antagonize him," Amber said, smiling. "If you could only hear his frustrations when you get involved in another crime."

"I can imagine." I sensed the children growing restless. "Time for gifts."

With Eric acting as Santa, all gifts were handed out. Turned out Tammy Olson had my name and gifted me with a wonderful oil painting of Caper in a dark wood frame. "I love it. I didn't know you could paint?"

She smiled. "I don't have as much time as I used to but try when I can."

"I'll treasure it. Thank you." I knew just the spot to hang the painting. It would fit perfectly between the two windows above the sofa.

I smiled as Kim Westford carried the cat sculpture to me. "This is lovely. Thank you."

"It reminded me of Sugar, in a sleek rather than fluffy way. There's also a plug in the bottom to use it as a secret hiding place. Maybe for when you get the collar and diamonds back."

"Don't tell Lee, but I've already received the collar back." She turned and headed back to her table, setting the sculpture in the center and fiddling with it for a moment, before returning to the front of the room where those participating in the sweater contest gathered. Her sweater with a cross-stitched resemblance of Sugar wasn't ugly in the slightest. At least not when put against Mags' pooh-brown sweater with elves and twinkling lights. My friend won the contest hands down and received the prize of a gift card.

"To buy a new sweater," Eric said, handing her the card.

"What's wrong with my sweater?" Mags arched a brow. "It wins every ugly sweater contest I've entered. I think I'll keep it."

An angry shout rose above the frivolity.

Conversations ceased as everyone turned to Kim.

Hands on her ample hips, she glared around the crowd. "Where is my present? Where's Lee?"

I whirled to face Davis. "Was Lee around when you returned the collar?"

"Yes. I gave it to them outside before the party started."

"Kim must have put it in the bottom of the cat and Lee saw her. He's the thief."

Davis darted outside, me on his heels, Eric and the others right on mine. Of course, Eric caught up and passed me on our race toward house number fifteen.

The shattered pieces of the sculpture lay on the front porch. One missed diamond sparkled from the wreckage.

"Stay here." Davis reached for the doorknob, halting as a car sped from the back of the house.

"He's gone." The taillights disappeared through the front gate. "You couldn't have known Lee was the thief," I told Davis. "Or you wouldn't have given them the collar."

"No, I thought it was Mike Royson. You know him as Jogging Man."

I narrowed my eyes. "How did you figure that one out?"

"Because he's a known thief, and a certain somebody described him as one who might have stolen a woman's ring." He groaned and marched back toward the clubhouse. "You should have come to me with your suspicions."

"I wasn't sure yet."

"Did you catch the rat?" Kim waited for us in front of the building.

"No, ma'am." Davis planted himself in front of her. "Do you know where he might have gone?"

"To his girlfriend's house, most likely."

"Do you have her address?"

"Of course, I do." She gave an evil grin. "Lee thinks he's sneaky, but I've known all along where he goes at night. I've got it written down at home. Her name is Ginger Smith. A stripper name, if you ask me."

We trooped back to her house. She muttered a curse when she saw the broken sculpture. "Lee had better not have let Sugar out."

"I'll get you another sculpture," I said, relieved to see her cat watching us from the kitchen counter when Kim opened the door.

Lee had definitely left in a rush. Several of his wife's figurines lay shattered on the floor. On purpose, maybe? Through the open bedroom door, I could see scattered clothes.

"I'm going to kill him." Kim opened a kitchen drawer and pulled out a flowered address book. From a slit in the fabric that covered the book, she pulled out a slip of paper and handed it to Davis. "Keep it. I have it memorized."

Davis handed her a business card. "Call me if your husband shows up or you see him anywhere around."

"I'll be standing over his corpse when I call."

"Ma'am, that is not funny."

"I'm not joking."

The two stared at each other for several long seconds. Davis was the first to break away. Outside, he ordered us not to follow him into town.

Fine. I returned to Kim. "Could you write that address down for me? If I find him before the detective does, I'll let you know."

"Promise?"

"I promise." While I'd let Davis know when Kim went to confront her husband, I didn't want the man dead, so I'd let her know right before I called the police.

She scribbled the address on a piece of paper. "It's a trailer park on the other side of town. Be careful. It's seedy." She handed me the paper and closed the door.

"You aren't going tonight, are you?" Eric asked.

I shook my head. "I've seen that side of town. It's scary enough in the daytime."

"That's my girl." He bent down and kissed me before walking me home. "Take Mags and her Taser with you when you go. Good night, sweetheart. See you tomorrow."

I let Caper out and leaned against the railing of my porch, hoping she'd hurry up with her business. The night had turned bitter cold, biting through my sweater. My painting. I'd left it on the table at the clubhouse. "Come on, girl. I need to lock the place up."

The trashcan overflowed inside the clubhouse. Some tables still held dirty dishes and wrapping paper. It might be past ten p.m., but I couldn't go home, leaving the place that messy. I bagged the garbage, pulled another trash bag from under the small kitchenette counter, and then cleared the tables, leaving the painting where it was. I'd fetch it after taking the garbage to the dumpster.

Caper moved around the room eating dropped bits of food until I took the broom from the closet and started sweeping. Hating the broom, she hopped up on a chair and curled up to stare at me with soulful eyes.

"Sorry, sweetie." I hummed Christmas carols as I worked, mulling over in my head what had transpired.

Lee Westford had stolen his own diamonds, hid the fact from his wife, hired someone to intimidate me, all because he had another woman in his life? I shrugged. Immorality caused people to do awful things. I'd seen it before. Too many times. It saddened me.

I did what I could to bring justice to the world, and while I'd suspected Lee, I hadn't figured out the whole thing. Now, the diamonds were gone again. I seriously doubted he or his girlfriend would still be around by morning.

Leaving Caper where she lay, I put the broom away, hefted one of the bags of garbage over my shoulder like Santa Claus, and headed for the dumpster. It took several swings before I pushed the heavy lid up and over. Then I headed back for bag number two.

Caper opened one eye, then closed it again. "You'll have to come home with me when I'm done, silly pup."

I grabbed the last bag and returned to the dumpster. It weighed less than the first one and only took one hefty swing. There. I could sleep well, knowing I didn't have the mess to deal with in the morning. I could have asked Roy to take care of it, but the man had enough work to do.

Turning, I froze at the figure of a man standing in the shadows. With a cry, I turned to run. He caught up with me and yanked me around to face him. His hands circled around my throat. Lee under the hoodie.

Shrill barking meant rescue was on its way.

Caper bit down on Lee's leg, shaking with her entire body. He released me and tried pulling her off. He aimed a punch at her head. She let go and he kicked her away. Cursing, he dashed back into the night, leaving me short of breath and grateful for my furry little protector.

I scooped her into my arms and sprinted for home, smart enough to know he'd come for me again when the opportunity presented itself. I couldn't be caught outside.

Chapter Eleven

"What happened?" Mags peered at my neck.

"I had a run-in with Lee last night. Caper saved me." I tied a scarf around my neck to hide the bruises. "We need to stop and speak with Davis before heading to the trailer park."

"Do you think Lee will be there?"

I shook my head. "I'm hoping his girlfriend, Ginger, will be there and feeling talkative."

"Did you tell Eric?"

"He was asleep when I arrived home, and now he's up in the mountain somewhere. I'll tell him later." He wouldn't take the news lightly. My man took it personal when I got in trouble as if it were his fault he wasn't there. It couldn't be easy being my boyfriend.

The receptionist at the police station informed us that Davis was out and wouldn't return for a few hours. That left us with no other course of action but to pay a visit to Ginger.

I drove to the address Kim had given us and studied the white mobile home with pink trim. Flowerpots, devoid of blooms because of the winter season, hung along a wooden porch erected to make the trailer look more like a house. Ginger might be a homewrecker, but she appeared to have some pride in where she lived.

"I don't see any sign of Lee, do you?" Mags leaned forward and stared. "I've got my Taser, though...just in case."

"Good girl." I didn't see any sign of the man or his car. "Let's see what we can find out."

I approached the house slowly, my gaze darting in each direction for signs of danger. It wouldn't surprise me to see Lee jump out from the evergreen bushes on each side of the porch. I touched the scarf at my neck, last night's events fresh in my mind. I wouldn't mind a little payback when I came face-to-face with Lee again.

"There's murder in your eyes," Mags said. "You might want to get rid of that look if you don't want to scare the woman away."

Good point. I pasted on a smile I hoped wasn't a grimace and approached the front door.

A red-haired woman opened the door before I could knock. She looked about forty, with maybe an extra twenty pounds on her frame— not exactly pretty but pleasant-looking enough. "If you're selling anything, I'm not buying," she said, taking a sip of coffee.

"No, ma'am. We're here to ask whether you've seen Lee Westford."

"Why are you asking? I already told the cops I haven't seen him in two days." A flicker of worry crossed her features. "He's in trouble, isn't he?"

I nodded. "He's guilty of insurance fraud and trying to kill me." I pulled the scarf away from my neck enough for her to see the bruises.

Her eyes widened. "He's gone off the deep end. Come in." She stepped back so we could enter. "Too many nosy neighbors."

I sent up a prayer that Lee wasn't waiting for us inside, then entered a cozy home smelling of vanilla from a nearby burning candle. A small tabletop Christmas tree added some holiday cheer. I felt as if Ginger and I could've been friends if we'd met under different circumstances.

Ginger motioned for us to have a seat on her floral sofa. "You must think me a horrible person, spending time with Lee when he's married."

"We aren't here to judge," I said.

Mags snorted and rolled her eyes. "I'll try to be charitable in acknowledging that Kim can be a difficult woman. Did you know what he was up to?"

"No." Ginger sat across from us. "Lee loves me—he really does. If I didn't know how much before, I do now. I've been diagnosed with cancer and need surgery I can't afford. Lee told me not to worry about a thing.

He had it all taken care of." Tears welled in her eyes. "I had no idea he'd resort to this in order to help me."

Drat. Now, I kind of felt sorry for the man. "The Westfords are financially broke. Or at least they were until Lee decided to steal the diamonds. I never did understand why they didn't sell them a long time ago."

"His wife refused. The cat's collar was a status symbol, I guess. A mask to wear to look prosperous." She wiped her eyes with the sleeve of her robe. "It's all for nothing. He'll go to jail, and I'll die."

Mags reached across and patted her knee. "Chin up. There's always a way."

"Do you have any idea where Lee might be?" I asked. While my heart broke for her, I couldn't let sympathy get in the way of justice. My sore throat reminded me of that fact.

"I have no idea." She broke into sobs. "He's been spiraling the last week, muttering things I didn't understand. Now, it's all clear to me." She fought for control and struggled to her feet. "You're right. I'll proceed with the surgery and worry about the cost later. I'll sell this place if I have to."

"Why don't you?" I stood and took her hand. "I've an empty house in Heavenly Acres that you can live in rent-free until you're back on your feet." Number ten had sat vacant for too long. My uncle wouldn't mind once he knew the circumstances. "Think about it."

"I will. Thank you."

"Will you be safe here alone with Lee clearly out of his mind?" Mags asked.

"He would never hurt me. I do think you should keep a close eye on his wife though. He really dislikes her and in his mental state—"

True. We needed to have protection assigned for Kim. I handed Ginger a business card. "Please, call me or the police if you see Lee."

She nodded. "Detective Davis came by last night. He also gave me a card, but I didn't spend much time talking to him. He searched the house and left. I hope you find Lee, I really do, and I hope he survives this ordeal. I'd rather have him in prison than dead."

As for me? I was torn between the two. An attempt on my life would do that. I thanked her and reminded her again about the house I had for her if she were interested, then headed back to the police station.

Davis must have pulled into the lot seconds before we did because he was marching up to the double doors when we pulled in. I tapped the horn. He turned and came to us.

"Find out anything?" He asked.

"Good morning to you, too." I grinned. "No, we haven't found out anything."

"Lee tried to kill CJ last night," Mags blurted out.

Davis paled. "I'd say that's worthy news."

I showed him my bruises. "Caper saved the day. Did you know Ginger has cancer and Lee promised to take care of her medical bills?"

He exhaled heavily. "You went to visit her?"

"Just left there. She said he's been different the last week or so. A lot on his mind."

"I'd say so. It can't be easy trying to steal from yourself, hide the fact from your wife, care for an ailing mistress, all while trying to act like the victim." Davis crossed his arms. "It would take a toll on any man. I'm glad you aren't dead, CJ, but you might not be as lucky next time."

"We think you should have an officer guard Mrs. Westford."

He nodded. "I'll have a squad car drive by on a regular basis. Go home and stay there. This case will be over soon, and Eric will kill me if something happens to you."

When he entered the building, Mags and I headed back toward home. "I'd hoped to find out more," I said, "but we did find out why Lee is doing this."

"Doesn't stop the fact he's gone bat crazy and needs to be behind bars."

"No, it doesn't." I glanced in the rearview mirror. "Don't look now, but speaking of the devil."

She turned in her seat. "He's coming up on us fast. Do you think he saw us at Ginger's?"

"I'd bet on it." I pressed the gas pedal. As I sped up, so did Lee.

"He's going to run us off the road."

"Most likely." I made sure my seatbelt was firmly in place. "I'm not a race car driver."

"You're barely a driver at all. Go faster."

"The faster we go, the harder we'll crash."

"So, you want him to catch us?"

"Not really." I increased our speed and tightened my grip on the steering wheel. Don't let us die, Lord, please.

My head snapped forward as Lee rammed us from behind.

Mags dropped her Taser and fumbled on the floor for it.

I whipped the wheel and spun the car around, speeding across the median and back toward the police station. Lee followed, cutting off a semi. The truck jackknifed and flipped. The man was definitely insane. Innocent people were going to get hurt before he finished his rampage.

"Got it." Mags held up her Taser just as Lee pulled alongside us and sideswiped us.

Horns blared. Cars careened out of the way. My small sedan was no match for his larger, older model.

"We can't beat him." My heart beat in my throat. "Call Davis."

Mags looked torn, then finally set her Taser on the dashboard and called her son-in-law. "We found Lee. That's the good news. The bad news is he's trying to run us off the road. He's already crashed a semi. We just passed mile marker 108." She nodded. "You'd better be faster than fifteen minutes. We might not make it that long." She hung up. "He's coming."

I swerved to avoid a slower car in front of me and ended up mired in the ditch. "We'll have to make a run for it." I shoved open my door as Lee skid to a stop beside us.

"Get in." He pointed a gun at my chest. "Both of you."

Something banged on the trunk of his car.

"Do you have Kim in there?"

"Sure do. Let's go. Now."

Mags and I scrambled into the backseat. "Where are we going?" I asked.

"Somewhere no will find three annoying women. Use those zip ties to tie each other's hands together. Don't try anything funny or I'll kill you slow and easy."

I did Mags' hands, then held mine out for her to secure mine. The longer we cooperated, the longer we would live. I fell back against the seat when Lee slammed his foot on the accelerator.

"Please tell me you have the Taser," I whispered to Mags.

"I did but dropped it again. It's under his seat."

"Shut up or I'll shoot you both right here."

We shut up.

Chapter Twelve

I stretched my foot, trying to dig the Taser out from under the front seat. Lee jerked the car to the right, slamming me against Mags and pressing her against the door. A yelp came from the trunk. Kim wasn't faring any better than we were. Still, the car would stop at some point and we outnumbered Lee three-to-one. No man in his right mind would go against three angry women.

We bounced down a dirt road and across a creek. I knew where we were headed. Lee was right. If he killed us at the quarry, our bodies would be easily buried.

He hit the brakes, sending us crashing against the back seat. I bent and fumbled for the Taser, wrapping my fingers around the handle, then sliding the weapon into my pants. It wouldn't be easy to retrieve, but it was the best thing we had.

I smiled knowing Davis would be able to track our phones. All we had to do was stay alive long enough for him to find us. Which he would. He had yet to let me down.

After Lee had me and Mags get out of the car, he opened the trunk and hauled Kim out. Not an easy task because of her size.

She stumbled to her feet, spitting mad. "I'm going to kill you, you worthless excuse for a man."

"Don't antagonize him," Mags hissed.

Kim whirled to face us. "Don't tell me what to do with my own husband."

"Maybe I should let the three of you kill each other." Lee laughed. "Stand on the edge of that giant hole in the ground." He motioned with the gun.

I stood and stared down, fairly certain I could survive the fall. If I jumped, how far could I get before a bullet struck me in the back? "You don't have to do this, Lee. You can't help Ginger if you're behind bars."

"What do you know about anything?"

"I know you want to help her with her surgery. That makes you a man with a good heart."

"He's as crazy as a rabid dog," Kim spit. "Where's Sugar?"

"Wandering around Heavenly Acres." He grinned. "Maybe she'll wander out to the highway. Play a little frogger with the traffic."

Kim lunged at him, her fingers curled into claws.

Lee fired the gun at her feet.

That was all the distraction I needed. I leaped forward and wrapped my arms around his neck, taking him into the hole with me. I twisted my body to put him on the bottom, softening the impact of landing in the packed dirt.

We both lay there gasping like stranded fish. I sucked in air and grappled for the gun as Mags and Kim scrambled down to join us.

Kim took the gun and aimed it at Lee. "I told you this would happen if I found out you stole the diamonds."

"Don't do this." I climbed to my feet, every inch of my body aching. "He isn't worth you going to jail."

"He's ruined us." Tears streamed down her round face. "I resigned myself to the fact he didn't love me anymore. We didn't even buy Christmas gifts for each other; that's how broke we are. I never thought he'd steal the only future we had left."

"It wouldn't have been so obvious if that dumb dog hadn't chased your stupid cat and pulled the collar off." Lee pushed to his feet. "I had the dickens of a time finding the collar and barely had time to remove half the diamonds before people started searching."

"Does this remind you of an episode of *Scooby Doo*?" Mags cocked her head. "'I'd have gotten away with it if not for those pesky kids'? Except this time, it's a little dog."

I bent and sawed the zip tie from my hands on a sharp rock, Mags copied. I reached into my pants and pulled out the Taser.

Mags seemed shocked to see where I'd hidden it.

"You can keep it now."

I rolled my eyes. "Kim, use this instead. I guarantee it will bring you satisfaction."

"Not as much as seeing him dead. He's ruined our lives and Christmas."

"Stop being so dramatic," Mags said. "Christmas is still coming. Think of the bright side. You won't have to spend it with him. Let's tie him up, shove him in the trunk, and go home. It's cold out here."

I agreed and stepped forward to threaten Lee with the Taser if he didn't cooperate. Two squad cars roared to a stop behind Lee's car.

Davis, Milton, and Eric sprinted toward us. Davis coaxed the gun from Kim, while Eric took possession of the Taser. "You did good, ladies," Davis said. "I'll take it from here. Mr. Westford. You're under arrest. You should have stopped with the diamonds. Trying to kill CJ means you'll go to jail for a very long time."

"You tried to kill this little snip of a girl?" Kim's face darkened. She doubled up her fist and landed an impressive right hook against her husband's jaw. "I want a divorce."

Eric gently untied my scarf and took a long look at my bruises. After kissing each one, he leaned his forehead against mine. "Will you marry me?"

"What?" My mouth fell open.

"Will you marry me?"

"So you can keep me out of trouble?" My lips twitched.

He laughed. "Darlin' I'm not a miracle worker."

I threw my arms around his neck. "You bet I'll marry you. Whose house will we live in?"

"Well, Anne is in your Grams's house, so I guess we'll put our two together." He pulled me into a hug. "I don't care. I'd live in a tent with you."

Mags clapped her hands. "It's about time. Look, Davis, Eric proposed."

Davis shook his head, pushing Lee ahead of him. "Strange time for a proposal."

"I've got to do it before something really happens to CJ." Eric took my hand. "Mrs. Westford, we'd appreciate a ride back to Heavenly Acres."

"I'm only going back there to find my cat." She stormed past us. "But you're welcome to the ride."

"I'll need you three ladies to come to the station and fill out a report," Davis said, putting Lee in the backseat of his car. "Mrs. Westford, don't leave until that's completed."

~

Christmas morning dawned bright and cold. Eric arrived as the sun came up and woke me with kisses. "Merry Christmas."

I stretched and smiled. "Merry Christmas."

He knelt beside the bed and opened a little black box. "Let's make our engagement official." Inside sparkled a diamond ring. "How does a New Year's wedding sound? I don't want a long engagement."

"That sounds wonderful. The sooner the better. I

want to get married in the chapel."

"Of course. There's nowhere else more perfect than that little building you fixed up." He pulled me to my feet. "Let's stay in today, just the two of us and the animals. After the last couple of weeks, I'm yearning for a day of peace."

I smiled and cupped his face. "That sounds marvelous." I couldn't think of a better day than snuggling on the sofa with my man and watching Christmas movies while the lights twinkled on my tiny Christmas tree.

The End

Don't miss the final book, <u>Caper Finds a Treasure</u>

COZY CHRISTMAS COLLECTION

Caper Steals Christmas
A Tiny House Mystery, Book Six
By Cynthia Hickey

Chapter One

I hung an ornament on the Christmas tree in the newly erected community hall. Now, we could have gatherings all year round, and our Christmas party would be the first big event.

The building took up the space where half the playground had been dug up after some serious issues with the local drug dealers a few months ago. Rather than repair the playground, we simply moved it over and built the community hall. Since the owner was my uncle, I could pretty much do anything I wanted with the place.

"CJ Turley," A voice scolded from behind me. I turned and smiled at my friend, Mags Snyder. "You know the tree should have some kind of a theme. This looks like a child decorated it. You've every color of the rainbow and then some."

I frowned, scrunching my nose. "These are my grandmother's ornaments. I like the ornaments to be a little of everything. You'll remember I did offer to let you take care of the décor, and you declined." I hung an obscenely large bulb at eye level just for spite.

Mags groaned. "I hope somebody steals that thing."

I whirled back to face her. "Take that back. Some of these are antiques." Maybe I shouldn't have used Grams's things, but I couldn't put a tree in my tiny house big enough for more than three or five bulbs. I wanted to share my treasures with those around me.

"Well, I think it's gaudy."

"It's gorgeous." Eric Drake, local park ranger and my boyfriend, entered the building as Mags continued her criticism. "But not as lovely as my girl." He lowered his head and kissed me.

"Hello to you, too." I smiled.

"Do you know where your dog is?" He stepped back. "Because she's causing trouble, chasing the new tenant's cat, or so they've complained."

I groaned. Caper only wanted to play, but not all four-legged, or two-legged, creatures for that matter, reciprocated my feisty pup's feelings. "Can you catch her and lock her in the house?"

"Already done. Just wanted you to know that house number fifteen isn't happy."

"Thanks. I'll stop by there when I'm finished here." I stepped back and surveyed the tree again. It was perfect. Grabbing my jacket, I headed for the door. "See y'all later."

A brisk wind blew off the mountain rising above Heavenly Acres. The winter sun sparkled off Blue Lake. I really loved where I lived, despite the recent crimes that had begun over the year I'd worked here as manager. Things had settled down for the time being, and life was good.

I climbed into my red and white golf cart and drove around the loop to house number fifteen. Hoping the couple who lived there, Lee and Kim Westford, were reasonable people, I hopped from the cart and knocked on their front door.

A fluffy white cat blinked at me from the windowsill. The pretty thing didn't look any the worse after Caper's romp with her, which eased my nerves.

Mrs. Westford, a slightly plump, well-dressed woman in her mid-fifties, answered the door. "What are you going to do about that dog?"

Okay, not reasonable. "I apologize. Caper is not normally away from me. Is your cat alright?"

"No thanks to that mutt, Sugar is just fine. I had to give her extra salmon to make up for the stress of the chase. When we rented this house, you assured us we could reside here in peace."

Caper was not a mutt. Well, I didn't know if she was purebred or not, but in my heart she was a show dog. "I'll do my best to fulfill that promise, Mrs. Westford." I glanced over to where the bored-looking feline licked its paw. "Sugar is very pretty."

"She ought to be. She's a Norwegian Forest Cat

with a long bloodline and cost us a thousand dollars. She's won awards." The woman actually lifted her chin and sniffed like an aristocrat.

Wow. I couldn't imagine spending that much money on an animal. "She, uh, looks worth every penny." No wonder they had to live in a tiny house. They probably spent all their money on the cat.

I shoved aside the uncharitable thought and turned to leave. Before I was off the porch, Sugar darted between my legs. I windmilled my arms and fell, bouncing down the steps. I'd call Caper and the cat even.

"Sugar," Mrs. Westford darted past me after the white ball of fur streaking down the road.

"I'm okay. I can get up by myself." I rolled my eyes and groaned. Nothing felt broken, thank God.

By the time I limped to my cart, Mags was speeding my way on her cart. "That cat is in your Christmas tree."

Oh, no. My ornaments! Sugar was starting to be a real pain in my behind, and that had nothing to do with my tumble down the stairs.

Shoving aside my aches and pains, I sped back to the community center. Thank goodness the tree still stood, but a white paw flicked out from inside the tree and batted at the large bulb I'd hung last.

"Mrs. Westford, please remove your cat from the tree." I put my hands on my hips and glared at the woman who sat, smiling, in a padded chair.

"She loves Christmas trees."

"These are my personal belongings that belonged to my grandmother. I'd really appreciate your cat not breaking them."

"Very well." She unfolded herself from the chair and carefully retrieved Sugar. "Have you considered a higher fence at the entrance here? I'm afraid Sugar can climb over or under the one we have."

"Mrs. Westford, I cannot put in a new gate for a cat." I fought the urge to roll my eyes again.

"This is going to be a long six-month lease." Back straight, she marched from the building.

I agreed with her. Six months would seem like an eternity if there were more days like today.

Less than two minutes later, Mrs. Westford returned. "Where is her collar?"

"Excuse me?"

"Sugar's collar is missing." She shoved the cat into my arms and made a dash for the tree. "I don't see it." Her frantic searching knocked several ornaments from the tree. One shattered, and the large bulb rolled across the floor and lodged under the tree.

"Be careful, please." I tightened my grip on the squirming animal and received a scratch for my trouble. "Could she have lost it on the way here? Do you have another one?"

She narrowed her eyes. "That one is crusted with diamonds!"

"Why in the world would you have a diamond

collar on a pet?" A jewel thief had once switched the rhinestones on Caper's collar to diamonds, but that was to hide the jewels in plain sight, not because my dog was spoiled.

"We bought it as a reward when she won her first ribbon." She took the cat from me. "She earned it."

"Let's fetch my dog and retrace her steps. Caper has a talent for finding jewels." Unfortunately for me in the past. I eyed Sugar. "Maybe we'll take her home first."

I drove Mrs. Westford to her house to drop off the cat, then she rode with me to retrieve Caper.

My little spaniel wasn't a genius or anything, but she definitely seemed to understand me when I talked to her. "Please hold out your wedding ring to her so she'll know we're looking for diamonds."

"Are you serious?" Mrs. Westford's eyes widened.

"Yes, ma'am."

Scowling, she held out her hand for Caper to sniff, recoiling as my pup's nose touched her skin. "I detest dogs."

"Be nice or she won't help." I knelt. "Find the diamonds, girl."

Caper barked once, wagged her tail, and took off with her nose to the ground. Diamonds, cats, and squirrels were what got my dog excited.

"What's going on?" Mags stopped next to us.

"An expensive collar fell off the cat's neck," I

said.

"She has a name, you know. Her name is Sugar." Mrs. Westford clamped her lips together.

"You sent Caper to find it?" Mags grinned. "That'll work. Hop in."

Mrs. Westford took the seat next to Mags, leaving me to hang onto the back. It wasn't the first time. Most of the time I actually enjoyed it, but my body was violently protesting my thumps down the stairs. I started to think I might have bruised my tailbone.

Caper slowed and glanced back at us, then continued forward again. She ran a circle around house number fifteen, then darted for the park, empty of children on the cold day. She squeezed under a bush and barked.

Bingo. I hopped off the cart and rushed toward her. "Okay, let me see." I pulled her out.

In her mouth was a collar with half the diamonds missing. "Looks like someone got scared and tossed this." I glanced around the area.

With no rain in a few days, there weren't any footprints. I didn't need anyone to know we had a diamond thief among us. Again.

Who and how did they know the diamonds on the cat's collar were real? And how did they manage to remove so many in such a short amount of time?

Chapter Two

Mrs. Westford yanked the collar from my hand. "I cannot believe this is happening."

Neither could I, to be honest. Theft and murder were getting old. At least it was just a collar. Hopefully, the woman had taken out insurance on something so valuable. Animals tended to get their collars hung on things when running around outside. "Time to call Davis."

Mags' grandson-in-law was our local detective. He wouldn't be happy, or surprised, about another mystery at Heavenly Acres.

Mr. Westford arrived at the community hall at the same time as Davis. While he had a worried look on his face, the detective looked more resigned than upset.

I went through the spiel of what had happened up to finding Sugar in the Christmas tree. Before I could finish, Davis had moved on.

Sighing, he parted the branches on the Christmas

tree, lowered himself to his knees, and looked up, then circled it twice. "I don't see anything."

"It's here." Mrs. Westford held up the collar.

Davis blinked a few times. "I thought it was missing."

"It was." She shook her head. "We found it with half the diamonds missing."

"If you hadn't been in such a hurry to be through with this," I said, "you'd know that I didn't have time to tell you the whole story." Seriously, was I that bad to be around that he couldn't stay long enough to hear all the facts?

"Sorry." Davis crossed his arms. "Mrs. Westford, kindly finish." When she did, he asked, "Do you have insurance on the collar?"

She looked taken aback. "Why would you ask?"

"Something that valuable should be insured."

"Yes, we have insurance," her husband said.

"But that doesn't bring back the fact this collar was a reward for Sugar's first blue ribbon. That is something we cannot replace." Mrs. Westford glared at me. "If it wasn't for your dog, this wouldn't have happened."

I raised my brows. "Your cat came here on her own. If it weren't for Caper, you wouldn't be holding at least some of the diamonds." I snuggled my pup under my chin. "You're a good girl," I crooned.

"Isn't there a leash law here?" Davis glanced from one to the other.

"Yes, but the cat ran out when I had the door open talking to Ms. Turley about her dog's horrible behavior." High spots of color appeared on Mrs. Westford's cheeks. "She's a high-strung animal and doesn't like a leash. The dog wasn't on one earlier."

Which reminded me. How did Caper get out in the first place? Since she seemed to find trouble when let loose, I always left her in the house, on her lead line, or on a leash with me. "May I go, please?"

Davis nodded. "I'll come by your place when I'm finished with the Westfords."

I stepped outside and glanced to house number seven where Eric lived. Seeing his jeep and his side-by-side parked out front, I headed in that direction. He opened the door before I reached the steps.

"Hey, gorgeous."

"Hey, yourself." I tilted my head. "Did you let Caper out earlier? Before you told me about her chasing the cat?"

"No, I saw the two running around, then Mrs. Westford flagged me down. Why?"

"Because I distinctly remember shutting her in my house." I went on to explain the rest of the day's happenings.

"Come on, Hershey. We're checking out CJ's house." He stepped aside so his chocolate lab could join us.

"You really think someone let her out?" It didn't make sense. Why? Usually when someone messed with my dog, it was because I'd poked my nose where it didn't belong.

He shrugged. "Let's go find out." He put an arm around my shoulders. "I was kind of hoping we could get through the Christmas season without a mystery."

"That would've been nice." I leaned into him, grateful for his warmth. "It's so cold today."

"Yeah, February cold, not December. No campers across the lake, so work is slow. Gives me time to get some things done around the house," he said, walking me home.

"What can you possibly do in a tiny house?"

"I've been watching shows. You know I like to cook, and one episode showed a tiny house with a pantry and spice rack that pulled down from the ceiling. I'm going to build one."

"Wow. That sounds amazing." I wanted one. I already had one in the floor storage where I kept things I didn't use much, but every inch of a tiny house could be utilized if one knew how. Maybe I needed to watch less true crime and watch what Eric watched to get ideas of my own.

"Stay outside." He put a hand on the mace clipped to his belt and pushed my door open. Unlocked. Had I forgotten again?

He glanced back and raised his eyebrows, holding the door open for the dogs to enter first.

My mouth opened and closed. "I got nothing." I really couldn't remember if I'd locked it in my excitement to decorate the tree.

Not hearing any barks or growls, Eric and I stepped inside. Nothing seemed out of place. I was good at putting things away when I'd finished with them. A house this size could clutter very quickly, so I could tell it was exactly as I'd left it. Strange. "Why let the dog out and not take anything?" I glanced around to locate my cat, Sherlock. He sat on the windowsill barely sparing us a glance.

"Are you sure nothing is missing?"

"Pretty sure. I don't keep anything valuable here." After the first rash of thefts, I'd rented a safety deposit box at the bank. Of course, I didn't really have a lot of valuables to begin with. My friend, Ann Lowery, cop turned private detective, rented my grandmother's house. I did have a few mementos there, but nothing someone would want to steal. I plopped on the sofa. "This has something to do with the diamonds." I heaved an exaggerated sigh and slumped. Sherlock leaped onto my lap. "Someone used Caper for their own rotten gain." Again. Why did this keep happening to me? "Sherlock could have escaped and been lost."

"Chin up, sweetheart." Eric sat next to me. "This is mild in comparison to some of our other adventures. Want me to call Anne?"

I rolled my head to face him. "Do you think we need to?" Anne always got roped into being my bodyguard when danger loomed over my head. "The Westfords seem to be the target this time. Someone just used my dog as a distraction." The thought made me feel a little better. No involvement meant no danger to me or my friends. "Want to stay for supper?"

"Sure. What are you fixing?"

"A hearty potato soup for a cold day like this."

A knock sounded at the door. Knowing Eric the way I did, I stayed put and let him answer. Always the gentleman, my man. He opened the door and let Davis in.

"Tell me again your version of the story, and you'll be done." Davis sat in the chair across from us.

I repeated what I'd told him. "That's it. Oh, and someone let my dog out as a diversion."

"What?" His eyes narrowed.

"I distinctly remember leaving Caper in the house when I went to the center so she wouldn't be under foot. Someone let her out. She chased Sugar. Sugar went home. I went to the Westfords, the cat got out. The cat ran to the center and climbed in the tree. Mrs. Westford retrieved said cat and noticed the collar was missing. We returned Sugar to the house and fetched Caper. You know how she loves diamonds." I smiled. "Then we found the collar with half of the diamonds missing. Voilà. End of story."

"Did the cat have the collar on when she darted out the door?"

"I don't know. She's pretty fluffy. It could have been easily hidden in her fur."

The pieces were clicking in his brain. "How far

behind you was Mrs. Westford?"

"She arrived at the building before me."

"Hm." He pushed to his feet. "Okay, let me know if you remember anything else."

"I will."

Eric escorted him out, then leaned against the door. "He's got a suspect in mind already."

"Good. I'm content to sit here." I propped my feet on the coffee table and crossed my ankles, then remembered I was supposed to be fixing supper and let my feet fall to the floor. With two dogs and a big man, moving to the small galley kitchen took some maneuvering. I loved this little house, but if I were ever to get married, I'd have to move back into Grams's house.

I couldn't help but wonder whether Davis would check the financial records for the tenants of house number fifteen. Not that I would ever have enough money to buy a thousand-dollar cat or a diamond-encrusted collar, but if I did, I wouldn't have anything left after. I glanced over my shoulder. "Do you think the Westfords could have done this for the insurance money?"

Chapter Three

I couldn't help it. I'd lain awake late into the night pondering how to find out whether the Westfords were trying to commit insurance fraud. Getting involved really was an addiction for me, one I had no idea how to break.

Ugh. I climbed out of bed and padded downstairs for a cup of coffee, doing some fancy footwork to keep from tripping over Sherlock who insisted on rubbing against my ankles.

I popped a pod into the coffee maker and stared out the window over the sink. The day looked as cold as yesterday. Frost covered the ground. Winters were slow not only for Eric, but also for myself. As manager of the campground and tiny houses, my main job was to lease the homes, or sell in some cases, and do one or two rides around the campground each day.

Some people might think my life boring, but I loved the simplicity of it. Coffee finished, I added creamer and folded down the two-person table from the wall. I set my laptop on top and booted it up to check for emails.

No new inquiries for rentals. Not a surprise this close to Christmas.

I closed my laptop and headed back upstairs to get dressed. Fifteen minutes later, I clicked a leash on Caper, checked and double checked that my front door was locked, and headed for the campgrounds in my cart with Caper wagging her tail beside me.

Just because there weren't any campers didn't mean there wouldn't be something that needed doing—kids partying, etc. It warranted me checking. Eric helped, but he had a much larger area to patrol.

I took the path past our little glass-walled chapel. The building was my pride and joy since its restoration. The cross that lit up at night could be seen from almost everywhere in the community and campgrounds. Everything looked fine.

Wait a minute... I stopped the cart and looked closer.

The chapel door hung open a couple of inches. I might forget to lock my own front door, and while the chapel was never locked, the door was always closed. I sighed. If people didn't take better care to keep the weather and critters out, I'd have to rethink the open-door policy.

"Come on, Caper." I led the dog inside the chapel and stopped to listen. No running footsteps, no slamming of the door to the storage room. All seemed in order, but I ventured forward anyway.

Footprints appeared halfway down the aisle. They led through the side door and disappeared. Whoever left them had gone into the woods behind the chapel. I called for Caper to follow, then let the footprints lead me.

It didn't take long for me to see the first sparkling, dropped diamond winking at me from the dried fallen leaves. Would the jewels leave a trail like Hansel and Gretel's breadcrumbs? Since I didn't know how far ahead the jewel thief might be, I returned to my golf cart. As I continued the drive to the campgrounds, I called Davis with my phone on speaker. "You know that path behind the chapel?"

"Yes."

"I found a diamond on the ground."

Davis sighed. "Please tell me you aren't getting involved."

"I'm not. I'm doing my job, noticed the door to the chapel was left open, followed the—"

"All right, I get it. I'll meet you at the chapel in twenty." Click.

I'd have to hurry to circle the campground. What I really wanted to do was stay at the chapel and follow the glittering trail. That would only result in more disapproval from Davis, and I'd had enough of that to last me a lifetime. It had been a very busy year.

I sped around the grounds, then circled back to the

chapel. The campground was asleep for the winter, and I hadn't spotted any signs of kids goofing around after hours. If I had, then Eric would step in, since enforcing the rules was his job. Breaking them was mine. I grinned and hopped off the cart to greet Davis.

"Come on, I'll show you." Rather than lead him through the chapel, we went around. "See?" I pointed to the gem.

"You only found this one?" He bent and used a cloth from his pocket to pick up the stone.

"Yes, I didn't go any further. I've learned my lesson about venturing out on my own."

"Sure you have." He glanced up the trail. "Let's see if we find any more."

Yay, he was letting me come along. A rare treat, indeed. I mean, I would have followed regardless, but it's nice to be invited.

"Stay behind me and be quiet."

Good ole Davis. Sweet as always. I took the end of Caper's leash to prevent her from running ahead and followed the detective, scouring the ground for anything sparkly.

We found nothing. The dropped diamond wasn't part of a trail.

"Keep your eyes open," Davis said. "The thief might be back."

"For the rest of the diamonds?"

"Maybe. The collar is at the station, but the thief doesn't know that."

"You think the Westfords are committing insurance fraud, don't you?" I arched a brow.

"What makes you think that?"

"A gut feeling."

"Don't ask any questions, CJ." He marched down the path, refusing my offer of a ride, saying walking helped him think.

Very well. I still needed to drive the loop of the community.

Roy Olson, our local handyman, stepped out of his house and waved for me to stop. "Number fifteen is really getting on my nerves."

"What are they doing?"

"They want me to build a see-through cat tunnel that goes up and around the house." He crossed his arms.

"That isn't your job."

"They seem to think I'm their personal servant. I need you to put your foot down. I'm hired to do repairs, that's it."

Yep. It was going to be a long six months. "I'll talk to them." Cat tower. Ridiculous. Plus, the Westfords were renters, not owners. They couldn't do major construction to the house, and I seriously doubted whether the other tenants would want a cat tower if the house wasn't rented.

I secured Caper's leash to the cart and approached the Westfords' front door. I knocked and stepped back, prepared to scoop up Sugar if she tried to escape.

A laughing Mrs. Westford opened the door. "Yeah?" She seemed to have gotten over yesterday quick enough.

"I must inform you that we cannot fulfill your request about the addition." There. That sounded official and authoritative.

"This place really doesn't care about the happiness of its residents." Her smile faded.

"You are renting, Mrs. Westford. That type of construction could prevent us from renting the house to someone else after you've vacated the property."

The woman stared at me, stony-faced, for a moment, then she slammed the door in my face. "Lee, you'd better figure this mess out so we can leave this horrible place," her voice echoed through the door.

Figure out what? How to retrieve their collar? The insurance money? Or something else entirely? I decided to keep a close eye on the occupants of number fifteen.

"What cha doing?" Mags pulled up alongside of me.

"Come back to the house and I'll tell you."

Back home, I made coffee for the two of us and told her about finding the diamond and the silly request of the Westfords. "Want to help me spy on them?"

"Do I? Silly question. Winters bore me to tears. With your Uncle Larry working such long hours at the youth center, he doesn't have a lot of time to spend with me." She blew into her mug. "What do you want to do first?"

"Stakeout?" I wiggled my brows. "It'll be cold, but we can wrap up in blankets."

"Let's do it."

Chapter Four

"This is like old times." Mags snuggled down in a thick quilt. We'd "borrowed" Larry's car since the Westfords wouldn't recognize it.

"Not enough time has passed for old times to fit here." I wrapped my hands around a thermos of hot coffee and stared at number fifteen.

The occupants still moved around inside at ten p.m. Sugar sat in the window. I'd bet she could see us, knew what we were doing. I shuddered. The cat might be beautiful, but her owner gave me the creeps.

"Say what you will." Mags cut me a sideways glance. "I miss having a mystery to solve."

"You're rarely the one almost killed."

"Nonsense. I'm usually right there with you. Except for the flight over the mountain. I'm too old for that."

I chuckled. Only Mags was allowed to mention her age. Not yet sixty, Mags wasn't old, at least I didn't think she was. Eccentric as she was, Mags was my best friend. I preferred older people, really. Especially after tending to Grams for so many years.

The door to the house opened. I squinted to see better. Mr. Westford closed the door and strode toward the front of the grounds, shoulders slumped against the cold. Who went for a walk this late on a frigid night?

"Come on. Let's follow him, but be quiet." I carefully opened my door.

Mags pretended to lock her lips, not that it would work, given past events. Still, she'd be silent for a few minutes before she couldn't help herself.

Staying low and keeping to the shadows as much as possible, we kept our eyes on Lee. The man stepped outside the gate and glanced both ways up and down the highway.

"He's waiting for someone," Mags whispered.

"Shh." I pulled her behind the dumpster and put a finger to my lips. Thank goodness it wasn't hot weather. The last time we'd hid here, we were surrounded by very unpleasant odors.

Lee pulled a cell phone from his pocket. "Where are you? Kim is going to notice me gone soon. I'd really like to put an end to all this." He listened for a few seconds. "Fine." He whirled and stomped back into the community.

I shrugged at the wide-eyed Mags. Who was on the other end of the conversation, man or woman? I motioned Mags forward and followed Lee back to his house.

His wife immediately started screeching, "Where were you?"

Uh-oh. The man wasn't very good at sneaking around.

"Just walking, dear. I've got a lot on my mind."

"You need to be worried about our investment in that collar." Her shadow through the curtains crossed its arms. "We're broke, Lee."

"I'm well aware of that, dear. That's one reason I've got a lot on my mind. Good night." His shadow headed up the stairs, I presumed.

"I'm not finished talking to you," his wife said.

We weren't learning anything here, other than the fact that things weren't rosy in the Westford household. Feeling bad for eavesdropping on a private, if unhappy moment, I pulled back.

A yeow sent me lunging forward. A white flash darted past me. Sugar had escaped when Mr. Westford either left or returned.

"Now what?" Mags asked.

"We catch the darn cat and return her. I'll say I was doing my last round before going to bed." As manager, it was plausible.

I gave chase, Mags quickly falling behind. Sugar ducked under house number six where the Flower family resided. Lucy would kill me if I woke up her kids.

"Here, kitty, kitty, kitty." *I'm going to wring your*

neck.

Sugar hissed and swiped at me. Of course, she wasn't declawed. My hand burned where her nail scratched.

"You like fish? I've got a can of tuna with your name on it."

The cat sprang away from me.

I sighed and crawled from under the house and continued my pursuit, passing Mags who now leaned against the car sipping her coffee. "Thanks for the help," I said, rushing past.

"No problem," she called after me. "I'm here if you need me."

I rolled my eyes and raced after Sugar as she headed for the community building. Now I had her. There was no way she could get inside. My shoulders slumped as she jumped and squeezed through a partially open window. Would I have to lock the building after hours? I'd hoped to provide a place for the teenagers to hang out of the cold.

Pushing open the door, I stepped into the dim room, lit only by the twinkling lights of the Christmas tree. "Here, kitty, kitty, kitty." *Please don't be in the tree again.*

She wasn't. Instead, she happily sharpened her claws on an easy chair in the corner. Destructive little beast.

I closed the window, turned on the overhead light, and unplugged the Christmas tree, already forming the notice I'd hand out tomorrow about how to leave the clubhouse before leaving. After shutting off all means of escape for the feisty feline, I headed to the corner.

"Come on. I've had enough of your shenanigans." As I stooped down to pick her up, my gaze landed on the back of chair where the upholstery had pulled away from the frame. How had I not noticed that before? I seriously doubted a cat could have torn it away.

I peered behind the fabric. Aha. A gift box. One of the fake presents I'd set under the tree as part of the décor. I pulled it out and opened it.

Loose diamonds blinked up at me.

Something hit me in the back of the head. The last thing I saw before blacking out was diamonds scattering across the polished wood floor.

The first thing I saw when I woke was a single diamond staring me in the eye. I put a hand to my head, relieved not to find any blood on my fingers, and inched to my feet before picking up the gem and dropping it into my pocket.

I groaned and stepped outside. Not seeing any sign of the trouble-making cat, I shuffled to where Mags still waited, although she'd moved to the car's interior.

"What happened to you?" She asked as I slid into the driver's seat.

I explained. "Did you see anyone?"

"No, but I closed my eyes for a few minutes." She pressed the button on her watch. "Look at that. It's after eleven. Way past my bedtime."

"I got hit in the head, but I'll call Davis in the morning." I drove home, which took all of two minutes.

"Should I stay with you?" Concern flickered across Mags' face.

"I'll be fine." It barely hurt, although I'd most likely have a dickens of a headache in the morning. "Call me at eight. If I don't answer, call the morgue."

"Not funny, Clarice Josephine." She shoved open her door and got out. "I'm going to call you every half an hour."

"Please don't. I'd really like a good night's sleep. I didn't get a nap like someone I know."

"Don't pout. It causes lines around your lips." She closed the door and entered her house.

Since I wasn't an idiot, I didn't go straight to bed when I got home. It was hard to resist teasing my friend. Instead, I let Caper out to do her business and leaned against the railing of my postage-stamp porch.

Whoever hit me hadn't targeted me. I was simply in the wrong place when they came to retrieve the diamonds. What bothered me was the fact I hadn't heard them enter the room. There were only two places to hide in the clubhouse. The bathrooms. The kitchen area wasn't closed off.

Had they taken Sugar, or had the cat ran out when my attacker did? I glanced toward number fifteen. I had to know whether the cat made it home safely. Pain in my rear or not, it was my tenants' beloved pet.

I reached into the house, grabbed Caper's leash off a hook, then clipped it to her collar. I wasn't going anywhere without a warning system, and my dog was perfect for the job. A few minutes later, I stood in front of number fifteen and stared at the open door.

Chapter Five

Here we go again. I'd landed smack dab in a mystery I didn't want.

Gravel crunched behind me. I gasped and whirled. Eric crossed his arms. "Mags called me. Why are you out here after getting knocked on the head?"

"I wanted to make sure the cat made it home. Instead, I see an open door. I was just about to call the police."

Appeased, he pulled me close. "Are you okay?"

"A dull headache. Nothing serious." I leaned against him, called the local police, and was told Milton, one of the officers on duty, would arrive soon. "Should we look inside?"

"No." Eric rested his cheek alongside mine. "We wait."

I understood going inside would contaminate a potential crime scene, but curiosity tugged at me like a laser beam. I stretched, trying to peek over the steps.

Eric chuckled. "Relax, Milton is here."

The officer pulled to a stop in front of the house. He shook his head as he strolled toward us. "CJ Turley, do you ever stop nosing around?"

"Trouble seems to find me." I grinned. "You police officers might get bored without me."

"You do keep us on our toes." He climbed the steps and paused in the open doorway.

I followed and peered around him. The house looked as if the occupants had merely stepped out and forgot to close the door. "Where's the cat?"

Milton glanced over his shoulder. "Outside if the door was left open long enough."

Caper yanked the leash out of my hand and raced to a nearby bush. She set up a frenzy of barking, sure to wake not only the dead but the living as well. "Caper, hush." I grabbed the end of her leash and pulled.

She yelped, then resumed barking harder. I separated the branches of the bush and spotted a very irate Sugar. "Found the cat."

"I'll get her." Eric reached down and smooth-talked the feline until she curled up in his arms and purred.

I glanced at Caper. "She doesn't usually act this aggressive toward another animal. These two must have gotten into a scuffle."

Milton exited the house and pulled the door closed. "Everything looks fine inside. They must have not closed the door properly. Anything else?"

Sighing, I told him about getting hit in the head.

"Lead on." Milton gave an exaggerated bow.

I went with Milton while Eric returned Sugar to her home. "The diamonds had been stuffed into that chair." I pointed to the one in the corner.

"Did Davis tell you there are teeth marks on the cat's collar? Have you checked your dog's pooh for diamonds?"

"You think Caper stole the collar and ate the diamonds?" I raised my brows. "Then why would someone hide the diamonds? Why hit me?"

"I don't have all the answers. It's just a theory. But that dog of yours has a thing for diamonds." He scoped out the room, then declared it empty.

True. Caper enjoyed sparkling things. "Now what?"

"We keep trying to find out what happened and keep you out of trouble." He flashed a grin and ushered me outside. "I'd make this a crime scene, but it's so contaminated now it would do no good."

"Don't go to any trouble on my account. It's not the first time someone cold-cocked me." I doubted it would be the last considering my penchant for snooping. Maybe I should start wearing a helmet when I leave the house. Since I'd been up long enough not to be concerned about falling asleep, I curled up on the sofa, covered myself with a crocheted blanket, and fell asleep as soon as my head hit the pillow. When I woke, both fur babies lay on top of me, I stretched, then padded my way to coffee. Couldn't start my day without it, especially since I'd had a very long day and only a few hours of sleep.

The Westfords' car sat in front of their house, so I made plans to let them know about the open door. I'd leave the fact that my dog might have been the first thief of the collar to Davis. My tenants didn't seem like fans of mine, so no need to increase their dislike.

Glancing to where Caper waited at the door to be let out, I couldn't help but wonder whether she was guilty of taking the collar off the cat's neck. I grabbed my coat and stepped outside so she could do her business. "A simple imprint of your teeth will tell, won't it?" I gasped.

If she were guilty, I wouldn't have to pay, would I? I couldn't replace one diamond much less half a collar's worth. "Oh, Caper, you've been a naughty girl." I called her back into the house and resumed my wakeup routine.

After showering, getting dressed, and eating toast and jam, I shrugged back into my coat, locked Caper in the house, double-checked the lock, and drove my cart to house number fifteen. Nine a.m. was a decent hour to knock on someone's door, right?

Before I got out of the cart, Danny, Roy Olson's son, ducked around the corner, then dashed across the street. The sixteen-year-old hadn't been in trouble since I took the job, but his behavior bordered on suspicious, like the time he'd stolen my laptop. I gave chase, cornering him against an empty rental.

"Hello, Danny."

"CJ." His features fell.

"What are you up to? I want the truth. I'm too busy for games, and if you're up to no good, I'll tell your father."

"I'm trying to solve the mystery." He scuffed the toe of his shoe in the dirt.

I tilted my head. "How do you know about that?"

"I overheard Mags talking to Larry."

"By listening outside her house?"

He exhaled heavily. "It's Christmas break. I'm bored, so I wander around. I can't help it if folks leave their windows open."

"You wouldn't hear anything if you stayed on the road. Get in." I motioned my head toward the passenger seat.

"Are you going to tell my dad?" He moved as if walking the Green Mile.

"Not this time, but I am taking you home." Summer break was easier on the boy since I'd hired him to mow the grounds here and at the camp. I'd try to find something constructive for him to do during the winter.

I stopped in front of his house, the largest in the community. It wasn't as large as the Flower family's house, but Roy did everything for Heavenly Acres that I couldn't. "Did you hear anything?"

Danny's face lit up. "I sure did. I overheard Mr.

Westford telling his wife that everything was going according to plan."

"That isn't much." I frowned.

"She replied that if that nosy manager would mind her own business, things would be smoother."

Aha. That would be me. What kind of plan did they have going?

"Then they started arguing about someone that Mr. Westford keeps sneaking out to see at night. That's when I left. I didn't want to hear anything gross."

"I don't blame you." I smiled and drove back to number fifteen once Danny slid from the cart. I'd used his eyes and ears before to help gather information, but if he were going to do it again, I needed to know at least, so I could watch out for him.

With no more interruptions, I knocked on the door. Mrs. Westford yanked it open. "What now?"

"Good morning," I sang, determined to be cheerful despite her surliness. "I'm here to inform you that your door was left open late last night, and nobody was home. I called the local authorities who came out to investigate. We found Sugar under a bush and put her back into the house." My grin widened. "I thought you would want to know."

"Lee?" She turned around. "You left the door open last night."

"Sorry," he called from the loft.

"Thank you." Mrs. Westford made a move to close the door.

"Is there any news on the diamonds?" I wanted to keep her talking to see whether she'd give me a clue as to whether she was behind my attack.

"No. Besides, it's no concern of yours any longer."

"Actually, it is." I told her of chasing Sugar into the clubhouse and finding a bag of diamonds. "Someone knocked me out and took them. You wouldn't know who, would you?"

"Are you accusing me of something?" Her eyes narrowed. "If Sugar was out, then you would also know we weren't home. Didn't you just tell me my door was left open?"

I shrugged. "Doesn't mean you couldn't have circled back. Have a good day."

That ought to flush her out, if she was responsible and/or committing insurance fraud. I'd found that antagonizing a suspect seemed to make them careless. The Westfords were the only suspects I had—the only ones the police had, too, unless Davis was withholding information from me. The only time he readily shared was if we were working together.

Maybe it was time to pay a visit to Ann. Since the prior cop was now a private investigator, she had access to information I didn't.

Chapter Six

"Hey, CJ," Anne greeted me with a smile when I rang her doorbell. "I wasn't expecting you."

"I took the off chance you'd be home." I removed my coat and hung it on the antique coat tree by the front door. "I have a favor to ask."

"I've heard of the latest mystery you've gotten involved in."

Ah. I'd forgotten about her boyfriend at the precinct. "I'm wondering if you can find out what Davis knows, and if there's any dirt on the Westfords."

"Sure. Want some tea?" She headed for the kitchen.

Returning to Grams's house always seemed a bit surreal to me. I'd spent five years caring for her as cancer slowly wasted her body away. That's probably why I couldn't live here yet. "That sounds wonderful. Thanks."

Tea in hand, I sat on the familiar tweed sofa and

told Anne everything that had transpired over the last couple of days. "Milton suggested Caper took the collar. That would mean the theft after was one of convenience. Which might blow my theory of insurance fraud."

"Not necessarily. Who could have taken advantage easier than the Westfords?" Ann sat across from me.

"I can't think of anyone. Anyway, I've accused her. Now to wait and see what happens."

Anne rolled her eyes. "Deliberately inviting danger."

"How else can I find out?" I wiggled my eyebrows. "I've been lucky so far."

"Luck has a way of running out."

True. "Let me know if you find out anything."

"I'll know something, even if only a little, by tonight. Want me to bring over a pizza?"

"That sounds great." I headed home to do some household chores while I waited. Mags was peeking out her front window, It wouldn't be long before she came over to see where I'd gone. It took two minutes. I wasn't even out of my car.

"Come into the house," I said, stepping out of my car. "I'll make coffee."

"Great. I'll fetch the leftover cake." She rushed back to her house.

By the time she returned, lemon pound cake in hand, I'd already let Caper out to relieve herself and waited on the porch for my friend. "I'm assuming you want to know the latest."

"I have to admit I'm surprised to see you out and about after being attacked." She pressed her lips together and sniffed. "You should have asked me to go with you."

"I only visited Anne." I popped a pod in the coffee maker.

"To have her dig up information?"

I nodded. "On the Westfords." I told her about the teeth marks on the collar. "I'm expecting Davis to take an imprint of Caper's mouth at any moment. I've openly accused Kim Westford of hitting me. The ball is rolling."

"Why not make it roll faster?" She grinned. "Throw a Christmas party at the clubhouse and have those interested draw names. Make sure you get Kim's. Then, make sure the gift you give her has something to do with her faking the theft. That ought to do it."

I laughed. "You have an evil mind, my friend." The idea did hold merit. "What could I give her?"

"A book on insurance fraud. Fiction, of course. If she's guilty, she'll get the picture."

"You should have been in law enforcement." I handed her a mug of coffee and prepared my own.

With one week until Christmas, I'd have to move fast to plan a party. "Could you ask Larry what kind of budget he'd let me have? I need to work on fliers and put them up right away."

"Sure. You know he can't refuse you anything." She carried her coffee to my table for two and sliced the cake. "You were already going to have a party. Why haven't you started planning?"

"I got sidetracked with the whole missing-collar thing." Now, time was running out, and I prided myself on community get-togethers. Once a month was what I aimed for.

A knock sounded on the door. I opened it to see Davis. "Hello."

"I need an imprint of Caper's teeth."

"What took you so long?"

He shook his head. "Milton has a big mouth." He pulled a flat piece of…something soft from his pocket. "I put bacon grease on it to make it more enticing. Here."

I took the whatever it was. "Afraid she'll bite you? Caper doesn't have a mean bone in her body." I knelt and placed the thing in her mouth. She bit down. "Good girl." Poor thing looked offended when I removed it. I handed it back to Davis and fetched my pup a real treat.

"How's the head?" The corner of Davis's mouth twitched. "Knock any sense into you?"

"Ha ha." I wrinkled my nose. "Don't you have work to do?"

"Yep. Mags, Amber and I would like to have you over for supper tonight. You and Larry."

"That sounds wonderful." She smiled over her

cup. "I'll bring dessert."

"I'm counting on it." He planted a kiss on her cheek and left.

"To think he wasn't always my favorite person," she said. "Regardless, he can't know of our plan to trap Kim Westford."

"He's more likely to get the tip from you than from me." I resumed my seat at the table and opened my laptop. "Let's do a potluck. As people respond to my invitation, I'll pair them up for the gift exchange."

"Or—" She held up a finger, "Why not do a week-long thing? A Secret Santa exchange, revealing the final gift at the party. You could really make Kim sweat."

"You're a genius." My fingers flew across the keyboard. Half an hour later, I'd sent out emails to every resident and printed a cute flier to hang on the community board.

"Larry said you had all the money you need within reason." Mags slid her phone into her pocket and pushed to her feet. "Let me know if you need anything else from me. I have to go bake a chocolate cake."

"Doing it potluck style won't cost much. We'll supply paper products and drinks."

"Let's have an ugly Christmas sweater contest, too. Those are always fun."

By the time Anne arrived with the pizza, and Eric showed up, since we usually ate supper together, I had an affirmative response from everyone. Even the

Westfords.

"You look pleased with yourself," Eric said, kissing me.

I explained why. "Now I need to find the perfect book for my secret pal."

"Mega meat." Anne set the pizza on the table. "Why wasn't I invited to this party?"

"You don't live here," I said.

"No, but my landlord does." She opened the box and plopped a slice on a plate.

"Why do you want to steal the joy of Christmas by giving a gift to someone that will only upset them?" He held up a hand to stop my protest. "I know she's a suspect, but...it's Christmas."

"If Davis is right about Caper being the original culprit, my dog might have already stolen Christmas. Especially, if I have to pay for the missing diamonds."

"You won't have to. You never had them, they've gone missing, yada yada," Anne said. "You can't fault a dog for chasing a cat."

"Especially *that* cat," I muttered, reaching for a slice of mega meat. "Did you find out anything on the Westfords?"

"They filed for bankruptcy. Lost a big house, a second car...they're involved in cat shows up the Yazoo. They've spent a lot of money on that cat."

"And intended for the diamonds to be their saving grace." I pursed my lips. "Steal them, get the insurance money, and have all that money back. But why not put rhinestones on the cat's collar and keep the money? No one would know the difference."

Anne shrugged. "People are weird."

Sherlock growled from the windowsill. His tail flicked back and forth like a pendulum.

Eric parted the curtains. "Sugar is out again."

"I ought to let Sherlock out so he can father some mixed-breed kittens. Wouldn't that rile Kim Westford?" I grinned. "I'm getting tired of chasing down that cat for people who can't take proper care to lock her inside."

"That's the pot calling the kettle," Eric said, smiling.

"Hey, I lock Caper up now. Someone else let her out this time." And I still hadn't found out who or why, other than to create a diversion. "If she was let out for the sole purpose of stealing the collar, then someone knows of her love of diamonds. This was all planned."

"Wasn't it mentioned in the newspaper during the diamond thefts?" Ann's brow furrowed. "Someone is following your infamous career in troublemaking."

"This must be 'pick-on-CJ' day." I bit into the pizza. A pepperoni slid off onto my chest. Great. A greasy stain on my favorite sweatshirt. I sighed and scrubbed at it with a napkin. I refused to let their jokes upset me. I'd solved worse crimes and lived to talk about them. This time would be no different.

Chapter Seven

The sound of my front window shattering jolted me awake. Caper darted downstairs, her barks ringing in my ears.

No shuffling for me that morning. Having something crash through a person's window woke them up faster than two cups of coffee. I dashed down the stairs after Caper and scooped her up before she could run across the broken glass.

A rock with a sheet of paper wrapped around it lay in the middle of the room. A blast of cold air came through the broken window.

"Hush, Caper." I closed her in the bathroom, then called Eric before heading back upstairs to get dressed in something warmer than my pajamas. By the time I came back down, my man stood in the living room, staring at the rock.

"If you get me a broom, I'll sweep this up." He bent and picked up the rock, unwrapping it. *"Stay out of it*," he read. "Maybe they don't know you after all." The corner of his mouth twitched.

"Ha ha." I handed him the broom. "Funny how this comes right after our conversation last night. Maybe someone stood outside the window and listened to us. It could have been Lee or Kim coming for Sugar."

"Makes sense. Someone must have heard us talking to know you were involved. Call Davis."

After I made the call and swept up the glass, Eric and I headed outside to search for clues. The lack of rain had left the ground hard as cement. No footprints appeared under the window.

I stepped back to the road's edge and raised my hand as if to throw something. "I think they were about here." Where would they have run to? I'd rushed down the stairs. They couldn't be far.

Hands on my hips, I surveyed the area while Eric studied the ground. "Eric?" I took off after a man in a dark hoodie. "Hey!"

He glanced back. I didn't recognize him. His eyes widened, and he took off at a run toward the front entrance.

Eric passed me with little effort. I was fast, but nowhere near as speedy as my six-foot-two boyfriend. As he caught up with the fleeing suspect, Davis pulled up.

"That was fast." I bent over, trying to catch my breath.

"I was close by." He marched to where Eric held onto a struggling teenager. "What's going on?"

"These freaks started chasing me," the boy said.

"Why'd you run?" Eric released him.

"When two strangers yell and come after you, you run." The boy straightened his hoodie.

"Why are you here?" I straightened.

"I spent the night with Danny Olson. Cheez." He glared.

Davis narrowed his eyes. "Know anything about a rock through this woman's window?"

The boy paled. "No."

"Did you see anyone outside besides you?"

"Sure. I saw a man jogging. He wore black sweatpants and a gray hoodie."

"What's your name?" Davis pulled a small notepad from his pocket.

"Ryan Johnson."

"Tell me everything you can about this man."

"That's it. He was jogging. I didn't think anything wrong about it. Look, I got a job, and I'm going to be late."

"Hold on." I glanced around the area, instinct telling me the boy lied. "How do you plan on getting to town? I don't see a car."

The boy whirled and sprinted for the road. Davis and Eric gave chase, leaving me to wait behind. I'd had enough exercise for the day, thank you, and it wasn't eight o'clock yet.

A couple of minutes later, Ryan was brought back by Eric and Davis, handcuffed, then put into the backseat of Davis's car. "The jogger paid him twenty dollars to throw the rock," Davis said. "He'd never seen the guy before. He stopped Ryan when he left the Olson house."

"The jogger could be anyone." Although I couldn't picture Lee Westford jogging. "If you got close enough to take money, you saw his face," I said through the car window.

"It was just a guy." Ryan hung his head.

"We'll question him some more," Davis said. "I suggest you board up your window and let me handle this. Things are escalating."

I nodded and stepped closer to Eric. "Want me to make pancakes?"

"Is that your way of bribing me to take care of the window?" He grinned.

"Yep."

"I'd do it for nothing." He put an arm around my shoulders, leading me home after Davis pulled away with Ryan in the back of his car.

"I know you would, but I doubt you've eaten."

"Nope. I threw on some clothes and came the instant you called me." He turned me to face him. "I'll always come to your rescue."

A slow smile spread across my face. "I know you will."

His kiss drove away the morning's cold, warming

me from the inside out. When we pulled apart, I leaned my forehead against his chest. I could stay there forever if not for the plaintive grumbling of my stomach.

We strolled hand-in-hand back to my place. I glanced at number fifteen. "Remember when house number ten was where all the action happened?" That lot still sat empty. "Obviously, it wasn't the house. It's time to put a new tiny house on that spot."

"Silly girl. It's always the people." Eric grinned.

I nodded, but after so many bad people living on that lot, I'd had the house removed. I wasn't superstitious, not really, but that house had seemed to be cursed. "Now, I need to get inside number fifteen and see whether Lee owns a pair of dark sweatpants and a grey sweatshirt. See if he has running shoes."

"I still can't see him jogging anywhere."

"Neither can I." The pudgy man looked as if the most exercise he got was from the sofa to the fridge. "But I want to make sure." Somehow, I needed a really good excuse for entering the house. As manager, I could at any time if I gave the resident a day's notice. Maybe it was time for an inspection.

Chapter Eight

In order to make things "fair," I sent fliers to every resident who rented about a cursory checkup in two days. No one cared. It was in their contract after all.

Bad thing was, my idea increased my workload. Good thing was, I got to see everyone's Christmas decorations, which I loved. Not that they could go full-out in such small spaces, but every bit of Christmas cheer brightened my spirits. Until I reached house number fifteen.

Mrs. Westford waited on the front porch, Sugar in her arms. "Make it quick." She stepped back from the door.

Darn. I'd hoped she wouldn't be home. Hard to snoop with her looking over my shoulder. "I will." I flashed a smile, hoping it looked genuine, and stepped into the house. They'd sure managed to fill it with clutter since moving in. I thought Mags' place was crowded with knickknacks, but this house with all its porcelain cats had hers beat.

"How do you keep Sugar from knocking over your things?"

"She is very sure-footed."

I headed for the bedroom at the back. Number fifteen was one of the few houses without a bedroom loft. "Does Mr. Westford enjoy jogging?"

"You're joking, right?"

I faced her and shrugged. "We're thinking of starting a jogging club. Just curious."

"The man goes to work, comes home, kicks off his shoes, and sits on the couch until bedtime. Then, after I'm supposedly asleep, he sneaks out to meet his mistress. Foolish woman." She laughed at my expression and sat on the sofa. "Of course, I know about her. I'm not blind."

I opened my mouth, then snapped it closed. Their marriage woes were none of my business. I riffled through the clothes in the closet, dug through the hamper, and didn't find any sign of sweats or running shoes. I couldn't spend too much time snooping, or Mrs. Westford might get up and come see what I was doing.

"Thank you. I look forward to seeing you at the party." I brushed past her, having second thoughts about whether the Westfords stole their own diamonds or not.

It was apparent neither of them jogged. I needed to find out whether Davis had gotten a description out of Ryan. It wasn't fair that the detective expected me to divulge every tidbit of information I dug up, but he could withhold from me. Law enforcement or not, he should share.

I was also having second thoughts about gifting Kim Westford a book on insurance fraud. Christmas was a time of kindness. I'd find another way to bait the Westfords. I rubbed my hands together. Time to go shopping. After picking up Mags, I headed to town. "I'm excited now."

"You're a strange one, CJ." Mags shook her head. "But I'm not one to turn down shopping in a gift shop."

Neither was I when it was for someone else. I didn't like clutter in my own home, but this shop carried porcelain cats.

I picked up a kitten ornament, an adult coloring book picturing cats, and a sleek twelve-inch sculpture. That would be the final reveal. I also couldn't resist two dog ornaments, one that looked like Caper and one that resembled Hershey. Cute and whimsical.

Mags bought enough animal miniatures to fill Noah's ark. "These are for me. I need to find fine teas for Tammy Olson. I drew her name for the exchange."

"Want to go to the coffee shop? My treat." I rarely turned down the opportunity for a frozen mocha. "Maybe you can find a special teacup for Tammy."

"Sounds good. We can sip our drinks and discuss the next step in Operation Fraud."

Mags bought several flavored herbal teas, then

joined me with her coffee at a round table. "That man keeps looking at you."

I turned in my chair. "Which one?" The place was crowded.

"Blue jacket with his back to you," she whispered. "He keeps glancing over his shoulder."

My phone buzzed, distracting me from the man whose face I couldn't see. I glanced down to read a text from Ann saying she had the jogger's description. Mid-thirties, white, dark hair, medium build, brown eyes. I sighed. That fit a lot of people. It also fit the man who apparently kept watching me.

I glanced up and met his dark-eyed gaze. When I narrowed my eyes, he turned back to the cup in his hands.

"So, how are we going to draw out the thief?" Mags tilted her head.

"Shh," I whispered. The man who'd been glancing at her stiffened and sat back in his chair at Mags' question. "I don't think this is the place to talk."

"People talk business around here all the time. No one cares what others are conversing about."

"He does." I stood. "Come on." I headed for the door and directed Mags around the corner of the building. I peeked around the corner to see the man exit the building and glance both ways. He was looking for us.

I withdrew and plastered my back against the block wall. When the man strolled by us, I grinned.

"Hello."

His eyes widened and he increased his pace.

"Did you have something to say to me?"

He kept walking.

"I don't think he likes the fact you figured out what he'd been doing," I said.

"Then he should have been more subtle." Mags hitched her shopping bag on her shoulder. "Let's get our treasures home. We can talk there."

We picked up sub sandwiches for lunch and went to my house. "How are you going to hand out your gifts?" Mags asked. "I haven't decided. I can't very well walk up and hand them to Tammy."

"Why not ask Rose Flower to take it and not reveal who sent the gift?"

"Good idea. Tammy might think Lucy is the Secret Santa. It will totally throw her off."

"I'm going to set mine on Kim's porch each night before going to bed." That way, I could also get a good look around the grounds. If I was lucky, I might spot our jogger up to no good.

"Have you heard anything from Amber about who Davis thinks is guilty?" I bit into my Italian meat sub.

"She won't tell me anything other than his original suspect doesn't look like a suspect anymore. Whatever that means."

I frowned. "That means he no longer thinks the Westfords are guilty."

"That puts us back at square one."

"Yeah." I set my sandwich down. All Lee was guilty of was seeing his mistress, a woman his wife knew about. Caper might have pulled the collar off the cat, but someone else knew the diamonds were real. How? Did the Westfords go around talking about how much the collar was worth?

"The cat show." I snapped my fingers. "That has to be where the outsider discovered the collar's worth." I searched the web for the next cat show. Tomorrow. "Want to see some fancy cats? I guarantee the Westfords will be there. It isn't too far of a stretch to expect the thief to be there, too."

"Sure. It might be fun." Mags grinned. "We should bring our cats and show those fancy felines what a real cat is."

I laughed. "Sherlock would not be pleased. He hates the carrier." I bore some scars to prove it. "From the photos, it looks fancy. People dress up."

"Like cats?" Mags' brows rose.

"No. In nice clothes." I rolled my eyes. My friend would wear something bright and monochromatic. Mark my words.

Mags stood and tossed her sandwich wrapper in the trash. "I'll be ready in the morning. Don't do any investigating without me."

"There isn't anything to do until the cat show. I'm going to study cats so I don't sound like a complete idiot tomorrow."

"Good luck." She laughed and went home,

leaving me shaking my head at her not-so-funny attempt at humor.

After cleaning up from lunch, I curled up on the sofa with my fur babies and my laptop to learn what I needed to pretend I knew something about cats other than that they purred and landed on their feet. The show the next day had the list of entries. Sugar Westford would be participating.

Good. Hopefully, I'd catch sight of someone overly interested in the Westfords' loss of the collar. Wouldn't the thief be interested in knowing how much information the police had? Wouldn't he want to know if there were any suspects?

I propped my feet on the coffee table and started researching. Yep, something would pass hands at the show, and I intended to be there when it happened.

Chapter Nine

The next morning, I dressed in wide-legged slacks, black flats, and a sparkling sweater. Since I'd never gone to an animal show, I had no idea whether I was overdressed or under.

After making sure Caper's and Sherlock's stomachs were full, I stepped outside. Mags strolled across the street in a bright fuchsia sweater dress with matching gym shoes. Around her shoulders was what I hoped was a faux mink shawl. I laughed. "Glad you didn't disappoint in your attire."

She preened. "I know how to dress for the occasion, young lady."

I stifled another laugh and climbed into the driver's seat. I'd already texted Eric where we were going, knowing he'd receive the message when he got to where he had service. Sometimes getting service on the mountain was impossible.

"Did I tell you when I went to leave my Secret

Santa gift for Kim, Lee was leaving? Again."

"I'd never stand for that behavior from my man."

"Neither would I."

"On a more pleasant note, I'm very excited," Mags said, petting her shawl. "Once I'm familiar with these shows, I may enter Callie. She's a purebred calico, you know."

"Maybe you could enter her into the Moggie category." I snorted. Mags' spitting cat was definitely not moggie material.

"What's that? The cat version of a muggle? You know, non-cat as opposed to non-magical? Non-magical people are called muggles…" I waved my hand in dismissal as I realized she had no idea what I was talking about.

"It's where the cat is judged on temperament." I grinned.

"Oh, she would win that for sure."

"Really? Callie makes Sugar look like a meek kitten. You do not have a nice-tempered cat."

"I suppose Sherlock would do better." She crossed her arms.

"I'm pretty sure he's a mutt, but he does have a nice personality." I pulled into the parking garage after an hour of Mags' cold-shoulder treatment. "Keep your eyes and ears open. I guarantee you the thief is here."

"I know what I'm doing." With a swish of her shawl, she exited the car and marched toward the entrance.

Running to catch up with her, I apologized. "Callie is a very fine cat."

"Hmmph."

"You no longer agree?" I bit my lip to keep from smiling.

"I'm done with this conversation. Let's catch a diamond thief." With great dramatics, she flung the double doors open, struck a pose, then strolled in as if she walked the red carpet at the Oscars. Crazy dress or not, I now felt very dowdy.

Heads turned, some stared, others looked as if they should know who Mags was, then shrugged when they couldn't place her. My friend should have been on the stage, the way she loved the spotlight. "Where do we start?" She whispered. "I can only act as if I know what I'm doing for so long."

"Let's find the Westfords." I paused in front of a tabby so still when its owner dangled a feather in front of it that I thought the cat was stuffed.

"Prince is very obedient," the woman said. "He always earns high marks."

"He's gorgeous." I smiled and continued to where a flat-faced, white cat hissed and swatted at everyone that walked past. Definitely not moggie material there.

We passed cats of all colors and breeds, in all stages of readiness for their moment in the judge's eye. We found the Westfords in the back of the building. Sugar sported a pink bow on her head and a new collar around her neck. I doubted the sparkling gems were real this time.

"I could have used you last night, Lee," Mrs. Westford glared at her husband and ran a brush through Sugar's hair. "You knew today was important, and not only to me and Sugar. I thought you wanted to recoup our losses with another big win."

"I do, but I feel claustrophobic in that tiny house." He studied the nails on his right hand. "I told you I have everything under control."

"Is it the house or me that makes you claustrophobic?" She clamped her lips tight when she noticed us.

"We came to wish you luck," I said, "but if this is a bad time—"

"No, it's fine." Kim resumed her brushing. "Sugar needs calming, though. Give her a pat and move on. I don't mean to be rude, but I need to focus."

I raised my brows and glanced at Mags, then patted the top of Sugar's bow. The cat ignored me like her owner and licked her paw. "Good luck." I forced a smile and stepped away.

"No matter how nice you try to be to her, she's rude." Mags sniffed and pulled her shawl off her shoulders.

"She's having a difficult time with the stolen diamonds and a cheating husband." I sent up a prayer for mercy for the woman. I might be testy too if I was going through what she was.

I stopped in an out-of-the-way corner and studied

the crowd for anyone seeming overly interested in the Westfords. I spotted the man from the coffee shop almost immediately. He stood behind a table on which sat the biggest cat I'd ever seen.

"That's a Maine Coon," Mags said. "My next cat."

"That won't fit in your house." But it was gorgeous. "It looks as if our eavesdropper is here legitimately."

"Doesn't mean he didn't steal the collar. Let's see how he acts when he recognizes us." Mags strode toward him.

The man's eyes widened, but since he couldn't very well leave his cat unattended, he couldn't run.

"What a marvelous creature." Mags scratched behind the cat's ears.

"Thanks." His gaze flicked to me. "You showing or looking? Cats for sale are in the other building."

"Just looking, not buying." I smiled. "Our neighbors are showing, and we're here for support."

"Right." Mags winked at me. "They've been through some trials lately." She leaned closer to the man. "Thievery and infidelity."

I didn't think it possible for his eyes to widen further, but they did, going almost googly-eyed. "We shouldn't gossip, but are you acquainted with the Westfords?"

"No." He answered rather quickly. "Only seen them at these type of functions."

"Thank you for watching Frederick." A woman in her sixties squeezed up to the stand.

"The cat isn't yours?" I arched a brow at the man.

He gave a quick shake of his head and melted into the crowd. Recognizing suspicious behavior, and going with my gut instinct, I went after him. "Hey."

Shooting me a glance over his shoulder, he ducked into the men's room. Drat. Making sure no one was watching, I followed him in, leaving Mags to guard the door.

"Seriously, woman?" He paled.

"Why are you so interested in me and the Westfords?" I crossed my arms and looked as stern as my miniature frame would allow.

"I'm not."

"Sure you are. At the coffee shop, you were very interested in the conversation I had with my friend. Now, you're here and you don't have a cat."

"Neither do you." He tilted his head.

"Are you the jogger who paid a boy to throw a rock through my window? Did you steal the collar that belonged to the Westfords' cat? Who are you?" I narrowed my eyes.

"Stay out of it. This doesn't concern you." He growled and shoved past me, knocking me to the floor.

My head hit the tiled wall behind me. I didn't even want to know what germs I might be sitting in. When Mags didn't come to my rescue, I used the strength of my legs to press my back against the wall and push to my feet. No way was I going to touch the floor with my bare hands.

After making sure I wasn't bleeding, I washed my hands and turned as a man entered. He jerked back and peered at the Men's sign on the door. "You're in the right place," I said. "I'm the one who is lost." I flashed a grin and stepped out.

Where was Mags? My heart skipped a beat. That man hadn't taken her, had he?

I dug my phone from my pocket.

"Can't talk. Chasing Mr. Jogging Man through the showroom." Click.

Where was the showroom? I thought we were in it. I asked someone wearing an official-looking vest.

"This is the prep room. The showroom is through those doors." She pointed across the vast room. "You're only allowed in the bleacher section, not the floor. The show starts in half an hour."

I nodded and rushed after my friend. She should never have taken off after the guy on her own. He had to be at least twenty years younger and a lot stronger. What if he turned on her?

I stepped into a room devoid of people. Either there weren't a lot of spectators at a cat show or folks waited until the last minute to pick their seats. I stood and listened, straining to hear past the silence for any sign of Mags.

There. The pounding of running feet.

I headed on a sprint in that direction, catching a

glimpse of Mags, dress hiked around her knees, racing across the red show ring. I guess no one told her that area was off limits. Making sure no staff was around, I took off after her. "Mags."

She stopped, breathing hard. "Thank the good Lord. I'm winded. You go." She pointed with one hand and handed me her Taser with the other.

I grabbed the Taser and ran.

Jogging Man barged through a set of heavy back doors. "Stop. I only want to ask you some questions."

He flipped me an obscene gesture and slammed the door behind him. Rude.

I went through the doors a little more carefully then he had. My head still ached a little from meeting the men's-room wall. I didn't want another concussion. Why did bad people think hitting me over the head was the way to go?

As I stepped outside, Jogging Man, now on the back of a motorcycle, sped past narrowly missing me. He had to be the one responsible for hiring Ryan. Whether he'd actually stolen the diamonds or knew the Westfords was left to be discovered.

I entered the main room. Cats and their owners took up position behind podiums. A quick scan of the small crowd in the bleachers located Mags easy enough, thanks to her bright-colored dress. I made my way to her, careful to stay on the outskirts of the show ring. "What were you thinking?" I shook my head. "He knocked me to the floor in the bathroom. He could have done the same or worse to you."

"You let him get away, didn't you?"

"He sped off on a motorcycle. I couldn't exactly keep up."

"Do you think he knows the Westfords?"

I shrugged. "No idea, but I'm pretty sure he paid Ryan to throw the rock. What I don't know is why, unless he's involved, which he must be." My shoulders slumped. We were getting nowhere fast.

She snapped her fingers. "I have an idea. At the party, we'll talk about what happened today close enough to the Westfords so they can hear."

"Yes." I smiled. "They'll think we know more than we do. If one of them is behind all this, it might draw them out. I'd really like this solved before Christmas."

"That would be nice. We don't want a cloud hanging over a special day." With a satisfied smile, she focused on the happenings below us. "Oh, good. Sugar got a blue ribbon. That should make Kim Westford happy enough to answer any questions you might want to ask. Are you delivering another gift tonight?"

"Yes, the last one before the party, but I go late so she doesn't see me. Questions will have to wait." I was pretty sure her good nature would carry over until the next evening. I no longer thought her capable of stealing the diamonds. My money was on her husband. Caring for a wife and a mistress had to be expensive.

All I had to do now was prove it.

Chapter Ten

The evening of the community Christmas party, I donned a red sweater with a felt reindeer head covering the front. Right in the center of my chest was a blinking red bulb to serve as the reindeer's nose. I might not win for the ugliest sweater, but I doubted this sweater would ever see the light of day again.

Eric picked me up in a sweater the color of pea soup with dogs wearing Santa hats running across the front of his chest. "I put the last of the supplies in the clubhouse. Ready?" His eyes widened as I turned on Rudolph's nose. "The men are going to be staring at your chest all night."

"What little I have, you mean." I wiggled my eyebrows and linked my arm in his. "Let's go catch a thief."

He grinned. "That has become your favorite sentence lately."

"Better than let's go catch a killer. This is much

safer."

Our laughter carried us across the road and to the community center. The party would start soon, but I had time to make sure any last-minute details were in order.

Mags and my uncle, Larry, arrived first, followed by Amber and Davis. They weren't members of the community, didn't expect to participate in the gift exchange, but did bring food. Davis figured I was up to something and wanted to be there to get me out of any trouble I might find.

"It's a party, Davis." I rolled my eyes and took the potato casserole from his hands. "Try to enjoy yourself, and don't look like a cop, please." He'd scare away the thief.

Soon, the laughter and excitement of the community's children filled the room, drowning out the adults' conversations. I eyed the stack of presents under the tree, grateful for Larry's donation for gifts for the children since they weren't part of the Secret Santa exchange.

The Westfords arrived last and sat at a table. Davis watched them with narrowed eyes, as did I. From their body posture, they weren't pleased with each other. I prayed a fight wouldn't break out and ruin the party atmosphere.

Soon all the tables filled with people and plates piled high with food. No one seemed to be acting suspicious at all. Maybe Jogging Man was the sole person responsible for the theft. I shrugged. The Christmas party would have taken place either way. I took my seat next to Eric and decided to enjoy myself and let what would come...come.

"People aren't doing anything but eating." Mags stabbed a meatball with her fork.

"Maybe we were wrong about the Westfords." I glanced up to see Davis's reaction to my comment.

He kept his focus on his plate, but a muscle ticked in his jaw. Interesting.

"Do you have a prime suspect yet, Davis?"

"Why do you insist on calling me by my last name? You know my name is Bill." He scowled.

"Habit." I grinned. "Well?"

"Yes, I have a suspect, and no, I'm not going to tell you anything more." He resumed eating.

"Maybe I won't tell you what I know." I dug into my pasta salad.

His plastic fork slapped against his paper plate with a dull thwack. "Since you've mentioned it, you'd be breaking the law by not saying anything."

"The two of you are more entertaining than a movie," Eric said, laughing. "But you might want to keep your voices low. You're attracting attention."

"CJ makes me lose all reason." Davis shook his head. "What do you know?"

I lowered my voice and leaned forward to tell him about Jogging Man. "I wasn't able to get his name."

"You were attacked and didn't tell me?" High

spots of color appeared on Eric's cheeks.

"No, I simply fell when he pushed past me."

"What's the difference? You were injured."

"Barely."

"Save it for later," Davis interrupted. "You said this guy followed you to the coffee shop?"

"Did he?" I glanced at Mags.

"He came in after we did," she said, "and took a seat at the closest table. But we didn't know he would be at the cat show."

"Could he have followed you there?"

"Possibly," I said. "We were busy looking for the Westfords. You know, to wish them luck."

"Right." Davis smirked and rose to his feet, then carried his empty plate to the trash bin.

"You really do antagonize him," Amber said, smiling. "If you could only hear his frustrations when you get involved in another crime."

"I can imagine." I sensed the children growing restless. "Time for gifts."

With Eric acting as Santa, all gifts were handed out. Turned out Tammy Olson had my name and gifted me with a wonderful oil painting of Caper in a dark wood frame. "I love it. I didn't know you could paint?"

She smiled. "I don't have as much time as I used to but try when I can."

"I'll treasure it. Thank you." I knew just the spot to hang the painting. It would fit perfectly between the two windows above the sofa.

I smiled as Kim Westford carried the cat sculpture to me. "This is lovely. Thank you."

"It reminded me of Sugar, in a sleek rather than fluffy way. There's also a plug in the bottom to use it as a secret hiding place. Maybe for when you get the collar and diamonds back."

"Don't tell Lee, but I've already received the collar back." She turned and headed back to her table, setting the sculpture in the center and fiddling with it for a moment, before returning to the front of the room where those participating in the sweater contest gathered. Her sweater with a cross-stitched resemblance of Sugar wasn't ugly in the slightest. At least not when put against Mags' pooh-brown sweater with elves and twinkling lights. My friend won the contest hands down and received the prize of a gift card.

"To buy a new sweater," Eric said, handing her the card.

"What's wrong with my sweater?" Mags arched a brow. "It wins every ugly sweater contest I've entered. I think I'll keep it."

An angry shout rose above the frivolity.

Conversations ceased as everyone turned to Kim.

Hands on her ample hips, she glared around the crowd. "Where is my present? Where's Lee?"

I whirled to face Davis. "Was Lee around when you returned the collar?"

"Yes. I gave it to them outside before the party started."

"Kim must have put it in the bottom of the cat and Lee saw her. He's the thief."

Davis darted outside, me on his heels, Eric and the others right on mine. Of course, Eric caught up and passed me on our race toward house number fifteen.

The shattered pieces of the sculpture lay on the front porch. One missed diamond sparkled from the wreckage.

"Stay here." Davis reached for the doorknob, halting as a car sped from the back of the house.

"He's gone." The taillights disappeared through the front gate. "You couldn't have known Lee was the thief," I told Davis. "Or you wouldn't have given them the collar."

"No, I thought it was Mike Royson. You know him as Jogging Man."

I narrowed my eyes. "How did you figure that one out?"

"Because he's a known thief, and a certain somebody described him as one who might have stolen a woman's ring." He groaned and marched back toward the clubhouse. "You should have come to me with your suspicions."

"I wasn't sure yet."

"Did you catch the rat?" Kim waited for us in front of the building.

"No, ma'am." Davis planted himself in front of her. "Do you know where he might have gone?"

"To his girlfriend's house, most likely."

"Do you have her address?"

"Of course, I do." She gave an evil grin. "Lee thinks he's sneaky, but I've known all along where he goes at night. I've got it written down at home. Her name is Ginger Smith. A stripper name, if you ask me."

We trooped back to her house. She muttered a curse when she saw the broken sculpture. "Lee had better not have let Sugar out."

"I'll get you another sculpture," I said, relieved to see her cat watching us from the kitchen counter when Kim opened the door.

Lee had definitely left in a rush. Several of his wife's figurines lay shattered on the floor. On purpose, maybe? Through the open bedroom door, I could see scattered clothes.

"I'm going to kill him." Kim opened a kitchen drawer and pulled out a flowered address book. From a slit in the fabric that covered the book, she pulled out a slip of paper and handed it to Davis. "Keep it. I have it memorized."

Davis handed her a business card. "Call me if your husband shows up or you see him anywhere around."

"I'll be standing over his corpse when I call."

"Ma'am, that is not funny."

"I'm not joking."

The two stared at each other for several long seconds. Davis was the first to break away. Outside, he ordered us not to follow him into town.

Fine. I returned to Kim. "Could you write that address down for me? If I find him before the detective does, I'll let you know."

"Promise?"

"I promise." While I'd let Davis know when Kim went to confront her husband, I didn't want the man dead, so I'd let her know right before I called the police.

She scribbled the address on a piece of paper. "It's a trailer park on the other side of town. Be careful. It's seedy." She handed me the paper and closed the door.

"You aren't going tonight, are you?" Eric asked.

I shook my head. "I've seen that side of town. It's scary enough in the daytime."

"That's my girl." He bent down and kissed me before walking me home. "Take Mags and her Taser with you when you go. Good night, sweetheart. See you tomorrow."

I let Caper out and leaned against the railing of my porch, hoping she'd hurry up with her business. The night had turned bitter cold, biting through my sweater. My painting. I'd left it on the table at the clubhouse. "Come on, girl. I need to lock the place up."

The trashcan overflowed inside the clubhouse. Some tables still held dirty dishes and wrapping paper. It might be past ten p.m., but I couldn't go home, leaving the place that messy. I bagged the garbage, pulled another trash bag from under the small kitchenette counter, and then cleared the tables, leaving the painting where it was. I'd fetch it after taking the garbage to the dumpster.

Caper moved around the room eating dropped bits of food until I took the broom from the closet and started sweeping. Hating the broom, she hopped up on a chair and curled up to stare at me with soulful eyes.

"Sorry, sweetie." I hummed Christmas carols as I worked, mulling over in my head what had transpired.

Lee Westford had stolen his own diamonds, hid the fact from his wife, hired someone to intimidate me, all because he had another woman in his life? I shrugged. Immorality caused people to do awful things. I'd seen it before. Too many times. It saddened me.

I did what I could to bring justice to the world, and while I'd suspected Lee, I hadn't figured out the whole thing. Now, the diamonds were gone again. I seriously doubted he or his girlfriend would still be around by morning.

Leaving Caper where she lay, I put the broom away, hefted one of the bags of garbage over my shoulder like Santa Claus, and headed for the dumpster. It took several swings before I pushed the heavy lid up and over. Then I headed back for bag number two.

Caper opened one eye, then closed it again. "You'll have to come home with me when I'm done, silly pup."

I grabbed the last bag and returned to the dumpster. It weighed less than the first one and only took one hefty swing. There. I could sleep well, knowing I didn't have the mess to deal with in the morning. I could have asked Roy to take care of it, but the man had enough work to do.

Turning, I froze at the figure of a man standing in the shadows. With a cry, I turned to run. He caught up with me and yanked me around to face him. His hands circled around my throat. Lee under the hoodie.

Shrill barking meant rescue was on its way.

Caper bit down on Lee's leg, shaking with her entire body. He released me and tried pulling her off. He aimed a punch at her head. She let go and he kicked her away. Cursing, he dashed back into the night, leaving me short of breath and grateful for my furry little protector.

I scooped her into my arms and sprinted for home, smart enough to know he'd come for me again when the opportunity presented itself. I couldn't be caught outside.

Chapter Eleven

"What happened?" Mags peered at my neck.

"I had a run-in with Lee last night. Caper saved me." I tied a scarf around my neck to hide the bruises. "We need to stop and speak with Davis before heading to the trailer park."

"Do you think Lee will be there?"

I shook my head. "I'm hoping his girlfriend, Ginger, will be there and feeling talkative."

"Did you tell Eric?"

"He was asleep when I arrived home, and now he's up in the mountain somewhere. I'll tell him later." He wouldn't take the news lightly. My man took it personal when I got in trouble as if it were his fault he wasn't there. It couldn't be easy being my boyfriend.

The receptionist at the police station informed us that Davis was out and wouldn't return for a few hours. That left us with no other course of action but to pay a visit to Ginger.

I drove to the address Kim had given us and studied the white mobile home with pink trim. Flowerpots, devoid of blooms because of the winter season, hung along a wooden porch erected to make the trailer look more like a house. Ginger might be a homewrecker, but she appeared to have some pride in where she lived.

"I don't see any sign of Lee, do you?" Mags leaned forward and stared. "I've got my Taser, though...just in case."

"Good girl." I didn't see any sign of the man or his car. "Let's see what we can find out."

I approached the house slowly, my gaze darting in each direction for signs of danger. It wouldn't surprise me to see Lee jump out from the evergreen bushes on each side of the porch. I touched the scarf at my neck, last night's events fresh in my mind. I wouldn't mind a little payback when I came face-to-face with Lee again.

"There's murder in your eyes," Mags said. "You might want to get rid of that look if you don't want to scare the woman away."

Good point. I pasted on a smile I hoped wasn't a grimace and approached the front door.

A red-haired woman opened the door before I could knock. She looked about forty, with maybe an extra twenty pounds on her frame— not exactly pretty but pleasant-looking enough. "If you're selling anything, I'm not buying," she said, taking a sip of coffee."

"No, ma'am. We're here to ask whether you've seen Lee Westford."

"Why are you asking? I already told the cops I haven't seen him in two days." A flicker of worry crossed her features. "He's in trouble, isn't he?"

I nodded. "He's guilty of insurance fraud and trying to kill me." I pulled the scarf away from my neck enough for her to see the bruises.

Her eyes widened. "He's gone off the deep end. Come in." She stepped back so we could enter. "Too many nosy neighbors."

I sent up a prayer that Lee wasn't waiting for us inside, then entered a cozy home smelling of vanilla from a nearby burning candle. A small tabletop Christmas tree added some holiday cheer. I felt as if Ginger and I could've been friends if we'd met under different circumstances.

Ginger motioned for us to have a seat on her floral sofa. "You must think me a horrible person, spending time with Lee when he's married."

"We aren't here to judge," I said.

Mags snorted and rolled her eyes. "I'll try to be charitable in acknowledging that Kim can be a difficult woman. Did you know what he was up to?"

"No." Ginger sat across from us. "Lee loves me—he really does. If I didn't know how much before, I do now. I've been diagnosed with cancer and need surgery I can't afford. Lee told me not to worry about a thing.

He had it all taken care of." Tears welled in her eyes. "I had no idea he'd resort to this in order to help me." Drat. Now, I kind of felt sorry for the man. "The Westfords are financially broke. Or at least they were until Lee decided to steal the diamonds. I never did understand why they didn't sell them a long time ago."

"His wife refused. The cat's collar was a status symbol, I guess. A mask to wear to look prosperous." She wiped her eyes with the sleeve of her robe. "It's all for nothing. He'll go to jail, and I'll die."

Mags reached across and patted her knee. "Chin up. There's always a way."

"Do you have any idea where Lee might be?" I asked. While my heart broke for her, I couldn't let sympathy get in the way of justice. My sore throat reminded me of that fact.

"I have no idea." She broke into sobs. "He's been spiraling the last week, muttering things I didn't understand. Now, it's all clear to me." She fought for control and struggled to her feet. "You're right. I'll proceed with the surgery and worry about the cost later. I'll sell this place if I have to."

"Why don't you?" I stood and took her hand. "I've an empty house in Heavenly Acres that you can live in rent-free until you're back on your feet." Number ten had sat vacant for too long. My uncle wouldn't mind once he knew the circumstances. "Think about it."

"I will. Thank you."

"Will you be safe here alone with Lee clearly out of his mind?" Mags asked.

"He would never hurt me. I do think you should keep a close eye on his wife though. He really dislikes her and in his mental state—"

True. We needed to have protection assigned for Kim. I handed Ginger a business card. "Please, call me or the police if you see Lee."

She nodded. "Detective Davis came by last night. He also gave me a card, but I didn't spend much time talking to him. He searched the house and left. I hope you find Lee, I really do, and I hope he survives this ordeal. I'd rather have him in prison than dead."

As for me? I was torn between the two. An attempt on my life would do that. I thanked her and reminded her again about the house I had for her if she were interested, then headed back to the police station.

Davis must have pulled into the lot seconds before we did because he was marching up to the double doors when we pulled in. I tapped the horn. He turned and came to us.

"Find out anything?" He asked.

"Good morning to you, too." I grinned. "No, we haven't found out anything."

"Lee tried to kill CJ last night," Mags blurted out.

Davis paled. "I'd say that's worthy news."

I showed him my bruises. "Caper saved the day. Did you know Ginger has cancer and Lee promised to take care of her medical bills?"

He exhaled heavily. "You went to visit her?"

"Just left there. She said he's been different the last week or so. A lot on his mind."

"I'd say so. It can't be easy trying to steal from yourself, hide the fact from your wife, care for an ailing mistress, all while trying to act like the victim." Davis crossed his arms. "It would take a toll on any man. I'm glad you aren't dead, CJ, but you might not be as lucky next time."

"We think you should have an officer guard Mrs. Westford."

He nodded. "I'll have a squad car drive by on a regular basis. Go home and stay there. This case will be over soon, and Eric will kill me if something happens to you."

When he entered the building, Mags and I headed back toward home. "I'd hoped to find out more," I said, "but we did find out why Lee is doing this."

"Doesn't stop the fact he's gone bat crazy and needs to be behind bars."

"No, it doesn't." I glanced in the rearview mirror. "Don't look now, but speaking of the devil."

She turned in her seat. "He's coming up on us fast. Do you think he saw us at Ginger's?"

"I'd bet on it." I pressed the gas pedal. As I sped up, so did Lee.

"He's going to run us off the road."

"Most likely." I made sure my seatbelt was firmly in place. "I'm not a race car driver."

"You're barely a driver at all. Go faster."

"The faster we go, the harder we'll crash."

"So, you want him to catch us?"

"Not really." I increased our speed and tightened my grip on the steering wheel. Don't let us die, Lord, please.

My head snapped forward as Lee rammed us from behind.

Mags dropped her Taser and fumbled on the floor for it.

I whipped the wheel and spun the car around, speeding across the median and back toward the police station. Lee followed, cutting off a semi. The truck jackknifed and flipped. The man was definitely insane. Innocent people were going to get hurt before he finished his rampage.

"Got it." Mags held up her Taser just as Lee pulled alongside us and sideswiped us.

Horns blared. Cars careened out of the way. My small sedan was no match for his larger, older model.

"We can't beat him." My heart beat in my throat. "Call Davis."

Mags looked torn, then finally set her Taser on the dashboard and called her son-in-law. "We found Lee. That's the good news. The bad news is he's trying to run us off the road. He's already crashed a semi. We just passed mile marker 108." She nodded. "You'd better be faster than fifteen minutes. We might not make it that long." She hung up. "He's coming."

I swerved to avoid a slower car in front of me and ended up mired in the ditch. "We'll have to make a run for it." I shoved open my door as Lee skid to a stop beside us.

"Get in." He pointed a gun at my chest. "Both of you."

Something banged on the trunk of his car.

"Do you have Kim in there?"

"Sure do. Let's go. Now."

Mags and I scrambled into the backseat. "Where are we going?" I asked.

"Somewhere no will find three annoying women. Use those zip ties to tie each other's hands together. Don't try anything funny or I'll kill you slow and easy."

I did Mags' hands, then held mine out for her to secure mine. The longer we cooperated, the longer we would live. I fell back against the seat when Lee slammed his foot on the accelerator.

"Please tell me you have the Taser," I whispered to Mags.

"I did but dropped it again. It's under his seat."

"Shut up or I'll shoot you both right here."

We shut up.

Chapter Twelve

I stretched my foot, trying to dig the Taser out from under the front seat. Lee jerked the car to the right, slamming me against Mags and pressing her against the door. A yelp came from the trunk. Kim wasn't faring any better than we were. Still, the car would stop at some point and we outnumbered Lee three-to-one. No man in his right mind would go against three angry women.

We bounced down a dirt road and across a creek. I knew where we were headed. Lee was right. If he killed us at the quarry, our bodies would be easily buried.

He hit the brakes, sending us crashing against the back seat. I bent and fumbled for the Taser, wrapping my fingers around the handle, then sliding the weapon into my pants. It wouldn't be easy to retrieve, but it was the best thing we had.

I smiled knowing Davis would be able to track our phones. All we had to do was stay alive long enough for him to find us. Which he would. He had yet to let me down.

After Lee had me and Mags get out of the car, he opened the trunk and hauled Kim out. Not an easy task because of her size.

She stumbled to her feet, spitting mad. "I'm going to kill you, you worthless excuse for a man."

"Don't antagonize him," Mags hissed.

Kim whirled to face us. "Don't tell me what to do with my own husband."

"Maybe I should let the three of you kill each other." Lee laughed. "Stand on the edge of that giant hole in the ground." He motioned with the gun.

I stood and stared down, fairly certain I could survive the fall. If I jumped, how far could I get before a bullet struck me in the back? "You don't have to do this, Lee. You can't help Ginger if you're behind bars."

"What do you know about anything?"

"I know you want to help her with her surgery. That makes you a man with a good heart."

"He's as crazy as a rabid dog," Kim spit. "Where's Sugar?"

"Wandering around Heavenly Acres." He grinned. "Maybe she'll wander out to the highway. Play a little frogger with the traffic."

Kim lunged at him, her fingers curled into claws.

Lee fired the gun at her feet.

That was all the distraction I needed. I leaped forward and wrapped my arms around his neck, taking him into the hole with me. I twisted my body to put him on the bottom, softening the impact of landing in the packed dirt.

We both lay there gasping like stranded fish. I sucked in air and grappled for the gun as Mags and Kim scrambled down to join us.

Kim took the gun and aimed it at Lee. "I told you this would happen if I found out you stole the diamonds."

"Don't do this." I climbed to my feet, every inch of my body aching. "He isn't worth you going to jail."

"He's ruined us." Tears streamed down her round face. "I resigned myself to the fact he didn't love me anymore. We didn't even buy Christmas gifts for each other; that's how broke we are. I never thought he'd steal the only future we had left."

"It wouldn't have been so obvious if that dumb dog hadn't chased your stupid cat and pulled the collar off." Lee pushed to his feet. "I had the dickens of a time finding the collar and barely had time to remove half the diamonds before people started searching."

"Does this remind you of an episode of *Scooby Doo*?" Mags cocked her head. "'I'd have gotten away with it if not for those pesky kids'? Except this time, it's a little dog."

I bent and sawed the zip tie from my hands on a sharp rock, Mags copied. I reached into my pants and pulled out the Taser.

Mags seemed shocked to see where I'd hidden it.

"You can keep it now."

I rolled my eyes. "Kim, use this instead. I guarantee it will bring you satisfaction."

"Not as much as seeing him dead. He's ruined our lives and Christmas."

"Stop being so dramatic," Mags said. "Christmas is still coming. Think of the bright side. You won't have to spend it with him. Let's tie him up, shove him in the trunk, and go home. It's cold out here."

I agreed and stepped forward to threaten Lee with the Taser if he didn't cooperate. Two squad cars roared to a stop behind Lee's car.

Davis, Milton, and Eric sprinted toward us. Davis coaxed the gun from Kim, while Eric took possession of the Taser. "You did good, ladies," Davis said. "I'll take it from here. Mr. Westford. You're under arrest. You should have stopped with the diamonds. Trying to kill CJ means you'll go to jail for a very long time."

"You tried to kill this little snip of a girl?" Kim's face darkened. She doubled up her fist and landed an impressive right hook against her husband's jaw. "I want a divorce."

Eric gently untied my scarf and took a long look at my bruises. After kissing each one, he leaned his forehead against mine. "Will you marry me?"

"What?" My mouth fell open.

"Will you marry me?"

"So you can keep me out of trouble?" My lips twitched.

He laughed. "Darlin' I'm not a miracle worker."

I threw my arms around his neck. "You bet I'll marry you. Whose house will we live in?"

"Well, Anne is in your Grams's house, so I guess we'll put our two together." He pulled me into a hug. "I don't care. I'd live in a tent with you."

Mags clapped her hands. "It's about time. Look, Davis, Eric proposed."

Davis shook his head, pushing Lee ahead of him. "Strange time for a proposal."

"I've got to do it before something really happens to CJ." Eric took my hand. "Mrs. Westford, we'd appreciate a ride back to Heavenly Acres."

"I'm only going back there to find my cat." She stormed past us. "But you're welcome to the ride."

"I'll need you three ladies to come to the station and fill out a report," Davis said, putting Lee in the backseat of his car. "Mrs. Westford, don't leave until that's completed."

~

Christmas morning dawned bright and cold. Eric arrived as the sun came up and woke me with kisses. "Merry Christmas."

I stretched and smiled. "Merry Christmas."

He knelt beside the bed and opened a little black box. "Let's make our engagement official." Inside sparkled a diamond ring. "How does a New Year's wedding sound? I don't want a long engagement."

"That sounds wonderful. The sooner the better. I

want to get married in the chapel."

"Of course. There's nowhere else more perfect than that little building you fixed up." He pulled me to my feet. "Let's stay in today, just the two of us and the animals. After the last couple of weeks, I'm yearning for a day of peace."

I smiled and cupped his face. "That sounds marvelous." I couldn't think of a better day than snuggling on the sofa with my man and watching Christmas movies while the lights twinkled on my tiny Christmas tree.

The End

Don't miss the final book, Caper Finds a Treasure

Website at www.cynthiahickey.com

www.cynthiahickey.com
Cynthia Hickey is a multi-published and best-selling author of cozy mysteries and romantic suspense/thrillers. She has taught writing at many conferences and small writing retreats. She and her husband run the publishing press, Winged Publications. They live in Arizona and Arkansas, becoming snowbirds with three dogs. They have ten grandchildren who keep them busy and tell everyone they know that "Nana is a writer."

      Connect with me on FaceBook
      Twitter
      Sign up for my newsletter and receive a free short story
      www.cynthiahickey.com

      Follow me on Amazon
      And Bookbub
Shop my bookstore on my website for better prices and autographed books.

COZY CHRISTMAS COLLECTION

Enjoy other books by Cynthia Hickey

COZY MYSTERIES

The Tail Waggin' Mysteries
Cat-Eyed Witness
The Dog Who Found a Body
Troublesome Twosome
Four-Legged Suspect
Unwanted Christmas Guest
Wedding Day Cat Burglar
The entire Tail Waggin' Series

Tiny House Mysteries
No Small Caper
Caper Goes Missing
Caper Finds a Clue
Caper's Dark Adventure
A Strange Game for Caper
Caper Steals Christmas
Caper Finds a Treasure
Tiny House Mysteries boxed set

A Hollywood Murder
Killer Pose, book 1
Killer Snapshot, book 2

Shoot to Kill, book 3
Kodak Kill Shot, book 4
To Snap a Killer
Hollywood Murder Mysteries

Shady Acres Mysteries
Beware the Orchids
Path to Nowhere
Poison Foliage
Poinsettia Madness
Deadly Greenhouse Gases
Vine Entrapment
Shady Acres Boxed Set

Nosy Neighbor Series
Anything For A Mystery
A Killer Plot
Skin Care Can Be Murder
Death By Baking
Jogging Is Bad For Your Health
Poison Bubbles
A Good Party Can Kill You
Nosy Neighbor collection

Christmas with Stormi Nelson

The Summer Meadows Series
Fudge-Laced Felonies
Candy-Coated Secrets

COZY CHRISTMAS COLLECTION

Chocolate-Covered Crime
Maui Macadamia Madness
All four novels in one collection

The River Valley Mystery Series
Deadly Neighbors
Advance Notice
The Librarian's Last Chapter
All three novels in one collection

Cozies not part of a series
Coffee, Tea, or Murder
Scones to Die For
Mischief and Mayhem

Romantic Suspense and Thrillers

The Sheriff of Misty Hollow
Girls' Weekend Survival
The Threat
Evil Returns
Drowned in Silence
Banner of Death
Christmas Burns

Cowboys of Misty Hollow
Cowboy Jeopardy
Cowboy Peril
Cowboy Hazard
Cowgirl Blaze

Cowboy Uncertainty
Cowboy Christmas Crisis
Cowboy Pitfall
Snowed in For Christmas With a Cowboy

Stay on the Ranch with the whole set

Misty Hollow
Secrets of Misty Hollow
Deceptive Peace
Calm Surface
Lightning Never Strikes Twice
Lethal Inheritance
Bitter Isolation
Say I Don't
Christmas Stalker
Bridge to Safety
When Night Falls
A Place to Hide
Mountain Refuge

Stay in Misty Hollow for a while. Get the entire series here!

Secrets of the South
The Lovers' Lane Murders
The Prom Night Hitchhiker
Up in Smoke

The Seven Deadly Sins series

COZY CHRISTMAS COLLECTION

Deadly Pride
Deadly Covet
Deadly Lust
Deadly Glutton
Deadly Envy
Deadly Sloth
Deadly Anger
Get the whole set here

Brothers Steele
Sharp as Steele
Carved in Steele
Forged in Steele
Brothers Steele (All three in one)

The Brothers of Copper Pass
Wyatt's Warrant
Dirk's Defense
Stetson's Secret
Houston's Hope
Dallas's Dare
Seth's Sacrifice
Malcolm's Misunderstanding
The Brothers of Copper Pass Boxed Set

Highland Springs

Murder Live
Say Bye to Mommy
To Breathe Again

Highland Springs Murders (all 3 in one)

Colors of Evil Series

Shades of Crimson
Coral Shadows
Indigo Nightmares
Read the whole set!

The Pretty Must Die Series

Ripped in Red, book 1
Pierced in Pink, book 2
Wounded in White, book 3
Worthy, The Complete Story

Lisa Paxton Mystery Series

Eenie Meenie Miny Mo
Jack Be Nimble
Hickory Dickory Dock
Boxed Set

Hearts of Courage
A Heart of Valor
The Game
Suspicious Minds
After the Storm
Local Betrayal
Hearts of Courage Boxed Set

COZY CHRISTMAS COLLECTION

Overcoming Evil series
Mistaken Assassin
Captured Innocence
Mountain of Fear
Exposure at Sea
A Secret to Die for
Collision Course
Romantic Suspense of 5 books in 1

Wife for Hire – Private Investigators
Saving Sarah
Lesson for Lacey
Mission for Meghan
Long Way for Lainie
Aimed at Amy
Wife for Hire (all five in one)

One Hour (A short story thriller)

Time Travel
The Portal

Historical cozy
Hazel's Quest

Historical Romances

Novellas
Runaway Sue
Taming the Sheriff
Sweet Apple Blossom
A Doctor's Agreement
A Lady Maid's Honor
A Touch of Sugar
Love Over Par
Heart of the Emerald
A Sketch of Gold
Her Lonely Heart
Abigail's Proposal
Sophia's Hope
Moira's Quest
Savannah's Trial
Josephine's Dream
A Most Reluctant Bride
Competing Hearts
A Teacher's Heart
Lesson of Love

SERIES
Finding Love the Harvey Girl Way
Cooking With Love
Guiding With Love
Serving With Love
Warring With Love
All 4 in 1

COZY CHRISTMAS COLLECTION

Finding Love in Disaster
The Rancher's Dilemma
The Teacher's Rescue
The Soldier's Redemption

Woman of courage Series

A Love For Delicious
Ruth's Redemption
Charity's Gold Rush
Mountain Redemption
They Call Her Mrs. Sheriff
Woman of Courage series

Short Story Westerns
Flowers of the Desert

Contemporary

Romance in Paradise
Maui Magic
Sunset Kisses
Deep Sea Love
3 in 1

The Red Hat's Club (Contemporary novellas)

Finally
Suddenly

CYNTHIA HICKEY

Surprisingly
The Red Hat's Club 3 – in 1

STANDALONES
Finding a Way Home
Service of Love
Hillbilly Cinderella
Unraveling Love
I'd Rather Kiss My Horse

Whisper Sweet Nothings (a Valentine short romance)

Christmas Romances (Contemporary and Historical)
Dear Jillian
Romancing the Fabulous Cooper Brothers
Handcarved Christmas
The Payback Bride
Curtain Calls and Christmas Wishes
Christmas Gold
A Christmas Stamp
Snowflake Kisses
Merry's Secret Santa
Holly's Hope
A Christmas Deception
A Christmas Castle

Heads up! Some of the links above are affiliate links. If you decide to buy through them, I may earn a small commission (thank you for supporting my work!). It doesn't change the price for you.

Printed in Dunstable, United Kingdom

74669630R00192